Born in Edinburgh in 1906, **John Innes Mackintosh Stewart** was educated at Oriel College, Oxford, where he was presented with the Matthew Arnold Memorial Prize and named a Bishop Frazer's scholar. After graduation he went to Vienna to study Freudian psychoanalysis for a year.

His first book, an edition of Florio's translation of *Montaigne*, got him a lectureship at the University of Leeds. In later years he taught at the universities of Adelaide, Belfast and Oxford.

Under his pseudonym, Michael Innes, he wrote a highly successful series of mystery stories. His most famous character is John Appleby, who inspired a penchant for donnish detective fiction that lasts to this day. His other well-known character is Honeybath, the painter and rather reluctant detective, who first appeared in *The Mysterious Commission*, in 1975.

Stewart's last novel, *Appleby and the Ospreys*, appeared in 1986. He died aged eighty-eight.

BY THE SAME AUTHOR
ALL PUBLISHED BY HOUSE OF STRATUS

The Ampersand Papers
Appleby and Honeybath
Appleby and the Ospreys
Appleby At Allington
The Appleby File
Appleby On Ararat
Appleby Plays Chicken
Appleby Talking
Appleby Talks Again
Appleby's Answer
Appleby's End
Appleby's Other Story
An Awkward Lie
The Bloody Wood
Carson's Conspiracy
A Change of Heir
Christmas At Candleshoe
A Connoisseur's Case
The Daffodil Affair
Death At the Chase
Death At the President's Lodging
A Family Affair
From London Far
The Gay Phoenix

Going It Alone
Hamlet, Revenge!
Hare Sitting Up
Honeybath's Haven
The Journeying Boy
Lament For a Maker
The Long Farewell
Lord Mullion's Secret
The Man From the Sea
Money From Holme
The Mysterious Commission
The New Sonia Wayward
A Night of Errors
The Open House
Operation Pax
A Private View
The Secret Vanguard
Sheiks and Adders
Silence Observed
Stop Press
There Came Both Mist and Snow
The Weight of the Evidence
What Happened at Hazelwood

MICHAEL INNES

OLD HALL, NEW HALL

HOUSE OF
STRATUS

This edition published in 2001 by House of Stratus, an imprint of House of Stratus Ltd, Thirsk Industrial Park, York Road, Thirsk, North Yorkshire, YO7 3BX, UK.

www.houseofstratus.com

Typeset by House of Stratus, printed and bound by Short Run Press Limited.

A catalogue record for this book is available from the British Library and the Library of Congress.

ISBN 1-84232-749-6

PART ONE

OLD HALL

1

It didn't seem much to have changed, Clout's authentic University, during the four years he had been away. Except, he remembered, that now it *was* a University, awarding its own degrees. When he had taken his finals it had been only a University College. That was why he was styled BA London, although he had never spent two consecutive nights in London in his life. C Clout, BA London, B Litt Oxford: it was precisely wrong – he robustly told himself as his walk ended and the familiar buildings came into view – because it obscured the basic fact that he was provincial and of the North. But it was right, or so he was hoping, for the business he had in hand.

Clout walked faster. It's better to arrive hopefully than to dawdle and have doubts. Besides, it looked as if it was going to rain. The sky had been clear when he set out from the town, but since then banks of black cloud had piled up, and sunshine was managing to shoot through them only here and there. This made the scene in front of him theatrical. The rather grandly bleak Georgian façades of Old Hall possessed, in their barely controlled disrepair, the rubbed abraded appearance of something done on canvas to an improbably stupendous scale. The sprawl of army huts, Nissen and Spider, on the one flank, and the raw brick boxes housing laboratories and workshops on the other, didn't look like anything that a responsible human being would pitch down beside an eighteenth-century mansion in a seventeenth-century park. But they might have been a run of fortuitously jostling sets waiting to be shoved severally

MICHAEL INNES

on-stage in some supernal theatre – that or the kind of *décor* that Hollywood knocks up by the acre.

Nevertheless, although the elements of the scene were heterogeneous, the suddenly lowering heavens were sweeping them powerfully together into a well-composed piece full of lurking alarm. Spirits Sinister and Spirits Ironic might be gathering in the wings for the purpose of appraising a drama lavishly accommodated to the principles of *Sturm und Drang*; and at the moment a single tremendous shaft of light was striking down upon a corner of the crumblingly balustraded terrace, so that one rather expected the striding forward of some principal personage, intent upon announcing that so foul and fair a day he had not seen. The whole prospect had taken on a momentary distinction, operatic and hallucinated. It was like a John Piper version of the unassuming adage that it's nice to see a little bit of sunshine.

These reflections, which had brought Clout to a halt, now made him impatiently shake his head. He had an idea that there is something debilitating in arty or booksy musings. One ought to see and feel things absolutely unmediated and direct. It was only in that way that they nourished, even modified, the sensibility.

But shaking his head made Clout self-conscious, and self-consciousness made him aware of being not alone. Somebody had got off a bicycle and was standing quite close to him. He glanced sideways. It was a girl. And there was no doubt about *her* coming to him direct and unmediated. For the first time in his life, his sensibility was modified so that he knew it without a period of conscientious introspection or serious discussion with friends. The only comparison was the occasion when somebody had put a knee in him in a barrack-room scrap and taken his breath away. The girl beside him had now done just that.

Suddenly, with the plain intent of signalizing Clout's new life, the heavens opened and the rain fell.

He discovered, rather to his own surprise, that he was carrying an umbrella. It was a concession to his recent sojourn in the South, for here such a thing would be considered rather soft in the hands of anyone below middle age. But it was a wonderful object to command now. Clout opened it, stepped forward, and held it over the girl. Very naturally, he had spent the second or so needed to perform this action in wondering about the words which should accompany it. Now he discovered that he might have saved himself this trouble. He was bereft of the power of speech. In fact he opened his mouth, found that absolutely nothing happened, and had the presence of mind to shut it again as quickly as possible. At least he needn't seem to gape. And fortunately, he wasn't in any sort of tremble or dither. He concentrated on holding the umbrella quite steadily and plumb-centre over the amazing girl.

This absence of civil phrase in Clout didn't seem to offend her. He even felt an obscure intimation of its pleasing her. But she wasn't awkwardly silent herself.

'Oh, thank you,' she said. 'Thank you very much. But please don't bother. These clothes won't come to any harm.'

And now Clout did slightly tremble. Not only was the girl's voice inexpressibly thrilling. It seemed to Clout that the words which she used had a choiceness, a perfect appropriateness, an exquisite tact and taste, such as must convey to any ear, not wholly unworthy of its office, full assurance that here outward beauty was abundantly matched by riches within. At the same time he saw that what she said about her clothes was prosaically accurate. She was dressed in tweeds – the sort that books call well-worn and good. So it seemed unlikely that she was a student. At the same time she was much too young, and immeasurably too rare to be conceivably one of the considerable number of learned ladies on the staff. Probably she had nothing to do with the University. She had got off her bicycle, here at the main gates, merely to take a curious glance at the place.

In Clout's excited imagination this conjecture made the girl less remote – or, if not less remote, at least more accessible. Her action had confessed an interest in something he knew about and had a share in. Perhaps it was only a fleeting interest in the picturesque turn the jumble of buildings could put up under this sort of sky. But even that was a start. And Clout found his tongue. 'It makes rather an unlikely fantasy, doesn't it, on a day like this? But when you strip away the atmospherics it becomes a bit of naked English social history. You might say a show piece, if that didn't suggest a museum. For it's not that. I mean, it isn't dead. It knows it hasn't a past, and it's bound to doubt whether it has a future. But, here and now, it's really full of life. I know. I belong to it.'

For a moment the girl was silent. But he was sure she wasn't disconcerted by these philosophical remarks, much less bewildered by them. If she had betrayed any faint surprise it was perhaps at his accent, to which his tie and his hair and even the way he stood on his two feet were no longer reliable pointers. His D H Lawrence phase had lasted well into the Oxford period, and during it he had zealously guarded his native intonations. By the time it was over – and himself once more clean-shaven – it would have been silly to start making a new set of noises. And indeed he could never be certain that the Lawrence business *was* utterly over. At this moment, at which his fate had declared itself with a certainty that ought to leave no room for foolery, he had a faint grotesque persuasion of himself as dressed in cap and breeches, as nursing a shot-gun, as feral and nobly savage, obedient only to some deep centre of consciousness somewhere behind his navel, and murmuring unprintable words with triumphant effectiveness into the ear of this upper-class woman. Here was a sad relapse into the booksy, and he would have blushed for it if he hadn't instead suddenly wanted to laugh at the glorious incongruity of this shadowy gamekeeper *persona* and the actual words upon which he had ventured. And then he *did* laugh. For some reason it seemed perfectly natural to do so. Clout shouted with laughter.

This time the girl *was* disconcerted. As she was huddled shoulder to shoulder under the dripping umbrella of one who had followed up a certain amount of sage sociological small talk with this inconsequent and maniacal mirth, it wasn't at all surprising that she should be. But at least she stood her ground and spoke entirely calmly. 'What's funny?' she asked.

'I am. But it would be difficult to explain.' Clout, who had become conscious of the girl's arm as touching his, and of everything else in the universe as fainting and fading, felt these to be wholly sufficient words.

'Then perhaps this isn't just the moment to try.' The girl peered out from under the umbrella. 'I think it's blowing over.'

Clout wanted to cry out that it would never do that; that things would simply fall apart if it did; and that in fact for ever and ever the rain would continue to descend, just missing her shoulder and just getting his neck, while the two of them, eternally side and side, gazed and gazed at an unremarkable, a makeshift university made strangely beautiful by a glint of sunlight through tumbling cloud. But to the girl (to whom, presumably, a like revelation to his own had not yet come) these would probably seem extravagant observations. 'We'd better give it another minute or two,' Clout said diplomatically. 'Just in case.'

'If you're sure you have the time.' The girl took up the matter where convention demanded. 'It's frightfully kind of you to be so patient. And I was an ass not to bring a mac.'

Clout was silent. Innocent of all but the vaguest appositeness, yet carrying with them the melancholy of love defeated by circumstances and time, lines of remembered verse were floating through his head:

> *Why didst thou promise such a beauteous day*
> *And make me travel forth without my cloak...*

He was realizing in a great horror that the shower must in fact entirely stop, the umbrella be furled, the girl get on her bicycle and prosaically pedal out of his life. As if to drive the point home in mockery, a raindrop, flicked by the wind, landed with cold precision on his nose.

> *'Tis not enough that through the cloud thou break,*
> *To dry the rain on my storm-beaten face...*

And it's not enough, he told himself savagely, to go poetical wool-gathering after Shakespeare and his lovely boy. Here is your own lovely girl going to slip from you if you don't wake up. Resource. Initiative. Enterprise. At least say something. 'Do you know the University?' he asked.

As a positive move made in a great crisis, it was pretty dim. But it did at least get a reply. 'No,' the girl said. 'I know hardly anything about it.'

'I thought perhaps you might be a student.'

This was a new low. It wasn't even true, since he had almost at once decided that she wasn't. Moreover she might regard it as derogatory. She was shaking her head. 'Oh, no,' she said. 'I'm not a student. I'm somebody's secretary.' Her tone was faintly self-depreciatory and yet more faintly ironical – so that he knew it was the product of some confident social background. 'What about you?' she asked.

Clout's heart gave a leap, so that the umbrella trembled and a shower of rain-drops fell in front of them. It seemed incredible that the girl herself should advance to this easy curiosity. 'I took my Arts degree here,' he said. 'Since then, I've been away for four years. And now I'm rather hoping to get a job – perhaps only just the ghost of one – in my former Department – the English Department, that is.'

'You can put down the umbrella.'

Very reluctantly, Clout accepted this suggestion. The girl took a step away from him, so that he saw her in a new focus and against an open sky. In spite of the shelter he had provided, drops of moisture glinted in her hair. Again he couldn't think of anything to say. Or rather he couldn't think of anything irrelevant to say. What was relevant would sound absurd and might be fatal. All he could do was to gaze. At the moment this was safe enough, for she was once more looking at the sprawl of buildings in the middle distance.

'Is your Department – English, did you say? – in the old part?' She turned to him in a way that made the question, indefinably, seem a shade more than merely casual.

'Yes. All the Faculty of Arts is in Old Hall – that and the administrative people. English isn't, of course, considered at all important, so it's right up near the top. At least there's a good view over the park, and you hardly notice the huts and the labs.'

'It sounds very nice.'

It seemed a highly conventional response. But Clout had an inspired glimpse of it as something to rise to. 'Would you care', he asked, 'to come and see?'

2

They walked up the avenue together in what was, for Clout, a daze of happiness. At first everything had become insubstantial, had sunk or swum away, except the girl herself. But now the sensible world had returned about him – and returned in a kind of glory, as if steeped in the colours of the Golden Age. The trees and the benches, the grass and the gravel and the fallen leaves, the little signposts saying *Women's Union* and *Strength of Materials* and *Gentlemen*: the veil of custom dropped from them all as he gazed, and their very essence was revealed. He recalled what he had read of the operation of certain drugs, and was sane enough to conjecture that the miracle of love at first sight had thrown him into a similarly hallucinated state. Nevertheless he gave himself wholly to this exalting experience, for he was sure that at the core of it was something in which he could entirely trust. And, at the same time, he was now confident that he needn't make an ass of himself. He talked, but not too much; he explained a few things about himself, but not too many; he frankly asked her questions, but not a single question that he oughtn't to ask. He had quite forgotten the Laurentian gamekeeper or groom, and was honestly C Clout, BA, B Litt. Only he didn't, in fact, volunteer his name, or even ever so indirectly fish for hers. Something told him that it was only on terms of a preserved anonymity that a girl like this would spend an hour with a casually contracted young man whose sole claim to her regard was the proprietorship of a serviceable umbrella.

Nor did this mutual reserve, with its hint that these were only fugitive moments and that nothing that wasn't wholly impermanent had happened – nor did this cast the shadow which it rationally might. The moments themselves were too entire. Envious time, though it might blunt the lion's paws and make glad or sorry seasons as they flew, had no power over them. But the girl, Clout was sure, had power over all who saw her. The Professor of Anglo-Saxon, shambling down the avenue and vaguely recognizing an old pupil, gave an uncouth nod and then, noticing *her*, straightened his shoulders and swept off his hat. The autumn term would begin in three or four days' time, and boys and girls lately disgorged from the grammar-schools of the city were straggling up to make their inquiries about this dreary course or that. The girls, awkward in their recent emancipation from gym-tunics and hideous felt hats, glanced at *this* girl round-eyed. The boys, some of whom on leaving home had absentmindedly performed the habitual action of jamming school caps on the backs of their untidy heads, stared insolently or shyly according to their several dispositions. Clout had no doubt that if the Vice-Chancellor himself had appeared he would have given some visible sign of being equally impressed.

They climbed by worn shallow stone steps up the broad terrace. Long rows of empty bicycle racks stretched on either side of them. Irregularly along the balustrade mildewed and eroded statues presided. Close by Clout one classical lady, her breasts and belly etched with lichen while her still immaculate buttocks glinted from the recent rain, held mutilated arms oddly and stiffly out before her, like a policewoman directing invisible traffic. Next to her an obese Hercules supported himself against the stump of a tree in an attitude suggesting a car-park attendant, badly out of condition, taking his ease against a lamp-post on a slack afternoon. Here and there the marbled divinities were pleasantly diversified with gigantic dogs and boars. In places the balustrade itself had vanished, and been replaced, for safety's sake, with a line of concrete posts linked together by a painted cable. The whole vista proclaimed its own departed grandeur with an obviousness that elicited irritation rather than melancholy.

11

'I'm not quite sure how you feel.' The girl had stopped before the central portico of the transformed mansion and was looking seriously at Clout. 'Do you regard it as a pity – or what?'

'You mean the social revolution, or whatever it's to be called, that puts places to changed uses like this?' Clout too was serious. 'When I first came here I used to think about that quite a lot. And I found that, although they weren't at all my sort, I was prepared to regret the passing of the kind of folk that used to live here. But since they've gone – or their ability to go on living here is gone – I think it's right to turn the place over to positive activities – even rather drab educational ones.'

The girl nodded. 'Of course it's happened everywhere. Stowe and Bryantson are public schools. And other places like that are mental hospitals and old folks' home and prisons without bars.'

'I think that's all right. It's sad, and the places are very literally disgraced. But the thing's not futile, like turning your house into a museum and living on the proceeds in the old servants' wing.'

'Yes, I agree. But here, I don't suppose the owners had the choice. It isn't grand enough for a show-place; it's not a great nobleman's seat. Just squirearchy at its most expansive.'

'And already a bit bogus. I don't expect a pile like this was built on the income from its own estate. Nabob money, probably. Or run up by a mahogany-coloured old gentleman who had done famously in Jamaica.'

'Probably.' She seemed amused – and rather in a fashion suggesting that she had seen a joke where he hadn't. But now she was moving forward. 'Take me in,' she said. 'And, if you've time, show me all of it.'

The enchanted progress continued, and so did their rational exchange of views upon impersonal topics. He felt certain that in all major matters they were divinely in accord, while at the same time in a thousand *trivia* of opinion and feeling they differed enough to provide a whole lifetime of stimulating discussion. It was true that every now and then the girl seemed a little absent, looking about her in terms of some train of thought which he couldn't quite elicit. But she listened to everything he had to say – he spoke sometimes caustically, but always with a decent loyalty nevertheless – about how the place was run. They looked at the Library, which consisted of the old dining-room and main drawing-room knocked together, and admired the way in which a large lecture-theatre, artificially lit, had been constructed in what must have been a gloomy and useless central court. Then they climbed to the English Department. He showed her the lending library of modern poetry that he had founded in his third year, and took her into the little seminar-room where he had mugged up for his finals things like *Piers Plowman* and the Miracle plays. There were group photographs on the wall, and she moved over to study them silently. He was there himself, standing perched on a bench beside an impudent looking girl with a mass of dark hair tumbling about her shoulders. He glanced cautiously at this, wondering if she would spot him, and was horrified to notice that he and the impudent girl were holding hands. He remembered the moment perfectly; they had done it out of bravado as the camera on its pivot had swung round towards them. But if this girl noticed it she didn't, of course, say anything, but moved on to another group. 'More women born than men,' she murmured.

Here was a further enchantment; she was a student of Yeats. 'There are always more women than men reading English,' he explained. 'Elsewhere, as well as here.'

'Ordinary girls like it, and ordinary boys think it a bit soft?'

'Just that.' What marvellous penetration she had!

'I wonder whether I know any of these people.'

These were the first words she had spoken that hinted at any sort of local connexion, and he waited for her to say something more. But she had spoken quite casually, and now she moved away. 'Come to the window,' he suggested, 'and look at the view.'

It was a good view, and he remembered it as having afforded considerable relief during his endeavours to conjure up Piers Plowman's beastly mist on Malvern hills. But she wasn't quite satisfied. 'Can't we get out on the roof?' she asked.

Clout hesitated, because this would be a misdemeanour and he was by nature extremely law-abiding. But he was, after all, an Old Boy, and he mustn't be abjectly pupillary. 'Yes, of course,' he said. 'I know how to do it. Come on.'

It meant going up a ladder and through a trapdoor. But she wasn't, he knew, the sort of girl to be deterred by that. And presently they were on the windy leads. She walked straight to the low stone coping and sat down on it. The flat surface was as broad as a park bench, but he felt a little nervous. 'I'd be careful,' he said. 'Everything's crumbling.'

'Things fall apart. The centre cannot hold.' For the first time, she looked at him in open cheerful mockery, and he realized that these scraps of verse, unlike his own Shakespearian maunderings, were ironically delivered. In fact she was making some sort of oblique fun of his self-satisfaction in the collection of Pound, Eliot, and what-not down below. But he wasn't at all resentful. He just continued to adore.

They were above the main front of the Hall. In front of them the straight avenue crossed the park at its narrowest extent, and just beyond were the outermost suburbs of the city that stretched, all smudge and smoke and watery glitter, to a horizon of chimney-stacks and miscellaneous industrial contrivances. But elsewhere the park faded imperceptibly into a sort of no-man's-land between country and town: fields creeping round abandoned manufactures, fresh manufactures devouring abandoned fields, hills in places immemorially wooded and in places scraped and scarred by mines and quarries.

'I suppose it's Satanic,' he said. 'But I like it.'

'I like it too.'

'Frightfully Wadsworth.'

For a moment she was puzzled. 'Oh, I see. I'd say Wadsworth is frightfully *it*.'

This rather prosaic correction was again something that didn't offend him. She had that fatal booksy-arty response better under control than he had. It would be no good sitting down at the typewriter to evoke this scene and simply tapping out the names of appropriate painters. One had to do something quite different. Pretend, for example, that it was a submarine landscape and work out all the congruous images. For a moment Clout was actually seduced from the girl by the impulse to get to work on this. But almost at once he gave over – it was a damned bad idea anyway – and sat down beside her. 'You see, it's as I said,' he began. 'The new buildings quite remarkably sink away, and the place looks almost undisturbed. When the old squire pottered up here fifty years ago, his park looked very much as it does now.'

'The old squire?' She was puzzled.

'A generic old squire. I don't know anything about individuals. I did once read it up. But I've clean forgotten.'

'Probably most people have.' She picked up a crumb of mortar and dropped it over the verge, leaning forward in an attempt to watch it fall. The action made Clout dizzy, but he felt it was up to him to do the same thing. For a moment they peered down together at the flagged terrace. Clout resumed his hunting for marine similes. If the grass beyond the terrace was like a gently heaving green sea, then the terrace itself became like the deck of an aircraft carrier, and the statues were personnel with the hazardous job of flagging planes on and off. Rotten again. 'Isn't there a barrow?' the girl asked.

He stared – and then saw that she was again looking out over the park. 'You mean the archaeological sort? I believe there is.'

'And a mausoleum?'

'There's certainly that.'

'And an ice-house?'

Clout was puzzled. 'I think an ice-house has been pointed out to me. They'd be grand enough to want to store ice through the summer, no doubt.'

'It's a big park. Bigger than I realized.' The girl spoke with a sudden odd gloom.

'Yes, it's pretty big. Rugger grounds and cricket fields and tennis courts are tucked away in it so that you just wouldn't notice. It's supposed to be one of the things in which we score over other provincial universities. The smart set even goes riding in it.'

'What do you mean by the smart set?'

'Does it sound so funny? There are some students, you see, who are the children of very prosperous local business people. They send their hopeful young here out of a strong sense of regional piety – but give them three times as much money as anyone else. It's highly democratic. And that's the smart set.'

'I see. Are you the smart set?'

'Of course not. If I was, I'd be in Dad's works or office by this time, and not scrouging round for a job in the University.'

The girl was silent for a moment. Then she stood up. 'I must be going,' she said. 'Steer me down and into the open, please. I might meet the smart set and feel shy.'

He led her down to the ground floor and out to the terrace. It didn't look like more rain, but nevertheless he supposed he would be allowed to escort her back to her bicycle. On the steps, however, she stopped with the plain intention of saying good-bye. He tried to speak calmly. 'We don't need the umbrella,' he said. 'But I'll just walk up the drive with you.'

She shook her head. 'I have an idea you've an appointment – about that job. And that perhaps I've made you late for it.' This was unfortunately true, so that for a fraction of a second he hesitated. 'I hope,' she went on, 'you get what you want. If you do, it will be possible to find you up there – among the modern poetry and the photographs?'

'Yes, of course. I'm...that is, I haven't told you – '

It was a moment of incoherence – for the suggestion that she might seek him out was at once astounding and something that he took as written in the stars. And when a moment later, still without any exchange of names, she shook hands and walked away, Clout found himself looking after her yearningly indeed but without dismay. And this was strange. In his twenty-five years, of course, he had built up several reassuring Clouts. First there had been Clout, BA (Ist Class Hons. English). Then there had been Clout, 2/Lt Army

Education Corps. And now there was Clout, B Litt. ('The Influence of Thomas Carlyle on the Thought and Expression of John Ruskin'). Yet the combined armour of these had not made plain Clout invulnerable to the slings and arrows of a disabling diffidence. He could never, during the introspective scrutinies he sometimes conducted in the watches of the night, have charged himself with an undue self-confidence. But now it was different. He had – he repeated it – a star. And he was certainly not going to have its orbit interfered with by Gingrass. He would get precisely what he required – what he now absolutely required – out of *him*.

Clout turned back into Old Hall and with quiet, unforced resolution climbed upstairs again.

3

Gingrass still had his uneasy setting. Most of the professors inhabited quarters having the appearance of lumber-rooms hastily three-parts cleared for them on their arrival. They sat on, wrote at, prowled amid, and balanced their books against junk that must have been mouldering *in situ*, little troubled by broom or duster, since the close of the Victorian age. It had been remarked that there was always dust on the seat of their pants, and that those who were over five foot eight commonly had cobwebs in their hair. In general all this became them very well. They were most of them genuine, if low-grade scholars, their persons distinguished by marmalade stains, missing buttons, improvised shoe-laces, and their minds directed upon distant and impalpable things. But Gingrass, who had married a lady with means and a shadowy past in interior decorating, owned a room designed to proclaim other affiliations. One of the walls was a deep violet. Against this Gingrass, now a pallid, flaccid fifty, showed like one of those reclusive fish that haunt the farthest ooze. Another wall was papered in thin grey stripes on a black ground. Viewed against this, Gingrass became a creature of nocturnal habit, prowling his cage in some darkened menagerie. A third wall exhibited, more deliberately, the man of learning, being clothed in massive calf-bound books – all impressively anonymous, since their spines were innocent of the slightest trace of lettering. Some maintained that these were a sham, and that pressure upon a concealed spring would cause them to slide away, revealing row upon row of lubricious romances. But this was undoubtedly a libel. So perhaps was the assertion that the litter of large dimly patterned pots, upon the originating Dynasties of which Gingrass would make obscure remarks when hard up for something to say, were in fact commercial ginger-jars obtained from a wholesale grocer's. Clout had always rather liked the pots. Indeed, he now found that he had a kind of affection for the room as a whole. Perhaps this was simply because his upbringing had been among objects that were sometimes hideous but always conventional, and this had been the first queer room he had ever entered.

He was late – the girl had made him undeniably late – but Gingrass didn't, as four years ago he would have done, look reproachfully at his watch. Instead, he put on one of his smiles – the one conveying his sense that your mere continued existence was part of the high comedy of things – and advanced with outstretched hand. 'Well, well,' he said jovially, 'so Colin Clout's Come Home Again.'

Clout tried a smile of his own. It was true that his Christian name was Colin, although it had been chosen for him by parents who had never heard of the poet Spenser. And it was natural that Gingrass should deliver himself of this crashing joke. No doubt Clout's proper course was to dredge up, from what memories he had of the poem thus wittily invoked, an appropriately gamesome reply. But Clout was determined to get ruthlessly to the point and stick there. If you took Gingrass that way, you probably had him. Or at least this was a theory worth gambling on. 'Yes,' he said. 'As I wrote to you, I'm looking for a job.'

'Quite so.' Gingrass, who had retreated against his violet wall, contrived a sideways drifting movement, rather as if a deep submarine current had caught him broadside on. 'Well, sit you down – sit you down.'

Clout sat down. 'Of course,' he said, 'I mean an academic job.'

'Oh dear! Oh dear!' As one vastly dismayed, Gingrass sank into a chair and produced from a pocket of his negligent but high-class gent's suiting a tobacco-pouch and a straight-grain briar. 'There's no money in it, my dear chap. Get that into your head at once.' He opened the pouch, and the scent of tobacco thus released was like the purr of a Rolls-Royce. 'I've been in it for thirty years, my dear Clout, and I haven't a penny. Not a penny!'

This was a known turn. Clout hadn't had it before, but he had heard of it. 'I don't feel', he replied with careful idiocy, 'that money's everything, sir.'

'To a studious young man it means very little, I agree. But, my dear boy, your circumstances will change. Unlikely as it seems to you now, you will meet a young woman.' For a moment Gingrass' gloom gave way to a roguish but kindly twinkle. 'And then, you know – marriage, insurance policies, shoe-leather. And your children, as dear Hilary used to say, will howl for pearls and caviar.'

Hilary was Hilaire Belloc. The extensiveness of Gingrass' acquaintance with the great – particularly those more or less recently deceased – was, Clout remembered, a circumstance altogether remarkable. But it wouldn't do to argue about this money-business. It must be ignored. 'And what I want, Professor' – Clout recalled that this was the proper way to address Gingrass from time to time – 'is something, even if it's not much in itself, that starts straight away.'

'I see, I see.' Gingrass did his sideways dither, this time, on his chair. 'But it's rather late, you know, for the coming term. Only a few days to go.'

'I wrote to you early in August.'

'Quite so, quite so. Unfortunately, last year's tutors are all staying on. So I'm afraid there isn't likely to be anything much *here*. But I do happen to know that at Leeds – '

'It's here, sir, that I'd particularly like to start.'

'I'm glad to hear it – delighted to hear it, of course.' Gingrass accompanied this assurance with a visible tautening of his unimpressive muscles, rather as a man might do who has achieved a provisional diagnosis of being closeted with a maniac.

'And I thought that if, perhaps, there was a research scholarship, or something of that sort, and I could do just a little tutoring on the side…'

'Certainly, certainly. Very reasonable.' Gingrass relaxed. 'Of course, there is the Alderman Shufflebotham. It goes to Council to appoint on Thursday. I could conceivably put you forward for that.'

'Thank you very much. Please do.'

Gingrass blinked, so that Clout thought for an anxious moment that this had been too fast a one altogether. But all was well. Gingrass merely pulled importantly at his pipe and nodded. 'Yes, I don't see why I shouldn't do that. Of course, there's Lumb. You remember Lumb?'

'No.'

'Ah – after your time. He took his degree last year. Exempt from National Service because of his squint and his terrible stammer. Lumb would be a very strong candidate – if I backed him, that is to say.'

Clout tried to keep his mouth shut. But a rash compunction forced his lips apart. 'I never heard of him. But I wouldn't like to get in the way of a chap who's all set for it, Professor.'

'Quite so, quite so. But I'm not at all sure about Lumb. The fact is, he wants to write. And it doesn't do, you know. It's not a thing that goes along with scholarship. Lumb has written a novel, he tells me. And that's bad, you'll agree.'

This time Clout managed silence without effort. The fact that his own novel (in the manner of Kafka) was now nearly finished didn't even give him a twinge. Lumb, clearly, was a demented person, incapable of decent reticence. He must accept the consequences.

'It's a thing I'm quite convinced of. As a matter of fact, my dear Clout, I've – um – proved it on my own pulse. I once thought of writing myself. I seriously considered the Novel.'

Clout judged it improbable that the Novel had ever seriously considered Gingrass. But he contrived to look respectfully interested. After all, he hadn't heard this for four years. The details might have changed.

'I took a long reflective holiday. You know San Vigilio?'

'I'm afraid I don't.' (Yes. It had been Toscalano last time.)

'A delightful place. Looks across to Sirmione. Catullus, my dear lad, Catullus!' Gingrass was silent for a moment, impressively lost in the reverie of a classically-educated man.

'The question was, you know: Had I got it? Had I *quite* got it? I sat by the side of the lake and read one or two things I was rather fond of: *Madame Bovary*, I remember, and *Anna Karenina*, and *The Wings of the Dove*. Then I put it to myself squarely. Could I, definitely and unmistakably, advance the form? Could I – to express the matter a shade picturesquely, no doubt, my dear Clout – seize the torch from the hand of James, or for that matter of Proust, and carry it over the next lap? I decided against myself. Rightly or wrongly, I said: No. The verdict went against me. I hadn't got it.' Gingrass paused. 'Not quite, that is to say.'

Clout supposed that he ought to murmur something about great courage. But there are limits, after all. 'I don't suppose', he said, 'that this Lumb can afford a reflective holiday on Lake Garda.'

'It was a hard decision.' Gingrass ignored the irrelevance. 'But I made it. And then I went straight to Cambridge and accepted a Fellowship at my old College. My life has been a scholar's from that day to this.'

'Did you say Alderman Shufflebotham?'

'Certainly. The Alderman Shufflebotham Award.' Gingrass evinced a natural reluctance in returning to this mundane topic. 'Instituted since your day. Two hundred pounds in the first instance, and renewable for a second year, at the discretion of Council. Of course they leave it to me. But I have a word, naturally, with Mrs Shufflebotham. That's the Alderman's widow. She takes a great interest. We hope she may even do a little more for us, one day.'

'I suppose I can have a room?'

'To yourself, you mean?' Gingrass again shifted uneasily on his chair. 'Well, you see, space is pretty – '

'I don't imagine Mrs Shufflebotham would like to think of the Shufflebotham Student, or whatever he's called, wandering homelessly around the corridors?'

Gingrass frowned. Indeed, he showed some signs of squaring up to this attack. 'There's always the Library,' he said. 'I don't recollect that Lumb proposed to make any claim for a room.'

Clout contrived to look contrite. 'I'm sorry, Professor. I forgot how tight space is. No doubt you can't command another room just for the asking.'

'Not at all, not at all. I need only speak to the Clerk of Works. If he made any difficulty, the Vice-Chancellor would give me his full support. You shall certainly have a room – *would* have a room, that is to say.'

'Thank you very much, sir. I suppose I'd better move in on Tuesday. No point in wasting time. It will be wonderful to get on with my research.' Clout hoped that he was managing a kind of learned glow. 'It's been rather held up lately.'

'To *get on* with your research?' Gingrass had removed his expensive pipe from his mouth and was giving his former pupil a slow uncomprehending stare.

'Franz Kafka and the tradition of symbolic fiction.' As he named this beguiling but still rather nebulous undertaking, Clout almost persuaded himself that it was already far advanced towards academic respectability. Everything, he felt, was coming his way – and it was the marvellous girl who was responsible. Only his determination not to be turfed into some corner of England remote from her light and presence had sustained him through this onslaught upon Gingrass. As for the demand for a room – hadn't she, amazingly, intimated something like a resolution to come and seek him out some day? Perhaps, with further luck, he could get an attic room, and they could again climb out on the roof, and sit together on the parapet gazing out over the park and the city and the distant countryside for ever and ever. For this was a degree of familiarity beyond which, at the moment, Clout's mind just didn't stray. But at the same time he was already organizing his bliss on economical and progressive lines. If he could simultaneously be improving his acquaintance with the girl and getting on with his novel, and winkling a good part of his living out of the Shufflebothams simply for writing what might turn out to be a second publishable book, a high-class critical one suitable, say, for Messrs Faber and Faber...

Clout had got as far as this in pleasing reverie when an uneasy sense came to him that perhaps he had admitted an element of *hubris* into his thinking. Certainly there was something in Gingrass' expression that suggested a dollop of nemesis coming his way. Or it might be fairer to say that Gingrass resembled a fifth-rate boxer who, having been forced right back on the ropes, suddenly sees his chance of getting in a dirty one to the kidneys. 'Kafka?' Gingrass was saying. 'Symbolic fiction? My dear Clout, you haven't got the idea of the Shufflebotham Award at all. You can't hold it simply to go on with some present bit of research. You have to embark upon something quite new.' Gingrass paused. 'And biographical.'

'Biographical? Well, I suppose that Kafka...'

'Put Kafka out of your head. There's a prescribed subject. The Alderman Shufflebotham Student must work upon the biography of a deceased eminent native.'

'You mean someone like Pocahontas, or Oroonoko the Royal Slave?'

'Certainly not. A deceased eminent native of the country. Or, of course, of the city. I made a particular point of that when the conditions were framed. If Council accept the biography as fit for publication, then the Alderman Shufflebotham Student is given the title of Alderman Shufflebotham Fellow.' Gingrass paused dramatically. 'Think of that.'

There was no doubt that Gingrass was now enjoying himself. And Clout couldn't really complain. Having bullied the wretched man into virtually awarding him the Shufflebotham, he must just submit to being nicely had over its conditions. 'Can I choose?' he asked. 'I mean can I nose out an eminent deceased native for myself?'

'I'm afraid not. The subject for research is nominated – or perhaps it's designated: I'd have to look that up – by the Professor. Of course, it has happened only once before.'

'And whom did you nominate then?'

'Naturally, Alderman Shufflebotham himself. Anything else would have been highly improper.'

'I see. And who did him – wrote the biography, I mean?'

'I did.' Gingrass appeared surprised at the question. 'It was considered the right thing – the handsome thing, you know. There's nothing in the conditions ruling out the appointment of a very senior man as Student.'

Clout's astonishment made him rash. 'You mean to say that you researched into the life of this Shufflebotham person, just for the sake of four hundred quid?'

'And the title – you forget that.' Gingrass was now in high good humour again, and entirely unoffended.

'You mean that *you* are – ?'

'Certainly. Professor of Literature and Alderman Shufflebotham Fellow. Until, that is to say, you succeed me, as I hope you will do. I shall then be Sometime.'

'Sometime?'

'Professor of Literature and Sometime Alderman Shufflebotham Fellow. I have a great regard for these traditional academic terms.' As he said this, Gingrass put on another of his smiles. This one was a blending of the merry with the ironic, and modestly intimated that Gingrass, like the Shakespearian Tragic Hero, was a being mysteriously, but definitively superior to his environment. 'Mind you, Clout, as a subject Shufflebotham had his limitations. It would have been disingenuous to exhibit him as a man of wide cultivation or extensive views. The salient feature of his public career was an implacable opposition to trolley-buses. He regarded tram-cars as virtually the only rational mode of public conveyance. One might even say the only morally and ethically defensible mode of public conveyance. It was a passion with him. He fearlessly put his great fortune behind it.'

'I see. How did he come by his great fortune?'

'By manufacturing tram-cars. Shufflebotham was a realist. I made that the theme of my biography. You will find your own man rather different.'

Clout felt that this could hardly be regretted. He was quite sure that the definitive life of – Shufflebotham would be beyond him. On the other hand he hadn't any large hopes that among those eminent deceased natives of the region who might be regarded as *en disponibilité*, this tiresome Gingrass would nominate or designate one with any very superior attractions. And apparently he had already done the job. Clout's own quarry had been singled out from the herd, and presently the Council of the University would give the formal signal for the chase to begin. It seemed rather an arbitrary arrangement, and Clout doubted whether, under such conditions, he would discover in himself much of the temper of the hunter. He looked at Gingrass, who had risen and was drifting about the room. This was one of the man's most irritating habits. In face of it, there seemed incivility in remaining seated, fussiness in standing up, and rashness in concluding that one was being blessedly dismissed. But on this occasion Clout decided to take it as definitely intimating leave to quit. He got to his feet. 'Can't I know yet?' he asked.

'Who your man is?' Gingrass shook his head. 'I'm afraid not.' He contrived to combine his roguish expression, indicative of cheerful conspiracy between kindred spirits, with a solemnity doing due deference to his own exalted position. 'Council doesn't like anything premature in these matters.' Gingrass sat down again and crossed his legs. 'Well,' he said, 'I must be getting over to a committee.'

As Clout had been edging towards the door and now actually had his hand on the knob, this ancient formula of Gingrass' was irritatingly gratuitous. But Clout would have judged his own disposition to be entirely shabby if he had felt, at the moment, other than vastly charitable. He was being restored – even if it was on mildly imbecile terms – to an institution in which the girl had shown interest, and to which she had intimated an intention of returning again. Clout made becoming noises to Gingrass and withdrew. He walked through the corridors – they were now the sacred corridors – in a daze.

His abstraction was so deep, indeed, that he cornered injudiciously and bumped into a young woman carrying a pile of books.

4

The young woman had a mass of dark hair tumbling over her shoulders. It would no longer have been quite fair to say she looked impudent, but she was certainly still the same Sadie. Clout was flushed as he scrambled up from recovering the scattered books. And Sadie Sackett, although she firmly hadn't stooped, was flushed too. 'Hullo,' she said uncertainly. And she added, as it were after a full stop: 'Colin.'

'Hullo, Sadie.' They oughtn't to be embarrassed. What if they had held hands for a group photograph? What if he had, in a highly experimental way, made love to her in the little room housing his select collection of modern literary masterpieces? You can't go far in such circumstances – not while on the glazen shelves keep watch Thomas and Ezra, guardians of the faith. It had all been extremely innocent. Still, she was the first girl he had ever kissed. And now they were both distinguishably agitated. 'I didn't think you'd still be here,' he said. The words struck him, on utterance, as a little lacking in the felicitous.

'I've got a job in the Library.' Sadie's books were now restored to her, and the pile was so considerable that she was keeping it in place by a downward pressure of her chin. Recovering his senses, Clout took the whole lot from her firmly. She found this perplexing – rather as if a foreigner had walked up to her, clicked his heels, and loudly pronounced his own name. 'And I'm going there now,' she said.

'Then, come along.' They went down first a small staircase and then a big one. There still weren't many people about. Their footsteps sounded with an awkward loudness on the uncarpeted treads. 'It's nearly four years,' Clout said. This time, he was positively horrified by his own speech – or rather by the tone of it, which was heavy with a maudlin sentimentality. In one who had met his eternal destiny practically within the hour, it was unbecoming, to say the least. But of course it was no more than a sort of reflex action. Those had been the accents which, at eighteen, he had supposed prescriptive in any incipiently amatory situation. And Sadie was associated in his mind with that.

But this time she wasn't put out. 'Did you get through?' she asked.

He glanced at her sideways – and with difficulty, since his own chin was now part of an awkward pincer movement. 'Get through?'

'The exam, or whatever it was. At Oxford.'

'Oh – I see.' Clout realized that he was, in fact, to some extent a foreigner, and that he was going to have intermittent trouble with the idiom. 'Yes, I got the degree, all right.'

'That's wonderful. I'm so glad!'

Clout experienced misgiving. Sadie was a very good sort of person. She had spoken with an honest, loyal satisfaction that made him feel potentially shifty. 'It's something entirely dim,' he said. 'Failure's pretty well unknown, even among the candidates from Lapland and Tierra del Fuego.'

If Sadie felt snubbed she didn't show it. But she did now allow herself a drift of cheerful, unsubtle mockery. 'And you haven't even come back talking like Gingrass or the BBC.'

'There's something to be said for old Gingrass.' For some reason Clout had become anxious to explain his own situation. 'He's getting me a niche of sorts about the place.'

'At the varsity? On the Staff?' Sadie's pleasure was again spontaneous – but this time he suspected that she had also a sense of a situation to be confronted. And for a moment she seemed glad of a diversion, for she had taken a couple of swift paces forward and opened the Library door. 'Just dump them down on the nearest table,' she said. 'I'll cope later. I'm off to lunch.'

'Come and have it with me, Sadie.' Now, at last, Clout was satisfied with the note he'd struck. It had expressed the exact truth: that Sadie was an old friend whom it was fun to meet again. 'In town, if the refectory hasn't started.'

'Oh, all right. And the refectory opened yesterday.'

Clout smiled at her. He remembered that this wasn't an ungracious speech; it was a formula indicating that Sadie intended to go Dutch, and would pay her own one-and-ten-pence. He realized, with proper mortification, that he had been forming the notion of taking her to a restaurant he couldn't afford, presumably simply to show off. This return-of-the-native business held some pitfalls that were entirely crude. 'That's fine,' he said. 'I'm down to Mum's last P.O.'

Sadie, as he had hoped, was delighted by this command of their ancient language. 'And mine's a book of stamps,' she said. 'But come on.'

The refectory, some sort of hangar that might have been reared to accommodate the last of the big dirigibles, was almost deserted. In no time they had shoved their soup and stew past the till and were facing each other across a narrow table. Clout told himself that it ought to be with a sort of humorous incredulity that he now recalled just what Sadie Sackett's first appeal had consisted in. She had been a creature infinitely mysterious and remote. How absurd! Or at least it seemed absurd now, when he had so powerful a sense that her attractiveness consisted entirely in her being familiar. Even as a physical object she would be that. The feel of her waist – supposing it wasn't ruled out by his late miracle – would be just a matter of cosy reminiscence. And how queer that he should once have judged enigmatical a girl who was so completely the girl next door. Twin semi-detached villas might have sheltered her family and his. They were looking at each other now with delighted – and of course entirely unexcited – understanding. They shared hundreds of assumptions – for instance, that soup should contain a lot of barley and chopped leek and exhibit an iridescent surface of free fat. It was true that he already had a rather similar feeling about his marvellous girl – for the first time Clout found himself involved in a comparison – but in that case it was an intuition of vast reaches of unexplored compatibilities that was in question. With Sadie both his agreements and his disagreements would be entirely circumscribed and homely. He was delighted to have tumbled upon her. He launched into a lively and satirical account of his late triumphant encounter with Gingrass.

Sadie had never heard of the Shufflebotham Award. She was sure almost nobody had. It must have been kept more or less dark while Gingrass himself was having the initial enjoyment of it. They fell to random and ill-informed guessing as to the identity of the eminent deceased native next to be celebrated. And then Clout remembered that the Award wasn't yet, after all, quite in the bag. He had a rival to whom Gingrass might conceivably still treacherously turn. 'Sadie,' he asked, 'do you know one Lumb?'

'Wun Lum – a Chinese?'

'No, no – a chap called Lumb! He'd like the Shufflebotham too.'

'Oh – George Lumb. Can't you both have the Shufflebotham thing?'

'No – just one of us. And I'm the chap.'

'Oh well, George can't want it too badly. He's got a job – cataloguing somebody's books.' Sadie was silent for a moment, and Clout discerned with unexpected annoyance that she was sorry to hear of this George Lumb's missing out on anything. 'You'd like George,' she added. 'He's terribly keen on Lawrence.'

Clout wasn't clear that he'd any longer find this a decided reason for liking anyone. 'You know him well?' he asked. 'Isn't he – ?' He was going to say: 'cross-eyed and a stammerer,' but had the good manners to alter this to: 'by way of being a writer?'

'Oh, yes. I'm sure he's going to be a good one. He and I went on an expedition in the vac, looking for cattle.'

'Why ever did you do that?' Clout finished his soup, reached for his stew, and stared at Sadie.

'Highland cattle. For me to dance to.' Sadie appeared perfectly serious. 'We wanted to see.'

'I can't think what you're talking about.'

'Colin, you surely haven't forgotten Gudrun dancing to the cattle in *Women in Love*?' Sadie was sincerely reproachful. 'George and I wanted to see if it would work. I was to do the slow, hypnotizing convulsion of the dance. And feel a terrible shiver of fear and pleasure. I was to dance right up to the cattle, and discover if I felt the electric pulse from their breasts running into my hands.'

'And this Lumb?'

'George was to watch the cattle, and notice if they breathed heavily with helpless fear and fascination.'

'How absolutely revolting. The man must be an imbecile.'

'He's very nice.' Sadie was suddenly angry without being in the least offended. 'And it was fun. But, of course, if you've become a prig, Colin Clout, it must sound silly.'

'Perhaps you danced for Lumb like Anna in *The Rainbow* too?'

This was an insulting question, and Clout was instantly ashamed of it. He rather feared that Sadie might quietly rise and quit. But she only frowned, as if making the effort to remember that he'd been away four years and probably picked up new ways. 'We haven't quite got each other's wave-length, yet – have we?' she asked. 'But never mind. By the way, are you married?'

This question, although it seemed merely absurd, in fact staggered him. It staggered him as suddenly revealing an unspeakable danger he had escaped. After all, he *might* already be married. Several of his fellow research students at Oxford had been, although goodness knew what they lived on. He might already be married – in which case what had come to him that morning would have been a hideous mockery. Clout felt sweat on his forehead at the mere thought of it. 'Of course I'm not married,' he said. 'What could put such an idea in your head?'

For the first time since their reunion, Sadie hesitated. 'I saw you earlier this morning,' she said. 'Before you actually bumped into me.'

'Oh.' Clout was wary.

'With a girl. And I thought perhaps she was your wife.'

A warm glow of pleasure suddenly suffused Clout's being. He recalled that he had always known little Sadie Sackett to have a strong streak of perceptiveness. Now she had been intuitively aware of the deep, deep intimacy which had so magically established itself between himself and the girl right at the first dawning of their acquaintanceship. And she had very naturally taken the tie to be already the marital one. 'Oh, no,' he said self-consciously. And he added as carelessly as he could: 'Just what made you think of such a thing?'

Sadie considered. 'Well, you seemed to be showing her round, and explaining the place. And she didn't really seem to be attending. Not, I mean, to you.'

'What do you mean – not attending to me?' Although he asked this question stupidly, Clout concluded that he must have entirely misheard what Sadie said. For her words, as he had picked them up, made, of course, no sense.

'She was seeming to attend to you, but really she was busy thinking of other things. And it's a way one sometimes sees married people – even quite young ones – behaving.'

For a moment invisible hands, very cold and very clammy, seemed to have felt their way beneath Clout's clothes, and to be clamping themselves about his body. Then he realized that he was in the presence of an absurdity requiring laughter – rather loud laughter, which, with a mingling of relief and embarrassment, he presently heard sound through the almost deserted refectory. Sadie was probably quite quick at understanding people like herself – or like him, for that matter. But the marvellous girl had a different sort of breeding behind her – not better but just different, Clout magnanimously interpolated to himself – and the outward and visible signs of it had led Sadie entirely astray. That was it. The marvellous girl had a poise, a delicious air of detachment, which Sadie had comically read as sheer inattention and absence of interest. Clout finished his stew with renewed appetite. 'I think you're terribly acute,' he said humorously. 'But you haven't got that one at all right. The girl isn't, as a matter of fact, anybody that I know at all well.'

There was a moment's silence. Sadie was looking at him curiously. It was as if she suspected that, one way or another, there had been something disingenuous in his last speech. And, of course, there had been. He was concealing the plain fact that, at that morning's breakfast, the girl had not yet existed for him. It came to him, with a hint of surprise and remorse, that although he had put in quite a lot of time with Sadie once, he had never been prompted to tell her the ghost of a fib. He stood up, went back to the counter, and fetched two cups of coffee. After all, this renewal of acquaintance was quite an occasion, and he could without ostentation offer Sadie a fourpenny drink. He rather expected her now to ask the girl's name, since it was one of the wholesome if unrefined conventions of the place that you uttered questions when they came into your head. And this question would certainly call his bluff. But Sadie said nothing. She simply took the coffee – some of which he had managed to slop into the saucer – as if it was a present she valued receiving. The cups were of some plastic substance that went squishy under heat; presumably they had been produced by the genius of a great nation at war, and taken over from a derelict NAAFI when the University started up again.

Sadie had a packet of cigarettes, and they smoked. 'As a matter of fact,' Clout said suddenly, 'I'd never seen that girl before. She was just peering in, so I took her around. I don't even know her name.' He sat back, relieved. That was honest. There was no call on him to go on, and announce his grand passion. He wasn't a bit less convinced of its existence, but he did have a clearer view of its extravagance. When Shakespeare had to put across a roughly analogous story about Romeo, he abandoned blank verse and slipped in a couple of sonnets. Clout could hardly continue his remarks to Sadie Sackett in elaborately concatenated rhyme. So he resolved on a change of subject. 'Is this Library job interesting?' he asked. 'Are you glad you've stayed on?'

'I'd call it not too bad.' Sadie was philosophical. 'It was either that, of course, or taking a Dip Ed and turning schoolmarm. I didn't want to do that – although I suppose it's not too bad, either.'

'I see.' Clout was aware of an obscure sense of guilt attending his perception that there was, for the time being at least, something missing from Sadie's life. He looked round the refectory almost in the hope of his glance falling on an adequate and biddable young man. But now there wasn't a soul in the place except themselves. 'Well,' he continued, 'I expect you made a wise choice. Books are no doubt a good deal less annoying than kids.'

'Oh – I don't know that I'd mind kids.'

Cloud was disconcerted by this. It sounded ambiguous. 'They're lively, of course,' he said hastily. 'And a library can't be that.'

'Not a university library, anyway. Public libraries are better.' Sadie appeared to be drawing upon stores of professional knowledge. 'They get eccentrics and drunks and even suicides.'

'Suicides?'

'Yes – we had it in a lecture. Apparently they open appropriate books – Schopenhauer or Sartre or Gissing or Hardy – at particularly suitable passages, and then swallow something. You're told to look out for anybody writhing or frothing or gushing asunder in the midst.'

'No doubt it makes a change. But you're not likely, as you say, to get any excitement in a university library.'

'Definitely not. Not anywhere in a university.'

'Exactly. They're dull places. Think of this Shufflebotham thing.'

'It certainly doesn't seem to promise much fun, Colin.' Sadie rose. 'Well, I'd better be getting back. It's nice that you'll be back.'

'It's nice of you to say so.'

For a moment they looked at each other in some faint uncertainty. Then they returned their squishy cups punctiliously to the counter – for they were both well-drilled children of the State – and left the refectory. They could have no notion how fallacious would prove the generalization upon which they had so sagely concluded.

5

Clout's attic was up to expectation. Indeed it was beyond that by some fifteen feet, being tucked away high in the gable of a surviving fragment of the original Caroline house which was buried in the Georgian one. In shape the room was a short triangular tunnel, running without fuss from the door at one end to the window at the other. On either side of the window, behind creaking cupboard doors, further triangular tunnels, crammed with lumber, vanished into gloom and distance. Clout had not ventured to explore these beckoning infinities, but it occurred to him that they would at least provide the mind with territory upon which to roam at large, should he later find his actual *Lebensraum* oppressive. At present he was very well satisfied with his quarters – or rather with having secured them. But when he looked beyond, he was conscious of some anxiety.

For one thing, his position around the place still appeared to be undefined. Gingrass, it was true, had shoved him in here, and told him of certain tutorial classes he would be expected to hold in a subject called the Higher Literary Form. But Gingrass had said nothing more about the Shufflebotham, upon which the whole financial feasibility of his new existence seemed to depend. And now the first day of Full Term had arrived. Its most obvious manifestation was echoing up the several staircases now; a throb, a soft pulse of menacing sound constituted by the heavy feet and unmodulated voices of the student body taking possession *en masse*. Presently there would be the ritual of the Pig Market. And Clout supposed that he ought to attend.

He took his gown from a hook behind the door and eyed it with misgiving. According to Dr Johnson's well-known poem, this lugubrious black object ought to exercise a strong contagion on any likely youth coming into possession of it, infecting him with the fever of renown. No doubt renown had come into Johnson's head chiefly because the word rhymed with the garment being celebrated. Still, the general proposition remained. Clout, as he wriggled himself into the enfolding subfusc, ought to be reflecting with excitement that he might go a long way in *this*. But did he? He doubted whether his publisher (when he had a publisher) would suggest adorning the dust-jacket of his novel in the manner of Kafka (when he had finished his novel in the manner of Kafka) with a photograph demonstrating that its author was indubitably Clout, BA, B Litt. Very probably Gingrass was right, and what applied to the wretched Lumb applied to him, Clout, too. Perhaps he ought to have retreated to Lake Garda, measured himself against *Buddenbrooks* or *À la recherche du temps perdu*, and decided about himself one way or the other.

But if he had done that, he might never have met the girl. Indeed, if ever in the course of his past life he had performed even a single trivial action other than he had in fact done, it was almost certain that from it there would have flowed a chain of consequences which would have resulted in his never meeting her. Clout found that he was meditating upon this almost metaphysical fact a good deal. It was a speculation that took his mind off the question of whether, after all, he was in the least likely ever to meet her again.

Deciding to take a plunge, Clout ran downstairs. The older-established students were standing about in large mixed groups of men and women, talking loudly. Simultaneously, and chiefly by intuitive processes, they were working out the cliques and couples into which they would presently sort themselves for the duration of the term. Some were confidently taking up again, at the precise point at which they had been broken off, the relationships of four months ago. Some had been planning a reshuffle, an exchange, a fade-out, an infidelity. Some were aware of difficulties ahead, precipitated by rash letter-writing during the boredom of suburban vacations. Cut off from all this of the passions and affections, the new students stood in rows before bewildering notice-boards, anxiously copying lecture-hours into large printed time-tables and then rubbing them out again. These still believed that a university is a home of the intellect.

It all made – Clout reflected – a wonderful field for the artist's brooding eye. He wondered if Redbrick realism was the line of his rival Lumb. What Kafka, of course, would 'do' – Clout remembered to put the magical word between its inverted commas – was the bewilderment: the ambiguities and the false casts and the *culs-de-sac*. Nobody would be quite sure whether anybody else was a student or a professor; and there would be intermittent doubt about the place being a university at all, and not, say, a maternity hospital or the municipal abattoir. And, in particular...

'Mr Clout, sir!'

Clout turned and saw advancing upon him an elderly man dressed in a frock-coat with enormous brass buttons. It was Gedge, the head porter. Gedge would have been no good to Kafka. Nobody could advance the hypothesis that Gedge was perhaps really the Vice-Chancellor or the Reader in Biometrics. Gedge was plainly too important to be either. And now Gedge had spoken. Clout's position was at last defined.

Mr Clout sir was decisive. Students, however senior or however affluent, were never other than plain *Mr Jones* or *Miss Brown* to Gedge. *Mr Jones sir* (or *Miss Brown miss*) at once elevated the person addressed to a position on the Staff. From the large twilight of young persons of indeterminate status – post-graduate students, senior scholars, part-time assistant demonstrators – it was the voice of Gedge that summoned to this clearer day. Clout was so overwhelmed by the voice thus having pronounced so early in his own interest that he was unconscious for a time of a large official-looking envelope which Gedge was now thrusting at him rather as if he were a pillar-box. 'With the Registrar's compliments, Mr Clout, sir.' Gedge reiterated the crucial formula plainly on the benevolent supposition that the young man couldn't, at present, hear it too often. 'Better take it in with you,' he added confidentially. 'The bell's just going to go.'

At that moment the bell went, as it did punctually at every hour throughout the day. It was an electric bell of almost incredible shrillness, guaranteed to dominate any uproar – and even (which was its principal function) to stop the most self-absorbed lecturer dead in the middle of a sentence. On this occasion it was the signal for a stampede. The new students, previously warned, knew that the moment had come at which they must present themselves for the approval of those professors under whom they aspired to study. Many had a muzzy notion that some sort of quota operated, and that they must use their elbows now if they were to be given the best chance of using their brains later on. And they all – Clout reflected as he received a jab in the chest – *had* elbows. He was borne along in the rush. But he managed to tear open his envelope and draw out a small sheaf of papers. He squinted at them and distinguished the word 'Shufflebotham.' So it was all right. The electric bell was still ringing.

'Abominable!' Another hurrying figure, gowned like himself, and whom he vaguely remembered as a lecturer in French or German, suddenly shouted in his ear. 'I've never got used to it. I'd rather have the bell in Greene's books – the cracked one.'

'The cracked one?' Manfully Clout bellowed back. 'Graham?'

'Yes – I mean no, It's the bell that's cracked.' The gowned figure reeled momentarily under the impact of a charging Amazon in spectacles. 'Always turning up in Greene. Cracked school-bell. Symbol of childhood's misery. But this one's a symbol of the misery of senescence... Aren't you Clout?'

'Yes – I'm Clout.'

'You've come back?'

'Yes – I've come back.'

'Good God!' Rather unwisely, the gowned figure made a theatrical gesture with his arms. At once he was adroitly savaged in his unguarded ribs, and disappeared gasping. There was a moment of maximum chaos as muscular young bodies jammed the double doorway of the great hall. Clout, whose instincts were modest, endeavoured to edge away from heaving bosoms and wriggling buttocks, and succeeded in standing on the toes of old Miss Harlock, the only woman professor. A moment later the *mêlée* thinned, and he found himself in the comparative security of the interior. The students, who had been jabbering excitedly in the corridor, fell silent here. The Pig Market was going to begin.

'Congratulations, Mr Clout.' It was possible that Miss Harlock had escaped without anything so positive as a fractured toe, for she appeared to bear Clout no malice. 'I have just heard about your appointment. Most interesting. It has always been my own ambition to write a biography, but of course it is something that doesn't come an entomologist's way. The ephemera are fascinating, but they would afford very little scope. Other forms of insect life – our friends in the Department of Education come to mind – have possibilities. Unfortunately I take the old-fashioned view that biography should conduce to edification, which entirely rules them out. What a large number of new students! The heart quite sinks. But happily students are a sort of mayfly too. Except those that hang on or drift back.' Having thus avenged herself, Miss Harlock gave Clout a kind smile and moved away.

Clout seized the opportunity of taking another peep at his papers. There was something about a Sir Joscelyn Jory. He knew that the name ought to convey something, but he couldn't remember what it was. And now Gingrass was waving to him. Gingrass had clearly got in early in order to set up his little pen cosily close to a steam radiator. On a trestle table in front of him were tidily disposed piles of syllabuses and entrance forms. Gingrass, although out to peddle these commodities to all comers, preserved an air of tolerant detachment, like a person of the largest cultivation who has taken a temporary job among high-class antiques. All round the sides of the hall similar pens, pounds, or booths had been set up for the several Faculties and Departments, and the professors and their dependent hierarchies were settling in to do business. The centre of the floor was occupied by the new students, who were expected to take on the role of peripatetic scholars, and move hither and thither in the endeavour to provide themselves with the ground-plan of a coherent education. Their efforts were somewhat impeded by the fact that, for their future teachers, this was a social as well as a learned occasion. The Staff was now united – if it was ever quite that – for the first time in months, and the peculiar arrangement of the Pig Market encouraged visiting. One or two enterprising ladies were making preparations to brew tea on primus-stoves, and thus establish themselves as centres of attraction when weariness descended half-way through the morning. Junior lecturers hailed each other with inquiries about sports-cars, Greek papyri, allusively designated girls, forthcoming scientific papers, or with proposals for meals, drinks, shared lodgings, or precipitate flight to one or another of the better remunerated forms of manual labour. It was all very familiar to Clout. Only he was seeing it from a new angle.

Jory, of course, was the family name of the former owners of Old Hall. Clout was relieved that he had remembered this in time, and not made a fool of himself by asking Gingrass. Sir Joscelyn was presumably a Jory who had attained to some celebrity, and the next most appropriate person after Alderman Shufflebotham himself for the purpose of biographical commemoration. His name suggested a romantic – conceivably, indeed, a heroic – ambience; one might come across such a one in the list of those who had sailed with Drake or ridden with Charles. But of course names were deceptive, and Sir Joscelyn might be quite a modern worthy – a manufacturer, say, of humble objects of domestic utility, knighted by Mr Stanley Baldwin for political and public services in the north of England. No doubt there would be some preliminary hint of the truth in the communication that had arrived from the Registrar.

Clout squeezed into a corner from which he could be summoned to assist his chief at need. But Gingrass had several henchmen of greater seniority, both male and female; and they were all having a wonderful time determining the destinies of the queue of young people applying to them. Clout was able to settle down with his papers. They didn't tell him much. Sir Joscelyn had flourished in the first half of the nineteenth century; and the Shufflebotham Student was to write a definitive biography in which there should be included a critical excursus upon Sir Joscelyn's scientific attainments. Some attention should be given to Sir Joscelyn's near relations and family circle. But his younger brother, Edward Jory, might with advantage be virtually excluded from consideration, since it was possible that his life might later lend itself to independent study. The Council of the University had ascertained that the writing of a life of Sir Joscelyn Jory would meet with the approval of his great-grandson, Sir John Jory of New Hall. Sir John had further intimated that he would give proper facilities for research to the University's nominee.

It didn't sound very exciting, but on the whole Clout was disposed to take a cheerful view. Probably Sir Joscelyn had been a bit of a bore, and his scientific attainments might well prove to have been in some field that was both dreary and incomprehensible. But he had owned Old Hall, the subsequent short history of which as a place of higher education Clout regarded with decent piety; and his descendants now owned New Hall, which was a substantial mansion about three miles away. It would be interesting to push in on that. With luck Clout might be able to fill several notebooks with observations on the habits of the landed gentry – a class of society to which his access had hitherto been frankly restricted. Clout's spirits rose. He was grateful to Gingrass for having himself weighed in and got Alderman Shufflebotham out of the way. Clout could already do Shufflebothams on his head, since their kind had sat immediately and obviously above his kind for generations. But Jorys would be something new. It occurred to Clout that his current literary venture was perhaps a trifle narrowly conceived (*The Examination* had, in fact, only one character, called C) and that after all there was something to be said for a panoramic fiction, confidently ranging over the several classes of English society. And to this a way was unexpectedly opening up before him. Excited by this discovery, he now turned and waved his papers at Gingrass. 'I say, Professor,' he called out cheerfully, 'what was the science my man went in for?'

'Aha!' Gingrass broke off his labours by simply waving away a seriously inquiring but heavily pustular youth whom he judged unattractive. 'So the news has broken, my dear boy, and the Jorys are all around you? I'm not sure whether Sir Joscelyn should be called a scientist or a scholar. However, I'm certain you'll find him interesting – although, mind you, it might be better fun to do Edward.'

'The one who's to be left out, because he may be written about by somebody else?'

'Just that.' Gingrass laughed – and his laugh was at once so robust and so benevolent that a girl waiting to enroll for French visibly lost her heart to it and immediately changed queues. 'But it's no more, you'll have recognized, than a form of words. I suggested it to Sir John myself. The truth is that Edward Jory was a bit of a black sheep, and even after a century the family isn't keen on throwing a limelight on him.'

'I see.' Being without old Miss Harlock's conviction that biography ought infallibly to conduce to edification, Clout at once felt rather defrauded by this imposed exclusion of Edward Jory from his purview. But he could, of course, find out about him even if it wasn't for the purpose of publication. 'But Sir Joscelyn', he asked, 'was entirely respectable?'

'Well, he was eccentric. He was a very considerable eccentric.' Gingrass turned away for a moment, grabbed several forms from waiting students, and initialled them without a glance. 'I don't mind telling you that's why I felt it wise to turn down Lumb. On sheer ability, of course, he'd have had to have the Shufflebotham, without a doubt.'

'Yes, of course.' Clout didn't find his feelings for the unknown Lumb growing any fonder. 'You mean – ?'

'That creative itch. If he set it loose on Joscelyn Jory – well, we might be in difficulty. A writer with a real sense of comedy, and a feeling for character, and a graceful and attractive style, would be too dangerous altogether.'

'So you decided on me.' Clout took some comfort in the fact that he didn't seem to be experiencing what is called deep mortification before these confidences; he simply had a wholesome wish to get behind Gingrass and kick. 'Were Sir Joscelyn's scientific interests eccentric?'

'Ah, that. Well, he was a tapheimaphil, as you know. He cultivated the grave. Edward was commonly interested in a less narrow bed.'

'Joscelyn loved tombs?' Clout was rather startled, and even wondered for a moment whether the whole project in which he was becoming involved was a product of Gingrass' ghastly notion of the humorous. 'You mean he used to go out and scrabble at them?'

'In a sense, yes. But a sublimated sense, as the jargon is. I don't think he was positively necrophilous. But he was an amateur archaeologist, and tombs were his great line. That's why he built the mausoleum, out there in the park.'

'Yes, of course – I've read about it. But it didn't stick in my head.'

'Go and have a look at the mausoleum now, my dear Clout. It has something of the stamp of your man's character, I dare say.'

'If you can spare me, I think I will.' Clout was quite glad to get away both from Gingrass and from the Pig Market. 'But what do I do then? I mean, how do I start?'

'Do some background reading in published sources, and read up about the family where you can. Then, when you've ceased being an absolute ignoramus, I'll give you an introduction to Sir John. He's not a bad fellow.'

'Thank you very much.' Clout got to his feet. 'Are there any other Jorys left, apart from this Sir John at New Hall?'

Gingrass shook his head. 'Not many, I believe. But Edward Jory has some descendants – legitimate descendants, that is – about the country.'

6

At a table near the door Sadie Sackett and two companions were issuing library tickets to such of the new students as thought to apply for them. Clout stopped on his way out. He had hardly seen Sadie during the past few days, and rather suspected that she had been avoiding him. But he was too full of his fresh information to stand on his dignity at the moment. 'Trade brisk?' he asked.

Sadie shook her head so that her dark hair circled her shoulders. 'Rotten. It hasn't come to them yet that they may need books. They think getting a degree is a matter of attending lectures and writing down as much of them as they can remember afterwards.'

'So it is.'

'Well, yes. But we can't admit it in the Library, or we'd all lose our jobs. How's Shufflebotham?'

'Come out and I'll tell you about him.'

Sadie hesitated, and took a circumspect glance round the Pig Market. There seemed to be nobody about who would take the slightest exception to her abandoning her unfrequented post for a while. 'Where to?' she asked.

'The mausoleum.'

Sadie stared. 'Why ever do you want to go there?'

'Because of the Shufflebotham. It seems my man was a tapheimaphil.'

'I never heard of such a thing.'

'I dare say. My guess is Gingrass invented the word on the spot. But think of Sir Thomas Browne, and what not. Some hang above the tombs.'

'Some weep in empty rooms.'

'I, when the iris blooms, remember.' Clout took Sadie by the arm as she came from behind the table – it was fun that she remembered bits of verse they used to chant at each other – and led her out to the terrace. 'Sir Joscelyn Jory,' he said. 'That's my man. He owned Old Hall. And built the mausoleum. And had a bad-hat brother I'm to ignore.'

'Are they the Jorys that live at New Hall nowadays?'

'Yes. The chap there is Joscelyn's great-grandson. I'm to delve into his family papers.'

'But surely that's what George is doing!' Sadie was perplexed. 'How very odd.'

'George?' They were walking down the broad avenue that led to the east side of the park, and they had already left the rows of labs behind them. But Clout now came to a halt. 'George?' he repeated suspiciously. 'Who's George?'

'George Lumb, of course. He's working at New Hall now. Not actually on family papers, perhaps – but cataloging the library.'

'But it's absurd. He nearly got the Shufflebotham, and didn't. But there he is – in on the Jorys, all the same. It must be one of Gingrass' idiotic tricks.'

Sadie shook her head. 'I don't think so. I believe it's just a coincidence. George was fed up with Gingrass, and went out and got this job on his own. Anyway, I'm glad.' Sadie spoke with less than her usual conviction. 'You'll like George. You'll be able to talk about – '

'Yes, I know.' The interruption came from Clout brusquely. 'We'll be able to jabber about D H Lawrence. What utter rot. And I'm quite sure Lumb's horrible.'

They walked in silence. 'I think I'll go back now,' Sadie presently said.

'Don't do that.' His tone was decently penitent. 'We're almost there. Let's just look inside.'

'Very well. But I think it's locked up. There was some fooling in it one night last term, and the V-C took a dark view. But we can try. I seem to remember it's not much more than a shell.'

'I've never had a look. And I don't know that there's much sense in poking about now.' Clout was suddenly depressed. Starting in to examine Sir Joscelyn's architectural folly seemed to typify the probable futility of the whole job that had been shovelled at him. And Sadie wasn't inspiring either. He rather wished he hadn't brought her. She only reminded him that his girl hadn't turned up again, and that he might stop here indefinitely, writing the lives of all the Jorys that ever were, without having the slightest rational ground for supposing that it would ever be otherwise. 'What a stupid affair!' he said. 'And it must have cost thousands.'

They had climbed a small hill, and the mausoleum was now in front of them. It had probably been modelled, Clout thought, on the celebrated affair at West Wycombe, but it had very little of the crazy impressiveness that Sir Francis Dashwood had achieved. It was a circular building, with half-hearted Ionic pillars engaged in the stone all the way round, and a dilapidated frieze of monotonously festooned urns on top. There was a single entrance closed by rusty iron gates, and here and there a few empty window-spaces, set very high up. These seemed to have no function at all, as the whole affair was without a roof, and one simply peered through them at the sky. Grasses and wild-flowers were sprouting everywhere between stone and stone, but this didn't lend anything that could be called a pleasing picturesqueness to the scene. Sadie studied it for some moments in silence. 'Stupid?' she said. 'Well, I suppose so. An enlightened landowner would have sunk the money in better cottages for the farm-labourers, or a row of alms-houses for the aged and deserving poor. But there's something to be said for a period in which rich men had the self-confidence to do queer things.'

'Nonsense – and, anyway, it's third-rate of its sort. Too late by nearly a hundred years. Not like the Hall.' Clout spoke rather roughly – perhaps because he found it obscurely tiresome that Sadie Sackett had no longer the large ingenuousness that he remembered in her.

Then he walked up to the gates and rattled them. 'But you're right about it being locked up. Let's go back. I don't think we'd get much kick out of a lot of mouldering Jorys.'

'But that wasn't the idea. Don't you remember? There's a bit about your Sir Joscelyn and his mausoleum in the University Handbook. I ought to have recalled it as soon as you said he was a thingummy.'

'A tapheimaphil?'

'Yes. He didn't intend the mausoleum for himself and all the future Jorys. It was to be a sort of museum of entombment upon historical principles. I suppose he was a collector as well as a student.'

'Of tombs and sarcophagi and grave-stones and things?' Clout looked at Sadie doubtfully. If she wasn't romancing, then he'd either entirely forgotten this odd bit of local lore or had never happened to acquire it.

'Yes, of course – and of canopic urns, and family vaults and baby mausoleums as well.'

'And, I suppose, a pyramid or two?'

Sadie nodded. 'That was probably in his plans. But it all didn't come to much. If it had, this would be a much more interesting place than it is.'

'Let's walk round it, and then clear out.'

They walked in silence. This corner of the park was very quiet. Nobody seemed to come near it. Suddenly Sadie stopped. 'I thought I heard something – from inside.'

'That's doves.'

Doves in considerable number were certainly cooing in the mausoleum. But Sadie didn't receive Clout's remark kindly. 'I know that's doves, you idiot. I think there's somebody moving about as well.'

'Impossible. You saw the gate's locked. Rabbits, I expect.'

'Look!' They had walked on again, and what had come into view was a ladder, its topmost rung resting against the sill of one of the window-like apertures high in the face of the building.

Clout judged Sadie's gesture unnecessarily dramatic. 'So what?' he said. 'Left by workmen, I suppose.'

'Look where it's been picked up from the grass. Clearly no time ago. Somebody's climbed in.'

'I don't see how they could – unless there's another ladder on the inside. And if they did, it's just some idiotic students. Come on, Sadie, for goodness sake.' Clout heard, with distaste, the quite unreasonable impatience in his own voice.

But Sadie didn't seem to mind. 'I'm going up,' she said. Before he could dissuade her, she had run to the ladder and was scaling it. Reaching the top, she swung her legs over the sill, sat down, and then turned to wave at him challengingly. 'Coming?' she called.

She was quite high up. He realized that if it was his lost girl who was behaving in this way he would be enchanted; indeed he was rather reminded of the way she had sat on the parapet of the Hall and dropped crumbs of mortar on the terrace below. Sadie now got to her feet and stood hazardously on the sill – apparently to get a better view of the interior. Clout ran forward to the ladder and climbed up beside her. At least there was no ladder on the other side. 'There you are,' he said. 'Nobody could get down.'

'But I've just seen somebody. A woman. She's disappeared somewhere below.' Sadie's voice was excited. 'She must have scrambled down this tremendous old ivy. Dusty but not dangerous. I'm going too.'

'I don't in the least see why you should.' The ivy had a trunk like a tree, and its branches seemed to niche themselves securely all over the place. So it certainly wasn't a particularly formidable descent. But Clout had some doubts about getting up again; and moreover if somebody was really exploring the mausoleum he didn't see why Sadie and he should barge in and interrupt. Sadie however was now clambering down, and he felt he had no choice but to follow. She had been right about the dust. He was coated in it and his lungs felt full of it by the time he arrived at the bottom. They stood side by side, looking and listening. Clout had a notion that Sadie wanted to take his hand – not by way of suggesting any reviving of their former flame, but because of an intuition that something was going

49

to happen; that the unexpected and disquieting was about to confront them.

It was warmer inside Sir Joscelyn Jory's mausoleum than it was without; their sensation as they looked up was of being at the bottom of a well so broad and shallow that the mild October sun reached down into it and soaked it. And the cooing of the doves was louder; they could be seen high up, comfortably tucked away wherever a stone had sufficiently crumbled to provide a shelf. It was evident now that this queer folly had never been completed. There seemed to have been a proposal to sheath it in marble that hadn't got very far; and four or five bays of arcading, with the beginning of a shallower arched gallery above, hinted at the sort of lay-out that this peculiarly funeral museum was to have assumed. The whole place breathed the double melancholy of achievement fallen into ruin and of intentions unfulfilled.

It was perfectly possible for more than one explorer to have withdrawn from observation – for the moment, at least – by slipping into one or another of the chapel-like recesses which had presumably been designed to house major exhibits. But nobody would remain invisible for long unless positively concerned to hide. They waited. There wasn't a sound. Clout turned to Sadie. 'You really think you saw somebody?' He found he was speaking in a half-whisper.

'Yes. A figure in grey – gliding silently amid the tombs. Do you think it would be a ghost?' Sadie, although she asked this satirically, had also lowered her voice.

'It might be Sir Joscelyn himself – but alive and in the flesh.' Clout's uneasiness for some reason prompted him to fantasy. 'All his life he had this obsession with the tomb. And it acted as some sort of inoculation – like Mithradates, you remember, and the poison. The poor old boy just can't *make* the tomb. It won't open for him. He lives on and on, haunting it.'

'Like the old man in Chaucer, striking the ground with his staff. "Leve moder, leet me in!" ' Sadie was delighted with this. 'But I think it's more probably a real ghost – a Jory one, of course. What about the bad-hat brother? I expect it's him. His spirit must be condemned to haunt the mausoleum, expiating some frightful crime. Let's conjure him, Colin.'

'Perhaps you'd like to try dancing for him.' Clout had recalled Sadie's exploit with the ridiculous Lumb.

But Sadie ignored this. 'Let's give a shout,' she said.

'Oh, rot. We'd better...'

'*Whatever Jory you are, appear!*'

Feeling herself challenged, Sadie had called out in a clear voice that rang through the mausoleum. And the effect was remarkable. Quite close to them, a young woman stepped into the open – a young woman in a grey dress. Clout took one glance at her, and stood dumbfounded. It was his girl. She took a step forward in the clear sunshine, and for a moment looked from one to the other with an equal lack of recognition. Then she gave an exclamation of surprise. Clout felt his head swim – it was now an old, familiar sensation – and realized that it was because she had smiled. 'Hullo,' she said quietly. 'Isn't this an odd way of meeting again? And how did you know my name?'

7

Rather curiously, Clout's first feeling was one of anxiety about Sadie. It was he who had proposed a walk to the mausoleum, and Sadie mightn't accept the marvellous girl's turning up like this at the end of it for the piece of pure chance that, in fact, it was. She might suppose that he had been planning to disconcert her in some way, or to exhibit her to his new acquaintance as something quaint and funny out of his past. It would be hateful if Sadie got anything like that in her head and was hurt by it.

But Sadie wasn't showing any sign of being disturbed; indeed, she was looking at the girl with a discreet curiosity that seemed entirely friendly. And she found something to say before Clout himself did. 'My name's Sadie Sackett,' she was announcing. 'And this is Colin Clout. But I don't at all understand what you've just said about *your* name.'

The girl was surprised. 'But I'm sure I heard you calling it. Jory. I'm Olivia Jory.'

Sadie laughed. 'And interested in your ancestors?'

'Well, yes – I am, rather.' Olivia Jory spoke with a shade of caution. 'Otherwise I wouldn't be poking about in this mausoleum.'

'Neither would Colin. You two have something in common.' Having said this, Sadie sat down composedly on a stone slab, put her knees and toes together, folded her hands in her lap, and assumed with a certain ironic obviousness the appearance of a disinterested spectator.

Clout didn't feel happy. He was wondering whether Olivia – it was the perfect name for her – had recognized in his present companion the impudent young woman whose hand he was holding in that wretched photograph. It seemed only too likely. Sadie's wasn't a very usual hair-do; and it was precisely now as it had been then. But that wasn't all. Since last seeing Olivia Jory, he had, by an amazing coincidence, indeed acquired an interest in her ancestors. But the Shufflebotham seemed to him a quite painfully fatuous thing to have to explain to her. And he couldn't be certain that she wouldn't find his suddenly accepted mission to research into the Jory family history impertinent rather than either admirable or amusing.

Yet all this, of course, was as nothing compared to the fearful joy of this unexpected and dramatic reunion. Moreover Olivia Jory, whatever she thought about Sadie, was looking at him now with open pleasure, as one might do on unexpectedly encountering an old and intimate friend. It was true that this wasn't quite the most satisfactory response that he could conceive; reserve, maidenly shamefastness, and a discernibly quickened respiratory system would be the ideal thing; nevertheless he might well be thankful for what he had got. And now it would be wise to speak up. This silent awe business was perfectly sincere. But a girl might feel a little of it was nicer than a lot. 'I'd better explain what Sadie means,' he said. 'You'll probably find it a bit odd. I'm to write a life of the Jory who built this place: Sir Joscelyn. It's part of my new job – the one, you know, I was hoping for.'

'How very interesting!' Olivia had started – but now she spoke with what seemed to Clout a disappointing air of polite unconcern. 'And is Miss Sackett to work on Joscelyn Jory too? Is it a partnership?'

'It has nothing to do with me.' Sadie remained composed on her slab. 'I don't go in for research. Mine's just a job in the Library. There's a small Jory collection there, by the way. I've just remembered it. It's tucked away in a small room nobody bothers about. Perhaps, Miss Jory, you'd like to have a poke about there, too?'

This wasn't so friendly. In fact the pause before that 'too' had been more barbed than anything Sadie commonly contrived. It was almost as if she had felt herself to have received a declaration of war. But Olivia – Clout noted with admiration – at once gave her an extra nice smile. 'That's very kind of you. Perhaps I'll come along one day. It's true that family history interests me very much.' She turned to Clout. 'You must think it funny. I didn't speak the other day of my connexion with Old Hall. But it would have sounded awkward. And, anyway, it's not a very direct one.'

'Are you a descendant of Sir Joscelyn's?'

Olivia shook her head. 'Oh no! Only of his younger brother.'

'Edward?'

'Yes – do you know about him?' She showed a swift interest. 'But I forgot. It's all part of your research.'

'Not Edward. I mean, I'm expressly not to do anything about him. Because somebody else may.'

'I think that very unlikely.' Olivia was amused. 'For one thing he didn't, being a younger brother, have Joscelyn's scope. He couldn't take it into his head – she waved at the mausoleum – 'to run up anything like this. Not that it's as amusing as I expected. I've always wanted to have a look at it; and I'd have asked you to bring me here the other day, if we'd had time. I'd imagined Joscelyn to have got rather further with it.'

Olivia stopped, as if aware that these remarks were somewhat disjointed. There was a short silence, which was broken suddenly by Sadie. 'Did you find the ladder like that, or did you heave it up yourself?'

'I heaved it up. Do you think it was very wrong?'

Sadie shook her head. She seemed concerned to ignore a faint mockery in this. 'Not a bit. Colin and I followed you, after all. But you do suddenly seem to be doing this ancestral home business with a will, Miss Jory.'

Olivia laughed. 'I may as well tell the truth. I'm going to write a book. Or try.'

Clout was simultaneously startled and delighted. 'A book! About Sir Joscelyn? Then this silly thing I'm required to do just mustn't get in your way.' He paused, a little disconcerted by the observation that

Sadie had provided herself with a daisy and was playing, with the appearance of a profound absence of mind, that simplest form of rural patience, *She loves me, she loves me not.*

'But it won't be anything learned.' If Olivia too had noted Sadie's occupation, she gave no sign of it. 'In fact, it's just going to be a historical novel.'

'Really?' Clout was properly enchanted by this further sign of a natural affinity between his mistress and himself. He had never, until this moment, thought very highly of historical novels. They belonged with commercial fiction, and had done ever since their invention by Sir Walter Scott, Bart. But now he suddenly saw that that was just it. The thing had been set going on the wrong lines, and so nobody seriously bothered about it. But, given a fresh approach...

'And what you're doing – real research – could be a tremendous help.' Olivia Jory had announced this with an air of sudden discovery and impulsive confidence. 'Of course, I wouldn't want to waste your time, or pick your brains...'

Clout's head was swimming again, and he was aware of himself as babbling enthusiastic words. Being a person of literary training, he was also aware, ever so faintly, that there had been some element of fatuity in his immediately preceding line of thought. But he couldn't remember what it had been, and he didn't a bit care. He would willingly have pitched every achieved page of *The Examination* (theme: the hero C's inability to discover whether he is the examiner or the examined) into the waste-paper basket if the action would in any way help to bring Olivia's less experimentally conceived masterpiece to birth.

'I suppose it's official?' Olivia had almost cut him short. 'I mean, the people at New Hall – Sir John Jory and his family – approve of your biography?'

'They approve of my having a go. Whether they'll approve of the result remains to be seen.'

'Have you met them yet?'

'No. It's only today that I've heard about Sir Joscelyn Jory's being my job. But it seems Sir John says he'll help with family papers, and so on.'

Sadie tossed away her denuded daisy. 'Is he nice – this good Sir John?'

Olivia hesitated. 'I hardly know him. I think he's all right.'

'You say he has a family. Grown up?'

'Yes. A son and two daughters.' Olivia was answering Sadie with charming patience. 'From what I've seen of them, I'd say they were all right too. But our acquaintance is quite casual. I don't go around a lot, that way.'

Clout remembered that at their first meeting Olivia had said something about being a secretary. He had been right in his guess about her social background; but it seemed likely that her own branch of the Jorys were quite poor, all the same. What might be called the badly landed gentry. This was a cheerful circumstance. Finding himself in love with any sort of minor heiress could be nothing but awkward. Clearly his marriage with Olivia was going to be ideally happy; and would be so, regardless of one sort of financial circumstances or another. Still, any man would find a slight tiresomeness in his wife's being free of more money than he himself was ever likely to earn.

This line of thought – which did credit to the solid morality on which he had been brought up – had distracted him for a moment from the rather odd catechism to which Olivia was being subjected. But Sadie's next question pulled him up. 'Do you', she was demanding, 'know George Lumb?'

'I don't think I do. What is he?'

'He's a writer. Another novelist.'

'Oh.'

'And he's working, oddly enough, at New Hall. Cataloguing a very neglected library. I think the idea is to see if the books are sufficiently valuable to have a fairly grand sale.'

'I see.' Olivia was frowning. 'I shouldn't be surprised.'

'You might have a go at George some time. I mean for more background for your romance.'

'I suppose I might.' For the first time, Olivia's tone was chilly. But not markedly so. Clout found himself enormously admiring her knowledge of how to drop the temperature, so to speak, just the requisite couple of degrees.

And this moderation was now thrown into relief by the answering brusquerie of Sadie's reaction. She jumped to her feet and gave Olivia Jory a straight, grave stare. 'Well,' she said, 'I'm going.'

'I suppose we'd better all go.' Clout offered this in a not very clearly thought-out desire to avoid friction. 'It's likely to be quite a scramble.'

'I'm going first. I've more of those library tickets to give out. And the climb isn't going to worry *me*. But of course Miss Jory, when she's finished her investigations, must be given a leg up.' Sadie's tone ingeniously contrived to make this last image sound highly ridiculous. 'So long,' she added – and took visible satisfaction in a form of words so socially unassuming. She turned and marched off to the ivy-clad wall.

Clout made a movement to follow her, and then thought better of it. Sadie, he remembered, had dangerous moods during which, if you got her wrong, she turned outrageous. Anything of that sort now would be most uncomfortable. He felt surprisingly uncomfortable as it was. He was going to be alone with Olivia once more, and the sense of this ought absolutely to exclude anything else from his head. But in fact he had – what was quite absurd – a lurking consciousness of infidelity. There was no sense in it at all. If Sadie hadn't happened to be still at the University on his coming back, her memory might never have recurred to him during all the rest of his life. And he hadn't the slightest reason to suppose that she would ever have thought of him. But here they were again, both with jobs in the same place – and it would take him, he saw, a little time to feel quite easy about it. It was that solid morality, once more. Presumably it asserted the duty of all men to marry the first child they kissed.

'What an awfully nice girl.'

Clout turned to Olivia and stared at her. If she had spoken satirically, or even if he had been positive that her remark was flatly conventional, he would almost not have liked her at all. But if she was just saying the right thing, then saying the right thing was so bred into her that it had the sincerity attaching to any spontaneous expression of personality. 'Yes,' he said, 'Sadie's very nice indeed.'

For a moment Olivia looked at him thoughtfully, and he had a notion that his unqualified agreement had somehow improved her opinion of him. Then she glanced back at Sadie, who was already half-way up the ivy. 'Will she be all right?'

'Absolutely. I can remember her as an undergraduate – a student – doing some famous climbs.'

'Rock climbing?' Olivia was interested.

'No. On buildings – for fun.'

'I've never done anything like that.' Olivia Jory said this with an air of deferring to some large and wonderful world unknown to her. And yet she couldn't really regard the University as other than a thoroughly provincial little place, swarming with up and coming young vulgarians, intent upon grabbing places and privileges that her sort was progressively letting slip. One couldn't deny, then, that her attitude was a bit artificial – but of course that was just one small part of her charm. Socially, her surfaces would always be marvellously smooth; it would always be gracefully that she would glide about among all sorts and conditions – without bumps, without friction. But he was sure that she had, at the same time, infinitely more than this. Strength of character, for a start. There was a tiny hint of that just in the masterful way she had marched in and taken the mausoleum, so to speak, in her stride. And now she was sitting down on the slab from which Sadie had risen. It was almost with a faint symbolism of assuming possession of something. She glanced upward. Sadie had vanished. 'What about you?' she asked. 'You've got a little more time to spare?'

'Yes, of course. What's going on today is a sort of preliminary ritual at which I'm quite superfluous.'

'And Sir Joscelyn?' She smiled at him. 'My great-great-grand-uncle?'

'I just haven't got on to him yet. I know hardly anything about him.'

'Later, you'll be able to tell me a lot.' Olivia Jory brought a cigarette-case from her pocket and opened it. 'Meanwhile, perhaps I can tell you a little.'

'That would be marvellous. I'd be most grateful.' Clout made this reply with a fervour that he could only hope didn't sound too imbecile. But, of course, she must really know. Olivia couldn't but know how he felt about her. And she wasn't in the least off-putting, although equally she wasn't faintly what Sadie would coarsely call come-hithering.

And it certainly wasn't with any facile flirtatiousness that she said a notable thing now. She was looking at him quite seriously – almost, indeed, with an effect of calculation. 'I think there's everything to be said', she pronounced, 'for our getting together.'

8

What he had heard, Clout told himself reasonably, was no more than a business proposition. But his imagination uncontrollably gave Olivia Jory's words a further sense. Above their heads, the doves cooed on a note that seemed to produce more than mere sound. The warm, still air inside the mausoleum throbbed and pulsed; and the effect was disconcertingly mixed up with something happening inside his own chest. His heart was pounding. He said rather feebly, 'Yes, of course.'

'Can you tell me anything about Miss Sackett's other friend?'

'Sadie's other friend?' The question seemed so odd and meaningless that Clout stared quite blankly at Olivia.

'The one working at New Hall. I think she said his name was Plumb.'

'Oh! Not Plumb – Lumb.'

'Lumb?' Olivia laughed. 'What queer names people have.'

'Yes – don't they?' Without being aware of it, Clout gave his beloved a repellent scowl. At last she had said something scarcely tactful. Moreover he was disgusted with the manner in which the unknown George Lumb kept bobbing up on him. 'I don't know anything about the chap,' he said. 'I never set eyes on him. But I know he stammers, and has a squint, and has been quite a prize student about the place.'

'Like you?' She laughed again. 'I mean only in being a prize student. But this job he's got with Sir John's books will have led to his taking an interest in the Jorys at large. He may be useful to you.'

'Perhaps. But it's not likely that Lumb has taken it into his head to work really intensively at the family history. Of course, if he shows a polite interest in the family, Sir John Jory will presumably give him a pointer or two.'

'The only pointer Sir John would be likely to give Mr Lumb would be one on four legs.' Olivia was amused. 'You see, Sir John doesn't much get beyond books on the Dog and the Horse. I'd say he knows nothing about family history, and cares less.'

'No doubt that's why he's agreed to an unknown young person at the local university writing a life of Sir Jocelyn.'

'That's certainly why.'

Clout took this frank rejoinder in good part. He couldn't quite make out what Olivia's questions and speculations were in aid of. 'What about you?' he asked. 'If you're planning this novel, I expect you've done a certain amount of digging things up?'

'Digging things up?' Olivia appeared startled – and then she smiled. 'That's an odd phrase – at least in its particular context. Joscelyn was always digging things up. It was his line. But I've done a certain amount of reading, and of what Miss Sackett calls poking about.' Olivia paused to stub out a cigarette. 'But this job of yours,' she said. 'It must have been arranged some time ago?'

Clout considered. 'Yes, I think it must have been. The man who decides – he's called Professor Gingrass – must have sounded Sir John some time back, and got him to promise access to papers and so forth in order to write this life of Sir Joscelyn. It's for a sort of prize at the University, you see. The Shufflebotham Award.' Clout got this out stoutly. 'When the thing's finished, one gets called Shufflebotham Fellow.'

Olivia nodded rather absently. She didn't appear to find this information ridiculous or even mildly funny. 'Then this Mr Lumb wouldn't have been working at New Hall for any length of time before this project of yours was fixed up?'

'I should imagine not. Actually, it was in Gingrass' head that he might set Lumb himself on the job. It was rather like that, when I barged in. But it seems that Lumb's being now at New Hall has nothing to do with that. It's just chance.'

'I see.' Olivia got to her feet with a movement that was slightly restless. It suggested a sense that time that might be in some way valuable was slipping dangerously by. She glanced round the mausoleum. 'I thought this would be a good place for a big scene,' she said. 'But now I'm not so sure.' She made as if to open her cigarette-case again, and then changed her mind and put it in a pocket. 'Did I hear Miss Sackett say that this Plumb – Lumb, I mean – is a novelist? Isn't he quite young?'

'He's certainly a good deal younger than I am. And I think Sadie simply meant that he *wants* to be a novelist.' Clout hesitated. 'A surprising number of people do.'

'Is that so?' Olivia appeared interested in this. 'How very odd.'

'Odd?' Once more Clout was puzzled. In the circumstances, Olivia's comment seemed quite as odd as the fact itself. At the same time he felt himself getting a sudden glimpse of what this was all about. There was some part of his mind, professional and uninfatuated, that told him Olivia's conception of prose fiction must be a good deal less sophisticated than much else about her. Having decided to write a historical novel embodying family material, she probably had the amateur's exaggerated sense of what would be good 'copy'. She had herself come upon something connected with Sir Joscelyn Jory that she believed would be the making of her story, and she was anxious that nobody else should get hold of it until she had exploited it in her own book. The news that the young man working at New Hall was himself a budding novelist had naturally rather alarmed her. And she must have been startled, too, when the nature of the Shufflebotham Award had become clear to her, by the similar possible threat constituted by Clout himself. And with all this she was now coping warily and well. Conceivably she could be charged with a little lacking candour. But then, although she must by now suspect the nature and even the degree of Clout's devotion, she couldn't positively know how utterly reliable it made him. It was all part of her attractiveness, of her coolness and cleverness and poise, that she was taking so cautious a line.

All the same, Clout yearned for confidence. It was only their second meeting; but their hearts, he felt, should be open to each other. He should tell her not only about the Shufflebotham but about *The Examination* as well. And she should tell him just what the wonderfully promising episode in the history of the Jorys was. If they could do as much as this before parting, it would be a promise of yet larger mutual trust to come. Suddenly he remembered that she had proposed beginning to tell him a little about Sir Joscelyn, preparatory to the deeper researches in which he must presently engage. And somehow this had got side-tracked. They must get back to it now. If he could get her to talk at all on the subject, she might go on to entrust her secret to him. 'What was chiefly interesting', he asked, 'about Sir Joscelyn?'

'I suppose you might say it was the singleness of his interest in this kind of thing.' She glanced round the mausoleum. 'If he'd finished it, it would have been terrific.'

'Why didn't he? Did he die, or run out of money?'

'I think money ran pretty low. But it wasn't that, and it wasn't that he died. There was some crisis that I don't yet clearly know about. Let's walk round again, Colin. Shall I call you that?'

'Yes, Olivia, please do.' For some seconds Clout had difficulty in distinguishing even the broad outlines of the structure in which they were to perambulate. The tremendousness of this latest development had positively dimmed his vision. He managed however to steer some sort of straight course beside his enchanting girl. 'What about Edward?' he asked. 'He didn't share his brother's passion for the winding-sheet and the shroud?'

'My great-great-grandfather preferred the quick to the dead. They were rivals, I think, in a way; and in the end they overdid it. Or that's what I seem to gather. Edward ended up with rather a crisis too.'

This, although scarcely explicit, was a start. Whether the crisis of which Olivia spoke was in fact the secret she was hoarding for her novel, or whether it was really something still quite vague to her, it was impossible to guess. 'I suppose', Clout said, 'that Sir Joscelyn was for most of his days a perfectly reputable amateur archaeologist and so forth, suitable for the stodgy sort of biography I'm supposed to write?'

'Oh, yes – he certainly was. The family picture is of just that, with perhaps a touch of amiable aristocratic eccentricity that grew rather pronounced at the end. He gave a collection of Etruscan stuff to the British Museum, which is a highly respectable thing to do. It certainly wouldn't occur to Sir John that an academic biography wouldn't be highly proper and becoming.' Olivia came to a halt. 'Here – just in the middle – there was going to be a *dakma*.'

'A what?'

'A *dakma* – the sort of tower upon which Parsees exposed corpses. They believed that either burial or incineration might pollute an entire element. But of course things happen to corpses left stuck up in the air. So there was provision for drainage into a central pit.'

'I see.' Clout was rather startled by this sudden turn by his beloved to mortuary considerations. 'And was Joscelyn going to have a central pit?'

'Certainly. And the corpses were to be in wax. All the corpses were to be that, and so were the horses and cows and crocodiles.'

'What on earth were they for?'

'Patagonians killed horses at the grave in order that the dead might ride to Alhuemapu.'

'Was that a nice place to ride to?'

'Beastly, I imagine. The cows and crocodiles – and, of course, cats – were for the Egyptians. The gallery up there was to be roofed and glassed in. That was for the collection of mourning garments. The Romans called them *lugubria*.'

'I bet they did.' Clout realized with something of a shock that dimly at the back of his mind there had been forming the notion that the present was a propitious occasion for advancing to actual love-making. Of course it could still be done. The personages of the Jacobean drama, for instance, were great hands at advancing amatory designs amid an oppressive décor of wormy circumstances. But it didn't seem quite right now – not when one had one's eye on a well-bred English girl with twentieth-century habits of mind. There was nothing to do but curse the Parsees and Patagonians, and bide one's time. 'You seem', he said a little morosely, 'to have been reading it all up.'

'It's interesting in itself. And don't you think, Colin, it would give just the right atmosphere for a historical novel that is at the same time contemporary?'

Clout found this difficult. He found it difficult, that is to say, to consider what might be called a technical and aesthetic question in a context so massively emotive as that created by the presence of Olivia. 'Yes, of course,' he said. 'That's to say, I'm going to be enormously interested in your conception of the whole thing. I just shan't be able to hear too much of it.'

She gave him a thoughtful look, and then rather abruptly moved on. 'What set Joscelyn going on all this', she said, 'was the fact that there's a barrow somewhere on the estate. I was asking you, you remember, about that.'

'Yes. It's on a small hill at the northern end of the park.'

'It had been opened and explored – and no doubt rifled – when he was a boy. And that's what gave his imagination its odd bent. I'd like to have a look at the barrow too, some time. Although apparently it's entirely bunged up again.'

Clout nodded. 'I know a bit about that. There's an archaeological society at the University, and I can remember their proposing to excavate the barrow. It was explained to them that the job had been done donkeys' ages ago, and that they'd find absolutely nothing. So they gave it up.' He paused. ' When you asked me about the barrow, Olivia, you asked me about an ice-house as well. What put that in your head? It's quite aside from this sort of business, isn't it?'

'Oh, entirely.' Olivia was decided. 'But it's a sort of relic of grand living that has an interest of its own. Can one get into it?'

'I'd hardly suppose so. Nobody's likely to have taken the slightest interest in it for generations, and it's probably all caved in. But I know where it is. We could have a look some time.'

'That would be fun. I feel we could do quite a lot of exploring – you and I.'

Clout's heart jumped again – for Olivia, as she said this, had turned and glanced at him. There was nothing out of the way in that. From the first she had never hesitated to look him full in the face, whether seriously, or in tantalizing mockery, or with her most delightful smile. But this time he was aware of something different. Or he thought he was. He might, of course, just be losing his head. 'Yes, rather!' he heard himself say, and broke off in confusion. For a second it was his absurd impression that Olivia had vanished. Then he realized that she had sat down again – this time not on any of Sir Joscelyn's abortive masonry, but on a small grassy slope that rose into the mild autumnal sunshine. She lay back on it and gazed up at the sky. He sat down beside her and remained perfectly still.

'Heaven is up there,' she said. 'That's why they bury us on our backs. Corpses are always made to face the direction it would be nice to go. In the old Scandinavian tombs nobody is ever found facing the frozen north. But of course, the dead are helpless, and have dirty tricks played on them from time to time. Think of being buried in a jar deliberately turned upside-down.' Olivia sat up again. 'Do you think I'm a bit touched?'

'No.' He shook his head and smiled. But in fact he was a little uncomfortable. It did seem possible that Olivia was rather obsessed.

'Let's talk of graves, of worms, and epitaphs.' Suddenly Olivia arched her back and stretched out her arms behind her. 'Or rather let's do nothing of the sort. Let's forget this is a mausoleum and think of it as something else – say, a temple.'

'Whose temple, Olivia?' He thought her a miracle of wit and beauty.

'Artemis, decidedly. Or have I got the name wrong? I was never good at them.' She was laughing at him. 'I think Joscelyn Jory's mania very amusing, and most attractive to write about. But I assure you I can have enough of it. I've less of Joscelyn in me, if it comes to that, than I have of Edward. And that's natural, since Edward was my great-great-grandfather. Who and what was your great-great-grandfather, Colin?'

'I haven't the slightest idea.' He was watching her, fascinated. They were both strangely relaxing; the faint warmth of the sun was soaking into them; there was no longer anything inhibiting in their queer surroundings. 'And I don't think it's important,' he said. 'But, very illogically, I rather hope my great-great-grandsons will know something about me.' He felt himself flush. 'I suppose that's extraordinarily silly.'

She at once turned quite serious. 'Are you talking about fame?'

'If I am, then I'm being terribly pompous. But it would be nice to leave something that would – well, be about for a while.'

'Of course it would.' Olivia spoke with decision, but something in her voice suggested that she had really been brought up against quite a new idea. 'You mean – writing?'

'Of course. You must feel just the same.'

'Naturally.' She said this in a small voice he hadn't heard before. He looked at her in surprise. She had plucked a blade of grass and was beginning to chew it moodily. 'How tiresome', she said, 'that honesty is one of the luxuries of the prosperous.'

He was so puzzled that he didn't manage to make any reply. What she had said sounded artificial and stupid; it might have been a *démodé* crack remembered from Bernard Shaw.

She threw the grass away and made an oddly irresolute movement that for a moment he didn't understand. Then he saw that she was putting out a hand to him. He realized their solitude in the middle of this bizarre stone circle, and he was at once awed and rather scared. 'Listen,' she said. 'When I told you…' She broke off abruptly, and he saw the hand which had been about to touch his raised suddenly in air and pointing across the mausoleum. They were in solitude no longer. A figure was climbing down the ivy just where Clout himself and Sadie had descended.

Clout felt an impulse to scramble to his feet, as if there were something improper or compromising in his being found reclining here with the girl. But he at once thought better of this and sat tight.

Olivia didn't stir either; only she gave an odd little sigh that might have been either exasperation or disappointment or satisfaction. 'Is it somebody come to turn us out?' she asked.

'I don't think so. That sort of person would have a key to the gate, and come in by it. Besides, I'm entitled to be here, even if you're not.' He grinned at her rather doubtfully, for he was in a confused state in which a faint sense of relief mingled with the robust annoyance that certainly preponderated in him. 'I was sent here by my professor to begin my researches.'

'And you've been interrupted, Colin, right at the start.' She gave him a quick smile that struck him as also being a confused affair. It seemed to mix up something rather new – which might have been compunction – with her familiar delicious mockery.

The scrambling figure touched ground and turned. It was a young man.

9

The young man walked over to them. 'G-g-good morning,' he said. He gave a swift glance at Olivia – it was almost as if she held no surprise for him – and then turned to take more deliberate stock of Clout. He was lanky – indeed he was slight to the point of weediness – but this didn't make him awkward. He had round glasses with rather thick lenses. The eyes that looked through them were bright with intelligence. They were also oddly set. In fact the young man had a squint.

So here was the detestable Lumb, who had watched Sadie Sackett dancing to the cattle, and who would have got the Shufflebotham if he hadn't added to his other disabilities a real sense of comedy and a graceful and attractive style. And what the hell was he doing here, anyway? Clout could only conjecture that Sadie had encountered him, and sent him along out of pure mischief. It decidedly wasn't a propitious introduction. 'Are you George Lumb?' he asked.

The young man nodded. 'Yes, I'm L-L-Lumb.' His own name appeared to give him particular difficulty.

'The Mr Lumb who is working at New Hall?' Olivia struck in swiftly with this.

For a second Lumb didn't reply. He seemed to be taking stock of some unknown factor in the situation. 'Yes,' he presently said. 'I'm working there for a bit.'

'We've heard of you. I'm particularly interested, because I'm a Jory – Olivia Jory. But not the New Hall Jorys – they're just kinsmen. I expect you know that this is Colin Clout. We've been exploring.'

Lumb nodded. 'So-so I s-see.'

Clout cast about in his head for some remark that would be extremely uncivil. He was aware of yet a further occasion for deploring Lumb. There was no special reason to suppose that the man would be interested in Olivia, or she in him. But they belonged to similar worlds – new-poor worlds. Clout (who, after all, was embarking on a professional career as a biographer) felt that the early life of Lumb was a field for quite secure conjecture. He had been at some small, dim public school, the fees for which his father – certainly a dear old vicar – had made untold minute sacrifices to achieve. Lumb was mild, gentle, friendly – and at the same time fanatical in anything he undertook: writing novels, or authenticating Lawrence on the musical capacities of cattle, or even cataloguing books. He would certainly have made an excellent job of a Shufflebotham – even of the first Shufflebotham on the deceased eminent Alderman himself.

What he was up to now was difficult to guess. But Clout seemed to know that his first conjecture had been wrong. Lumb wouldn't come along like this – or be sent along – just for the sake of his nuisance-value. He probably hadn't known at all that there was anybody in the mausoleum. He had come on some independent mission. Perhaps he had tumbled on the same basis for a novel that Olivia had, and like her had come to investigate an important part of its setting. But Clout found that he had his doubts about this. He took another glance at the stammering, squinting Lumb, and acknowledged to himself that he was impressed. Lumb didn't look at all the sort of man who would suddenly become enthusiastic about celebrating early nineteenth-century Jorys in a historical novel. Lumb was up to something else.

The opportunity to say anything scathing had passed. Olivia was clearly determined on giving Lumb a friendly reception; she had offered him a cigarette, and was talking to him with the easy, delightful frankness that Clout had admired in her from the first. This was very tiresome in itself. And it was yet more annoying that Olivia was talking about *him*. She was explaining to Lumb that he,

Clout, would presently be appearing at New Hall in quest of biographical material on Sir Joscelyn Jory. 'And I', she said, 'met Colin quite by chance, on the very day he came back here to hunt up something of the sort. Isn't it odd?'

Lumb agreed that it was odd.

'As it happens, I'm very interested too – both in Joscelyn Jory and in my own ancestor, his brother Edward. I'm going to write a novel about them.'

'A n-novel?' Lumb frowned.

'Yes – don't you think it might be fun? And I hope that Colin, when he joins you at New Hall, may find out things that may be useful to me.'

Lumb's frown remained. He was clearly thinking. It was something, Clout divined, that he did rather well. And suddenly Clout felt a senseless panic. It seemed to proceed from an obscure intuition that Lumb was about to perform some dreadful act – or at the very least to utter some atrocious sentiment.

And something of just this sort did now happen. Lumb turned to him. 'Do you b-b-believe this n-nonsense?' he asked.

The doves didn't stop cooing, and the sun continued to shine. The universe is a strictly neutral affair, neither beneficent as some poets have proclaimed, nor malign as numerous novelists have darkly hinted. No bolt descended from the blue upon the miserable Lumb, nor did Olivia's grey dress fall away from her to reveal the burning limbs and gleaming vestments of an offended goddess. A sense of the cataclysmic, indeed, seemed confined to Clout himself. Lumb's expression was mildly inquiring – which was clearly what was most habitual with him. Olivia might have been described – but only by an observer more in possession of himself than was her outraged lover – as engaged in composed calculation.

'Nonsense?' Clout heard himself say. He had risen to his feet, and even amid his just indignation was aware of himself as rather fatuously putting on a ham-fisted turn. 'You miserable little…'

'Be quiet, Colin!' Olivia made an impatient gesture. Then she turned to Lumb. 'You've broken our agreement,' she said quietly.

Clout couldn't believe his ears. 'Your agreement?' he demanded – and felt that he might take to stuttering worse than Lumb. 'You know him? You've met before?'

Olivia ignored this. 'And you're the sort', she continued to Lumb, 'that's supposed to know about playing fair.'

Rather disconcertingly, Lumb turned to Clout with a grin. 'Women,' he said.

And once more Clout felt foolish panic. He had a nasty conviction that he would have to be very smart to cope with Lumb. If Lumb had said 'women' satirically or witheringly or in anger there would have been nothing remarkable about it. But in fact he gave it the air of gently perceptive comment upon one large aspect of the human situation; and this was unnerving. It seemed to Clout that Lumb was what they had used to call, at school, a Great Brain – meaning those in a different class again from boys who, like Clout himself, sat comfortably at or near the top of the sixth form. Not that Clout thought any coming show-down with George Lumb to be necessarily a lost battle. Except for these momentary visitings of nasty doubt, he was full of confidence – both in himself and in Olivia. If Lumb had been up to something with Olivia, she must be rescued forthwith. He resolved to speak with firmness. 'I'd like to know, please,' he said, 'what this is all about.'

'I was quite p-p-prepared to stretch a p-p-point.' Lumb paid no further attention to Clout. 'Although p-p-pretending to this chap that you and I had never m-m-met was a bit thick. I'd accept it as the l-l-luck of the game that you've p-p-pocketed him just when he's going to write this biography. It gets him into New Hall as your spy. That's all right by me too. But I won't stand for him as your d-d-dupe. All this about a n-n-novel.'

'Her dupe!' Clout was again unable to refrain from hinting immediate physical violence.

'Do be quiet, Colin. I quite see Mr Lumb's point.' Olivia seemed unperturbed. 'No doubt it will be best to have a few explanations.'

'You see his point? Why, the man's outrageous!'

Olivia laughed. 'Not a bit. He's highly reasonable. Aren't you, Mr Lumb? By the way, may I call you George?'

'P-p-please do.'

Clout was really staggered by this – not more by the monstrousness of Olivia's most untimely advance to familiarity with the wretched man than by the sudden revelation in Lumb of common human frailty. It was clear that he was still indignant with Olivia. But at the same time he was goggling at her in a manner betraying nothing less than disgusting infatuation. Clout had realized from the first that Olivia was a girl who must knock men over wherever she went. But this was the first specific exemplification of the point. It was just one more jolt.

'But George doesn't like imposture about novel-writing. The craft's sacred to him. And I expect, Colin, it's the same with you. Anyway, the novel-business was a mistake. I could never had kept it up. You'd have spotted me as a fraud in no time. Any extremely clever person would.'

This speech naturally occasioned something like a revolution in Clout's mind. He realized that Olivia had been for some reason disingenuous, and he noted the outrageous stroke of flattery to which she had finally had recourse. He realized that the person with whom he had been in love was substantially his own invention. He realized with equal force that the real woman – tricksy, resourceful, and unscrupulous – was even more enchanting. Like Lumb, he was indignant. But, like Lumb, he goggled. Olivia glanced from one young man to the other, and was plainly satisfied with what she saw. 'I'm so glad', she said, 'that it's going to be possible to have absolute frankness. We shall have to take sides, I suppose. But that will be part of the fun.'

'I'd like to be on your side if it was p-p-possible, Olivia. But I have to guard the interest of my employer.'

Olivia looked up swiftly. 'You haven't told Sir John anything yet? You haven't broken *that* bargain?'

'I shan't tell him anything until I'm convinced it isn't a m-m-mare's nest. He isn't very bright, and it would only fuss him.'

'Sir John has no legitimate interest, anyway. Remember the swap. It's my whole point.'

'I know it is.' Lumb nodded vigorously. His stammer, Clout noticed, tended to fade away as he warmed up. 'But the evidence for the swap is even thinner than the evidence for the t-t-treasure.'

'For the *what*?' Clout looked from Lumb to Olivia in bewilderment. 'Whatever has treasure got to do with it?'

'Everything, Colin my dear.' Olivia's laugh rang delightfully through the mausoleum. 'This is all about treasure – a perfectly enormous treasure. And we may be sitting on it now.' She patted the grassy bank on which they were all perched. Then – unexpectedly, gracefully, with an enchanting fling of skirt and glint of knees – she was on her feet in front of them. 'Do you know what I think will be best? That I leave George to explain. Then he can say absolutely anything he likes. That's fair. And it's only fun – isn't it? – if one plays entirely straight.'

Clout stared at her in dismay. The thought that Olivia might vanish again quite precluded his feeling anything a trifle steep in her last sentiment. 'You mustn't go!' he said.

'St-t-teady on, Olivia!' Lumb was equally upset

'You can talk it out – a couple of men together.' She glanced from one to the other in impartial mockery. 'So – as your Sadie says – So long!' She turned and ran for the ivy.

Neither Clout nor Lumb stirred. Abject and ashamed of it, they didn't even follow Olivia Jory with their eyes as she rapidly climbed. But they did presently look at each other cautiously – and each found himself viewing so dismal a sight that they involuntarily exchanged rueful smiles.

'One could scarcely make a grab at her,' Clout said.

'No. She knows her own m-m-mind.' Lumb dug a heel gloomily into the turf. 'It's easy for you, C-C-Clout. You can b-b-back her b-b-bald-headed.'

'Can't you?'

'D-d-damn it, no!' Lumb was angry, although it was difficult to distinguish with what. 'It would be a breach of t-t-rust. But I'd better do what Olivia said, and t-t-tell you what I can. For the sake of what she c-c-calls fair play.' He paused, brooding darkly. 'Women,' he said again.

10

'I begin with a personal narrative.' George Lumb had turned over on his stomach and was peering into the grass as if it was a jungle. 'This will quite quickly bring me to my first meeting with Olivia, and to the situation as it stands at present.'

Clout saw that he mustn't interrupt. When Lumb could ignore the existence of other human beings, using articulate speech only as for the purpose of soliloquy, he didn't stammer at all. So Clout kept quiet, and found that he was coming to view the prone figure before him with mixed rather than pure feelings. Lumb was a pest – but there was also something engaging about him. He was even shabby in an engaging way – a way, that is, that Clout understood. His jacket was threadbare and the seat of his trousers was very shiny. There could be no doubt that Lumb was excessively poor.

'When I'd taken my degree, I felt I must get down to serious writing at once. The real thing seemed to be coming to me at last.' Lumb, who couldn't be more than twenty-one, paused broodingly for a moment, as if reviewing long years of unsuccessful creative struggle. 'Lawrence had been a great influence with me. And, after Lawrence, some modern Continental writers – and notably Kafka. At last I felt I was through with all that pupillary phase. I dare say you know what I mean.'

This time Clout had no difficulty in keeping silence. Clearly, it would be dreadfully humiliating if Lumb ever got to know about the existence and yet-unfinished state of *The Examination*.

'So I looked about for a job on which to keep going. I rather think Gingrass might have found me something. But, of course, it's fatal for a writer to mess about with the academic life. He ought to get clear of it as soon as he can, don't you think? Well, what I wanted was a local job, so that I could live at home, and at the same time pay my way there. My father – he's the parson of a parish called Bardley, less than four miles from here – found me the very thing. Our Squire is Sir John Jory, and New Hall is just over the vicarage wall. It seemed the library was in a great muddle, and Sir John had a vague notion there might be quite a lot in it that is valuable. He offered to take me on. Of course I explained that I hadn't the right bibliographical training. But he very decently said he'd have me, all the same. That's where my obligation to him begins.'

Lumb paused at this, and gently waved his heels in air. Even to this idle action, it seemed to Clout, he contrived to give rather a special air of intellectual distinction.

'Sir John didn't say anything about this biography of his great-grandfather that it seems you've been turned on to. But I thought I ought to know about the building up of the library, and that made me think about the family history in general. There have been Jorys for quite a long time, but they've never been what would be called a distinguished family. They've never produced anything tip-top – not, that is to say, until Olivia.'

Clout had one of his fits of alarm. There was something unnerving in this indication that Lumb – Great Brain Lumb – was as deep in as he was.

'But at least there had been this rather eccentric archaeologist, Joscelyn, who had been almost the last of the Jorys to live at Old Hall. His dates are easy to remember. He was born in the same year as Wordsworth and died a decade earlier.'

'In fact, 1770 to 1840.'

'Y-y-yes. Well, he sounded quite interesting, and I did poke about and discover some facts. Joscelyn drifts in and out of various memoirs of the period – in addition to figuring in the transactions of learned societies, and so on. He was a specialist in this business of tombs and burial customs. That's where, towards the end of his life, he differed from the professional learned chaps in that line. They went after tombs as historical evidences – for what they might reveal about a long-past living culture. Joscelyn liked them for their own sakes. He wandered about the world, haunting them in all their melancholy variety. And then he hit on the notion of having them, so to speak, artificially thick on the ground; of assembling a collection of them in his own park. Hence, as you know, this mausoleum. It brought him up against quite a lot of trouble.

'Even in post-Napoleonic Europe, which was still a wonderful place for rich people to fool around in, there was sometimes difficulty in walking off with a tomb. Joscelyn was usually prepared to pay cash down. But the ownership of tombs is often, it seems, disputed between private persons. And, if the things are sufficiently grand, governments may step in and be extortionate or obstructive. After a good deal of experience of all this, Joscelyn, as far as I can make out, went on the black market. Sometimes, even, he appears to have proceeded to plain theft. And in the end there was a row.'

'So big that all this' – Clout made a gesture – 'stopped off?'

'I d-d-don't know, C-C-Clout. This place was nearly completed, and Joscelyn had a lot of stuff ready to move in, when the obscure row happened. Quite soon after that he seems to have dropped the whole thing, and a few years later he died. Perhaps as his own dissolution approached, other people's tombs held less attraction for him. Perhaps he just took a craze for something else.'

'And that's all you've found out?'

'It was all I'd found out up to the day that Olivia came to tea.'

'Olivia came to tea with you?'

'N-n-no. She c-c-came to tea at New Hall, although she only has a slight acquaintance with the Jorys there. But I was p-p-present.' Lumb paused and gently sighed. 'Oh! when mine eyes did see Olivia first,' he breathed, 'methought she purged the air of pestilence.'

Clout didn't find this at all odd. 'That instant was I turned into a hart,' he rejoined simply, 'and my desires, like fell and cruel hounds, e'er since pursue me.'

There was silence. The two young men looked at each other seriously and with a kind of melancholy respect.

'D-d-did you ever believe', Lumb presently asked, 'that sort of Zuleika D-D-Dobson business ever really happened? Of course, it's in other b-b-books too.'

Clout made no immediate reply – and when he did speak it was to return to a subject less absolutely mysterious. 'Well, then,' he said ' – about this treasure, and so forth?'

'Olivia and I went wandering through the gardens at New Hall, and had a lot of talk. I quickly saw that she wanted to pump me.' Lumb's gravity was here broken in upon by his highly intelligent grin, so that Clout marvelled at how much it must have been with his eyes open that he had fallen in love. 'She wanted to know if Sir John's library had much in the way of old family papers – letters or diaries, perhaps, of the first half of the nineteenth century.'

'But she didn't say she was going to write a historical novel?'

'N-n-no. She couldn't have imagined I'd believe anything so absurd.' Lumb offered this opinion quite inoffensively. 'She told me about a family tradition – a sort of legend. She'd had it from an old nurse. According to this tradition, her great-great-grandfather, Edward Jory, had won something like a fortune from his brother, Sir Joscelyn, by some sort of queer bet. Or rather, it was first a bet, and then a bit of barter.'

'What Olivia called the swap?'

Lumb nodded. 'Yes. But she admitted it was all quite obscure – and also rather scandalous. The bet was that each brother was to bring back to Old Hall, within twelve months, the masterpiece of his career as a collector.'

'Edward Jory collected things too?'

Lumb shook his head. 'Edward didn't collect *things*. Edward collected w-w-women.'

Again there was a long, serious silence between the young men. Being in love, they viewed the frailty of Edward Jory with tolerance indeed, but at an infinite remove. 'A Regency hang-over,' Clout presently said.

'Yes. And B-B-Byronic stuff. Beautiful Circassians, and that sort of thing. The isles of Greece. It was from one of them, in fact, that the story says Edward brought his exhibit.'

'And Joscelyn?'

'A tomb from the Caucasus. And a friend was going to decide between them. Do you know about ancient Caucasian burial customs?'

'Of course I don't.' Clout was momentarily impatient. 'And I don't believe you did either, Lumb, until this business hit you.'

'P-p-perfectly true. Well, it appears they didn't attend to Sir Thomas.'

'Browne?'

Lumb nodded. 'Let monuments and rich fabrics, not riches, adorn men's ashes. It seems that in the Caucasus great ladies had all their jewellery buried with them, as well as their best frocks. What Joscelyn boned – it seems the right word – was a whole tip-top set-up of that sort.'

'Tomb, corpse, jewellery, and all?'

'Just that. And then, according to Olivia's story, there was this swap. Joscelyn, who had put in half a lifetime messing around with the dead, was suddenly struck all of a heap by Edward's all alive-oh Grecian girl. He offered Edward his Caucasian treasure – it really did amount to a treasure – in exchange for her.' Lumb frowned. 'The m-m-morals of these people were very bad.'

'Clearly. And Edward agreed?'

'Edward handed over the girl at once. But he didn't get the treasure.'

'You mean Joscelyn cheated?'

'Olivia doesn't know. Her old wives' tale broke off there. But there seems to have been an awful row, and some sort of panic. Edward went abroad again in a hurry, leaving his wife and some children behind him, as he always did. He died of fever in Syracuse about a year later. And at about the same time Joscelyn appears just to have dropped his hobby. And now, Clout, you can see Olivia's notion. She believes that Joscelyn hid the treasure and did Edward down.

She believes that it can be found – that it may have been hastily buried in this very mausoleum – and that her branch of the family is entitled to it.'

'But surely the law...'

'She doesn't bother about the law. If Joscelyn had the Grecian maid...'

'Maid?'

'Well – g-g-girl, if you like. If Joscelyn had her, then the Caucasian treasure was due in honour to Edward. Olivia's out to get it. She put all this to me, and asked my help. It put me in a difficulty, as I've explained. Being employed by Sir John, I am, to a certain extent, in a position of trust. So I couldn't give her any unqualified promise of help. Even, you know, if I hadn't been working at New Hall, I'd have had to make reservations. Olivia's a w-w-wonderful girl. But you mustn't let a girl be silly. You must see that a girl t-t-toes the line.'

'That's so.' Clout, although he managed to deliver himself of this agreement firmly, was again experiencing his nasty feeling of lurking awe in the presence of George Lumb. 'So you simply promised not to give her away?'

'Yes. I said I must leave my course of action undetermined until I had investigated the story myself. It was painful not to become Olivia's ally, wholly and at once. But, the more m-m-marvellous the girl, the more essential it is to step off on the right f-f-foot.'

'Of course. And have your own investigations come to anything?'

Lumb looked at his watch and scrambled to his feet. 'Nothing much. There aren't many family papers, as far as I can discover, preserved at New Hall. But I have got a little further. Olivia's story isn't all moonshine.' Lumb moved off towards the ivy by which they might climb out of the mausoleum. 'Too late to do any real nosing about here now. We'll come again. That is, if we're going to c-c-collaborate. Do you think we are, Clout?'

'No. I think we're going to be rivals.' Clout found no difficulty in saying this decidedly.

'I see. Well, we must play fair. Which isn't' – Lumb gave his intelligent grin – 'what Olivia calls playing fair. I'll t-t-tell you what,

Clout. When you come to New Hall, I'll tell you all the rest of what I know. As I say, it isn't much. And then we can see. You're bound, after all, to get ahead of me on the whole thing, since you're commissioned to go ahead, full-time, on Sir Joscelyn's life.'

Clout nodded. 'Would you agree, Lumb, that it's more my business than it is yours?'

'Joscelyn and the treasure and so on: yes. But not Olivia. I m-m-met Olivia first.'

'She was calling me Colin before she called you George.'

'H-h-how long before, Clout?'

'At least half an hour.'

'I think', Lumb said, 'that with Olivia we'll admit an equal interest, and st-t-tart all square.'

PART TWO

NEW HALL

1

The autumn term, although not destined to be wholly uneventful, got going quietly enough. The new students assembled once more in the Great Hall, and listened to the Vice-Chancellor delivering his customary address: 'Modern Universities and the Heritage of Greece.' Were we justified, he asked them, in speaking of the Socratic equation of Virtue and Knowledge? They must often have wondered; but they should wonder again. He would stress the importance of wondering; it was something at which they should put in a a lot of time – and the professors and lecturers, let them remember, were there to help them do it. Perhaps, although they had often read the *Protagoras*, they had never gone on to the *Meno*? He earnestly advised them to do so. But, above all, let them remember that knowledge was truly knowledge only when it was followed absolutely for its own sake, without thought of practical consequences or worldly advantages. With that thought he would leave them.

And at this the Vice-Chancellor went off to lunch, and the new students filed out. At the doors each was presented with a small pamphlet setting forth the various examinations they must pass if they were not to be deprived of the sundry State and County Scholarships on which for the next three or four years they must subsist.

Thus prefaced, the familiar round began. Professor Gingrass gave the first of his twenty-four lectures on the Literature of the Victorian Age – a course famous for the mellow patina which it had taken on with time. Clout, closeted in his attic with the small group of students allotted to him, tackled the Higher Literary Forms with all the bright speed of the tyro, so that within a fortnight he had dispatched the Epic, got well launched on its successor the Heroic Poem, and was beginning to put in anxious hours peering ahead at Tragedy, Comedy, the Ode, the Lyric, the Essay, the Sermon, and anything else that might pass as sufficiently elevated. One of the men was awkwardly learned, and two of the girls were incipiently flirtatious – an inopportune circumstance, since the divine vision of Olivia Jory excluded all thought of other women from Clout's mind.

There was a further minor worry in the fact that Sadie Sackett was now discernibly estranged from him. And for this he had to thank George Lumb – or rather, what was really vexatious, a combination of George Lumb and a certain weak lack of forthrightness in himself. He had tried, with Sadie, to play down the extent of his own absorbed interest in Olivia; and he had also thought he had better not confide to her the extraordinary possibility that Sir Joscelyn Jory might have left a considerable treasure buried somewhere round about Old Hall. But Lumb, it appeared, had told Sadie the true state of the case – no doubt under some vow of secrecy – and at the same time had made a formal statement of the manner in which his affections were now engaged. How much Sadie liked, or had liked, Lumb wasn't clear to Clout. It was pretty clear that she didn't at all like Olivia. But the result of this direct dealing of Lumb's was that he and Sadie were now as thick as thieves. Lumb turned up pretty frequently at Old Hall, and the two of them would have lunch together in the refectory. Their air of serious conference for some reason annoyed Clout very much.

Not that Lumb seemed at all flourishing or happy. Had Clout's dealings with the Higher Literary Forms comprehended Neo-classical Drama, it might have occurred to him that here was a striking instance of the Corneillian hero, torn between *inclination* (or *amour*) and *devoir* (or *loi*). Passion prompted Lumb to second Olivia Jory in her proposal to locate and appropriate a substantial buried treasure. Conscience bade him refer the matter to his employer. In this painful dilemma even being a Great Brain didn't apparently much help. Lumb's perplexed cogitations found ease only in the society of Sadie, whose brain, Clout supposed, was just above decent average.

Clout himself was in a position of some advantage. He hadn't yet been presented to Sir John; and it didn't seem to him that the University's having turned him on to Sir Joscelyn for the purposes of the Shufflebotham in itself put him under any obligation to Sir Joscelyn's great-grandson. If Sir Joscelyn had really played some dirty trick on his younger brother, hiding away substantial wealth that had become due to him, then Olivia was entitled to locate it and secure it for her branch of the family if she could. Or at least she was morally entitled so to do. Clout had no notion what the law would say about the ownership of a collection of jewellery carried off from an ancient Caucasian tomb. And he decided not to inquire. Mature consideration – or what he persuaded himself was that – had convinced him that it would be merely poor spirited not to back Olivia all-out.

Unfortunately Olivia had faded away again. Her inspection of the mausoleum had perhaps made her feel that it gave no indication that any particular part of it might profitably be attacked with pick and spade. She had presumably gone off, for the time, on another line. Remembering her interest in the ice-house, Clout located it in the half-hope that he might there run into her. It appeared to be no more than a species of short tunnel dug into the side of a hill, with heavy wooden doors that were massively overgrown with briars and quite immovable. But a hundred years ago it had presumably been in working order, and quite a prominent object. No moderately intelligent man could then have thought of it as at all a cunning place in which to hide anything away. On the two or three occasions upon which Clout visited it there was, of course, no sign of Olivia. He formed a strong conviction – not on the strength of any ponderable evidence – that she was occupied in improving her at present slight acquaintance with her kinsmen at New Hall – while at the same time doing her best to subdue the conscience of the already amorously enthralled Lumb. This was a conjecture which might have been thought to establish Olivia decidedly in the character of an adventuress. But Clout found that he didn't have to put in much time justifying to himself these devious courses in his beloved. He had got it firmly fixed up that her proceedings were highly romantic and enterprising. In fact he thought there had been nothing so good in that line since the maidens of Shakespeare's mature comedies.

It was desolating to be out of contact with her. And he still didn't even so much as know her address. Of course he could find it now if he wanted to. The number of Jorys in either town or country was limited, and he could quite quickly be on her doorstep. But if he was to call – which he certainly hadn't been invited to do – it would be nice to take, so to speak, a present with him. He must overtake and pass George Lumb in the pursuit of Jory family history. He must do more. He must try to locate the treasure. That, pin-pointed on a map, would be the really adequate gift to lay at Olivia's feet.

Reduced emotionally to this near-besotted condition, Clout didn't, oddly enough, experience any diminution of his quite respectable intellectual capacities. Assisted by Gingrass, who proved surprisingly helpful, he got up the known history of the Jorys expeditiously and well. He would at least cut a respectable figure when presented to Sir John as the budding biographer of his distinguished forbear.

Meanwhile it occurred to him one day to inspect what was called the Jory Collection. He had no great hopes of it. The University Librarian, an austerely scholarly young man not much older than himself, explained that it was no more than so much junk: small heaps of books abandoned here and there about the mansion when the Jorys had departed. He supposed that the University at the time of its humble beginnings, having received permission to hold on to these literary sweepings, had given them their impressive title while experiencing delusions of grandeur. No one ever went near the stuff. But no doubt it was incumbent on Clout, having undertaken the curious piece of research he had, to go and have a look. The Jory Collection was in the basement, in the small room next to the boiler.

Clout took himself off without enthusiasm to the quarter indicated. If there was anything of the slightest significance, it was quite certain that Lumb and Sadie wouldn't have missed out on it. Still, he had better stir the dust and see what was doing. The so-called Jory Collection ought at least to give some indication of the sorts of books and topics which the last of the Old Hall Jorys set particularly little store by. And no doubt that, in a way, made part of his research.

He had no difficulty in finding the room he was looking for. The door was much blackened by fumes from the neighbouring heating-plant, but it was just possible to distinguish that the words *Bibliothecula Joriana* had once been inscribed in gilt letters on the lintel. This was the delusions of grandeur again. Clout turned the handle and shoved, expecting to find semi-darkness and solitude. But the small book-lined room was brilliantly lit by a single naked electric bulb. And at a table beneath this, absorbed in what appeared to be a manuscript catalogue, sat a middle-aged scholar.

Clout was to be sure afterwards that there had been something instantly ominous about this encounter. It was certainly dis-concerting that the Jory Collection should be frequented at all. The middle-aged scholar had grey hair worn rather short; rimless glasses with a glint of gold at their sides; and a face of monotonous pallor, of which the chief feature was a mouth which might have been supplied by a single deft stroke of a knife. His clothes were good and quiet and loose and casual. He had a modest air of high distinction. Clout concluded that he came from either Princeton or Yale.

The elderly scholar got to his feet – without fuss, but with as little hesitation as if Clout had been the lady of the manor. 'How do you do, sir?' he said. 'My name is Milder. Milton Milder. Is it possible that I am speaking to Dr Clout?'

'Yes, I'm Clout.' Clout was a good deal staggered at being known. 'But I'm not a Doctor.'

The stranger received this disavowal with a slow benevolent nod. 'Of course,' he said, ' – of course. In my country most professors have at one time taken the Doctor's degree. But it is different here.' The stranger advanced with outstretched hand. 'It is a privilege and pleasure to meet you, Professor Clout.'

'Yes, of course. That is – I'm delighted.' Clout found himself not at all good at coping with this formality. 'Have you been here long?'

'I have only just arrived.' The stranger walked across the room, possessed himself of a second chair, brought it over to Clout, and with a courteous gesture invited him to sit down. 'I have been lunching with your Vice-Chancellor. A learned and delightful man.'

'Yes – isn't he?' Clout, aware that only the common forms prevented his instantly disputing both these epithets, sat down. He wondered if he should offer the man a cigarette.

'He told me about your present research. I was extremely interested – and for a reason which I shall explain right now. He also introduced me to your colleague, Professor Gingrass. Mr Gingrass is a learned and delightful man.'

'Yes – isn't he?' This time Clout was hardly aware of disagreement. He suspected that colloquy with Professor Milder was insidiously hypnoidal in its effects.

'And I believe Mr Gingrass is coming right along at this moment. I was honoured to meet him. He is a great authority on' – for a fraction of a second Milder appeared to hesitate – 'on his subject. It is a great stimulus to meet leaders in one's own field. And to see something of the great English universities. Yours is a most interesting university. It is not one of the old universities, but it is most interesting. In England you have a great deal that is old. In the States we have little that is old.' Professor Milder had sat down again, and his voice had taken on the soft purr of a well-oiled and perfectly adjusted machine. 'We must remember that the Americas were not in fact colonized until the close of the sixteenth century. So we have no medieval architecture.'

'I suppose not.'

'In England alone you have almost a score of great cathedrals. Consider York.'

'York? Yes – of course.'

'The cathedral at York is known as the Minster. Some sixty miles to the north you have Durham. As an example of Romanesque architecture, Durham is excelled nowhere in Europe. Of the later Gothic style there is perhaps no finer instance than Salisbury. The spire is of particular note, and is celebrated in many of the canvases of John Constable.' Professor Milder paused. 'And so we come, by a natural transition, to an allied topic – the riches of English painting. Consider your National Gallery.'

This time Clout merely nodded dumbly. It was clear that Professor Milder had evolved principles of discourse which approximated his conversation to the behaviour of bodies in outer space. Once launched, there was no reason at all why it should ever stop. One could almost feel, indeed, the presence of a physical law positively obliging it to go on for ever. From the National Gallery he would come, by a natural transition, to the allied topic of the National Debt – and after that it was anyone's guess. Clout tried to let his mind wander, but the murmur of Professor Milder's voice continued at once to lull and to compel his ear. He had known other learned men capable of the almost continuous enunciation of platitude. But their resources had been mostly in the sphere of received and approved opinions. What distinguished Milder's performance was its pronouncedly factual slant. He was now simply enumerating the principal English portrait painters in chronological order. But he wasn't doing this dispassionately. His words were so uttered that they carried the sense of a tremendous effort to soothe and compose. It struck Clout that Professor Milder might have been an ingeniously contrived robot, designed to be set at the bedside of incipiently maniacal patients in an asylum. Why he should be lurking here in the Jory Collection was a mystery. But Clout didn't feel it to be a mystery to which any very absorbed interest could attach. Nobody could conceivably be *interested* in this man, or in his concerns. On the other hand, Milder couldn't quite be treated like the traffic, or the neighbour's wireless. When operating, he would always constitute part of the surface awareness of one's mind. Clout, as he sat dumb before his new acquaintance, felt his eyelids growing heavy – but without hope that he would positively drop to sleep. Probably one sank into something like this condition when placed *vis-à-vis* Niagara Falls. When the door of the Jory Collection opened and Gingrass walked in, Clout turned to him as to a liberator. It wasn't a kind of sentiment he had ever felt towards Gingrass before.

'Aha! So the authorities are already in conference?' Gingrass spoke with robust cordiality. At the same time he gave Clout his conspirator's smile, thereby indicating that for the two of them there was to be great fun ahead. 'But you won't find anything here. I went through it all years ago. New Hall's the place for both of you. I've just rung up Sir John. We'll all three drive out there now.'

2

It didn't take them long in Gingrass' large car. Very quietly and gently, Professor Milder talked all the time, so that one could scarcely have got in a word had one wanted to. Nevertheless Milder's tone was constantly that of a man accepting and amplifying observations just made to him. Clout was still wondering how on earth he came into the picture. It was certainly true that in American universities there was always an enormous amount of what might be called Shufflebotham business going on. But it didn't seem plausible that the most abstruse of transatlantic researchers should propose to devote himself to the Jorys.

This mystery, however, was presently resolved by Gingrass. Gingrass' line with Milder was to attend to him in a spirit of whimsical connoisseurship. Everything that was sturdily provincial in Clout condemned this. It was true that Milder appeared to be less a man than a wandering catastrophe. But as he had wandered in, so would he wander out. In the meantime one had better put up with him – dumbly and glumly if one must, but not in a pose of ghastly superiority. However, Gingrass did, after his own characteristic fashion, a little explain the man. 'I suppose', he said merrily to Clout, 'you know the Professor's work?' He spoke not in a pause in Milder's discourse – for there wasn't one – but underneath it. 'No doubt you've read his books?'

'No, I don't know his work. And I've never seen any of his books.'

'Ah – you must keep up, my dear Clout. That hour before breakfast with the learned journals. That couple of hours after dinner with your batch of books from the London Library. Nothing is more important.'

'What are his books, anyway?'

'Oho!' Gingrass was jocose. 'That would be cheating – eh? No short cuts in research.'

Clout was silent. It was quite plain to him that Gingrass had never had a volume of Milder's in his hands in his life; that he had probably heard of him for the first time, indeed, that morning.

'But of course it's quite fair to tell you what he's doing now. Liberation in the Romantic Age.'

'Godwin and Shelley stuff, and Byron at Missolonghi?'

'Not precisely. Not precisely liberation in that sense.' Gingrass raised his voice, and boldly cut into Milder's murmuring. 'What is the title, Professor, of the work you're engaged on now?'

'That's a question that I find a little hard to answer at this stage.' Milder's tone as he offered this answer positively exuded poppy and mandragora, much as if he apprehended that Gingrass was on the brink of nervous paroxysm. 'The chronological limits haven't yet clearly defined themselves. Provisionally, I figure it might be "English Aristocratic Depredation in the Later Eighteenth and Earlier Nineteenth Centuries". But perhaps that's a mite clumsy.'

'Not at all, not at all!' Gingrass was delighted. 'On the contrary, my dear Professor, I judge it most felicitous. And now Clout understands the sense in which we are speaking of liberation.'

Clout thought he did. 'Lord Elgin liberated those marbles from the Parthenon?'

Gingrass nodded. 'Exactly. An excellent – indeed, the transcendent instance.' Sitting back at the wheel he began to recite in his special lecturing voice:

'Let Aberdeen and Elgin still pursue
The shade of fame through regions of virtu;
Waste useless thousands on their Phidian freaks,
Misshapen monuments and maim'd antiques;

And make their grand saloons a general mart
For all the mutilated blocks of art...'

He paused. 'But better, of course, is the epigram:

Noseless himself, he brings home noseless blocks,
To show what time can do, and what...'

'A brilliant couplet – certainly a brilliant couplet.' Milder had interrupted – seemingly in the interest of propriety. 'So Professor Clout will understand why I am interested in Sir Joscelyn Jory. Of course his depredations weren't on Lord Elgin's scale. He didn't walk off with much of the world's greatest sculpture. Still' – Milder was soothingly judicious – 'he is a very interesting late instance of the form of social behaviour I am proposing to study. He should certainly have an appendix to himself, if not a chapter. And that's why I'm taking time to look him up.'

Clout said nothing. At least he now understood about Milder. It seemed a little hard on Sir John Jory, that, having innocently agreed to one literary detective getting to work on his great-grandfather, he should incontinently be saddled with another in the shape of an American proposing to honour Sir Joscelyn with a minor niche in a species of thieves' gallery. The absoluteness with which Lord Elgin had stolen those celebrated marbles Clout had forgotten, or never known. Certainly Byron had denounced him roundly enough. But no doubt a lot of that sort of thing had gone on, and Sir Joscelyn's later methods of acquiring tombs and the like had merely taken him a little late into the swim. The whole subject would doubtless lend itself to a quietly amusing book. But Milder would never be amusing – or he would be amusing only to one who, like Gingrass, had a perverted sense of humour. As one who should bring Sir Joscelyn Jory to life again Milder wasn't a serious rival. Even fewer people would read his book than would read Clout's biography. And perhaps nobody at all would ever get as far as the appendices.

At this point in Clout's speculations Gingrass swung his car off the high road and up the short drive to New Hall.

The grandeur of the Jorys couldn't have lasted long. From Old Hall, which had replaced an unpretending earlier residence, they had withdrawn to New Hall within a few generations. New Hall was a good deal older than Old Hall, since the real Old Hall was the Caroline building which had virtually disappeared. New Hall was, in fact, Queen Anne, but there was a late Victorian wing, run up decidedly on the cheap, which rather spoilt its modest elegance. All this had to be explained to Professor Milder – and had then to be fed back by Professor Milder to his companions – before they climbed out of Gingrass' car. It was then necessary to pause.

It was necessary to pause and regain one's nerve. The front door of the house was open, and from it there had emerged as they drove up a black spaniel dog. The creature had advanced and stood inoffensively at gaze with them; whereupon another, and identical, dog had come out behind it. What was disconcerting was merely the fact that this process was continuing indefinitely. There were now some twenty dogs: all jet black, but all with the natural mournfulness of their kind enhanced by a faint powdering of grey about the muzzle. For a few seconds they stood in a wide semi-circle before the visitors. Then they converged upon them – without haste and without sound.

'Black spaniel dogs,' Professor Milder said informatively. 'A large number of black spaniel dogs.'

'Do you think they're all right?' Gingrass clearly wasn't a doggy man, and his voice was apprehensive.

From somewhere amid the score or so of dogs there rose a half-hearted growl. Clout couldn't resist this. 'I don't like it,' he said. 'I don't like it at all. Far too many of them. They might get utterly out of control.'

'Do you really think so?' Gingrass eyed the dogs in incipient panic. They continued to advance. 'Good dogs!' he suddenly cried out desperately. 'Good doggies! *Goo-ood* doggies!'

At this, the spaniels stopped as one dog. They all bore expressions of sombre *hauteur*. Gingrass continued his abject propitiatory noises. 'Good old doggies-woggies!' he screamed – and fell to clicking his fingers as if eagerly solicitous that the brutes should crowd around him. At the same time he began to edge backwards towards his car. But the spaniels were now in movement again. This time they were drifting sideways and away. It was demonstrable that they had turned the visitors down.

'The dogs are going away,' Professor Milder said – and added, as an afterthought: 'Black spaniel dogs.'

At this moment Clout became aware that a lady and gentleman had come out through a french window at the end of the house. They must have observed the scene which had just transacted itself, and they were now coming forward with courteous haste. At the same time it was obvious that they were exchanging perplexed speculations. Sir John and Lady Jory were probably unused to persons given to calling spaniels doggie-woggies. It didn't seem a terribly good start to the afternoon.

Lady Jory provided tea in a long, low drawing-room upon which Clout at once fell to making conscientious mental notes. It sounded what he recognized from his reading as the authentic note of a derelict landed class. The curtains were so frayed and the chintzes so faded that in his mother's house they would long ago have been abandoned as not respectable. There were a good many pieces of really beautiful eighteenth-century French furniture; and on the walls there was an extraordinary mingling of darkened oil paintings, wishy-washy watercolour sketches (presumably by ladies of the family), and innumerable photographs of people clasping swords, reading books, smelling flowers, sitting on horses, talking to dogs, gazing at mountain scenery painted on canvas, or represented simply as bodiless busts hovering in a void. Over the fireplace there was a portrait of a melancholy, long-faced man, depicted as deciphering an inscription incised on a stone slab embellished with blubbering infants. Clout eyed this with a somewhat unenthusiastic proprietary interest. It was undoubtedly Sir Joscelyn.

Lady Jory's conversation was conscientious but admitted of numerous pauses. During these she appeared to be running over in her mind the names of all her acquaintance in the hope of hitting upon one that any of her visitors might know. Her interest lay in the present whereabouts and activities of specific persons, and any advance to more general topics found her rather at a loss. Her husband seemed to suffer from absence of mind – in just what sense Clout felt it would as yet be difficult to say – but combined this rather unexpectedly with a perfect attention to the material wants of his guests. He had the sort of moustache that can be chewed with ease in ruminative moments. But at the moment he was confining himself to buttered toast. One favoured spaniel was admitted of the company. The creature lay with its head flat on the hearth-rug, peering out through a sort of tunnel formed by its enormous ears.

'No doubt you know my daughters, Jane and Elizabeth.' Lady Jory addressed herself to Clout. 'No doubt you have met them at dances, and so on. They were at the Dangerfields' at Christmas, for instance.'

'I wasn't.'

'But now they are abroad.' Clout noticed that Lady Jory didn't really take much account of anything he said. 'But Jerry, our son, is at home. I am surprised he hasn't come in to tea. But tell me' – and Lady Jory leant forward and appeared to believe that she was lowering her high, clear voice – 'is your friend in the brown suit a foreigner?'

'Professor Gingrass?' Clout was surprised, since he had gathered that his chief was in the enjoyment of the Jorys' intimacy. 'Oh no – I believe he's quite English.'

'I supposed he must be a foreigner because he was frightened of the dogs.' Lady Jory made this incursion into the sphere of logical inference with some air of intellectual triumph. 'But your other friend? Surely he is a foreigner?'

'Yes. He's a professor from America.'

'From America? How very interesting. He may know the Van Burens. Or the Reichenbachs. It is always interesting to meet Americans. It makes a change.'

'Yes, doesn't it?'

'As a girl, I lived for some time in France. There were a great many American girls. They rode very well.'

'Is that so?'

Lady Jory was silent for some moments. The mental roll-call was on again. It prolonged itself while she consulted the interior of her teapot. Then plain inspiration came to her. 'I think', she said, 'you know George Lumb?'

'Yes – although I met him only quite lately.'

'Of course we have known George since he was a child, and are very fond of him. I understood he was to be here to tea.' Lady Jory turned to her husband. 'John, surely George Lumb was coming to tea?'

'Certainly. Ought to be here now. Has something to say about the – um – business that has brought these gentlemen to visit us.'

'Business? Oh, yes – of course.' Lady Jory spoke with gentle relief, as if the events of the afternoon were now slightly less mysterious to her.

'Getting out this book-affair, you know, about Joscelyn Jory. Seems to be a sudden interest in all that.' Sir John looked a little misdoubtingly at his guests. 'Taken up by the University.'

'The University, John?' Lady Jory was puzzled.

'The College, m'dear. Old Hall. Place Lumb put George to. Calls itself the University now. Quite proper. Go-ahead sort of place in its own way. Run by Principal Gingrass here.'

Gingrass, thus oddly promoted, was jovially explanatory. Milder, who had been taking stock of his surroundings, began describing them to Lady Jory in detail. Lady Jory was at first bewildered, but quickly became attentive. Presumably large new realms of conversational resource were opening out before her. She even forgot to ask about the Van Burens and the Reichenbachs.

Sir John came over and sat beside Clout, thoughtfully bringing a plate of plum-cake with him. 'Know', he asked, 'about this Shufflebum business?'

Clout was nonplussed. He didn't know whether this perversion of the late alderman's name was inadvertent and to be discreetly corrected, or whether it was a jest with that eighteenth-century flavour in which a baronet of ancient lineage might suitably indulge. 'Yes, sir, I know about it,' he finally said. 'In fact, it's me who's to do the writing.'

'You Clout?'

'Yes, I'm Clout.'

'Odd. That Gingrass fellow said you were clever but unpresentable. How would you account for that?'

Clout thought it discreet not to try. So he merely shook his head.

Sir John lowered his voice – more successfully than his wife had done. 'Bit of an ass, isn't he?'

Clout, although he felt this judgement upon Gingrass to be highly perceptive, resolved to continue on the note of discretion. 'He's a little disconcerting at times.'

'Ah! Fellow your head man?' As he asked this question, Sir John gave Clout, rather surprisingly, a shrewdly appraising stare.

'Yes, he's my professor.'

'Um.' Sir John took a bite of plum-cake. 'About this book on Joscelyn. You'll do. Go ahead.'

Clout, who hadn't at all realized that a *viva voce* examination was in progress, felt for a moment the simple joy which he had experienced throughout life as he successfully cleared another rung of the interminable educational ladder. Moreover Sir John had spoken so incisively that he felt it almost incumbent upon him to produce a fountain pen and proceed to sketching out Joscelyn Jory's early life forthwith. 'I'm afraid', he said cautiously, 'that there's a lot of spade-work still to do.'

'Spade-work?' Sir John appeared not to follow this. 'That was Joscelyn's line, certainly. Always digging up this and that, it seems.

Learned, you know. Credit to a family – once in a way.' He paused. 'I wish George would come.'

'George Lumb?'

'Yes. Been finding out a thing or two, it seems. Intellectual lad. Preach a better sermon than his father, if you ask me. And now he says there's something that should be matter of general communication.' Sir John paused. 'Talks like that, you know. Might be reading it out of a book. But a nice lad.'

'Yes – he seems all right.'

'Been doing a very decent job for me. Couple of fellows on the estate want Dutch barns. Perfectly reasonable. And Smith at the Home Farm needs a milking-parlour. Quite right. Go-ahead chap. So George is seeing what we might get out of the books. Friend of mine tipped me the wink on that at the Cavalry Club.' Sir John turned as the door opened. 'Ah – here is George.'

3

Sir John, however, was mistaken. The newcomer was a man of about his own age, dressed in dark, professional clothes. Shown in with a sort of modified ceremony by a parlourmaid, he walked up to Lady Jory and shook hands. 'Good afternoon, Lady Jory.'

'How nice to see you, Doctor. More hot water, please, Evans.'

The stranger turned to Sir John. 'Afternoon, Jory.'

'Afternoon, Jory.'

The two men had nodded at each other, apparently well pleased. They were not positively familiars, but they were too familiar to shake hands. General introductions followed – but even before these had taken place, Clout had tumbled to the truth. Something familiar in Dr Jory's features no doubt helped him to it. This was Olivia's father, Edward Jory's great-grandson. He was a visitor, so to speak, from the limbo of younger sons. He looked much more capable than Sir John, and his appearance didn't suggest that the junior line had taken any marked tumble in the world.

'I rather expected to find my girl here. She's been improving her acquaintance with you, I gather.'

'Jerry had been improving *his* acquaintance with *her*.' Lady Jory uttered this expertly as a gracious correction. 'Jerry likes clever people. Old Lord Dangerfield says he can't understand why the boy has gone into the Diplomatic.'

Sir John was hospitably bringing forward the toast. 'Foreign Service,' he said. 'New name. And examination wallahs, every one of them. Dangerous – eh?'

'We've got along with it in medicine for some time.' With business-like dispatch, Dr Jory took three pieces of toast. 'Of course, other qualities are desirable as well.'

At this Professor Milder, who for some minutes had been surprisingly silent, found his form again. 'The degree of positive correlation between competitive tests and subsequent distinction in the business and professional world', he said soothingly, 'is a topic that certainly opens up a wide field of reference. To take first the figures from Minnesota – '

'But how *very* interesting!' Lady Jory slightly moved her chair, and with the effect of immediately drawing off Milder into *tête-à-tête*. Clout saw that the action was virtually automatic, and he was duly impressed. That was how, with a detected bore, a practised hostess behaved. And yet Lady Jory was certainly a quite stupid woman. Clout discovered that he was enjoying himself. Clout, BA, B Litt, mightn't, after all, be so terribly clever himself. But learning was second nature to him. And at present he felt he was learning all the time.

Dr Jory, who had finished his toast, leant forward for a piece of plum-cake. And he made this the occasion for a confidential murmur to his kinsman that Clout just caught. 'I say, Jory. I don't want to speak out of turn. But I had a notion you might be expecting me. A friend of Olivia's – a young fellow called Crumb' – he took a bite of cake – 'or perhaps Plumb – '

'That's right.' Sir John nodded, bewildered but encouraging. 'Name is Lumb. Parson's son here. Doing a job for me. Nice lad.'

'Well, he tipped me to come along. I've a notion my girl is up to something.'

'That so?' Sir John, himself a parent, received this communication with ready sympathy. 'There's certainly something in the wind, if you ask me. I'm waiting for this George Lumb now. He wants some sort of family conference. Puzzling – eh? But George Lumb will get it straight. Capable boy.'

It was clear that Sir John had come to place a large confidence in the Great Brain. Clout's reaction to this discovery was unfavourable.

It came back to him forcibly that Lumb was a pest. He was also inclined to suspect that Jerry Jory was a pest too. Sir John's heir was in the Foreign Service. One knew what *that* meant. And if he and Olivia had been meeting each other, it was a foregone conclusion that here was just one further male tagging after the girl. Clout realized that special hazards, as well as a great glory, must attach to the pursuit of a mistress so decidedly magnetic as Olivia. Her nature was, of course, altogether superior to feeling any special attraction in the fact that a young man was a budding diplomat and the heir to the family baronetcy. But Clout didn't like the sound of Jerry Jory, all the same.

He liked it neither figuratively nor in plain fact – as he discovered when, in the middle of these ruminations, hurrying feet and laughing voices made themselves heard through the windows of Lady Jory's drawing-room. It sounded almost as if some mild sky-larking was in progress. A minute later, Olivia came in – very decorously, and accompanied by a young man, whose gravity was unflawed. Jerry Jory was like his father, but he was even more like Sir Joscelyn over the fireplace. He had the same long and melancholy face, which would lend itself admirably to being sketched against a background of funerary urns and sarcophagi. Alternatively – Clout morosely thought – he would photograph well as a minor member of his profession, standing solemnly behind a Foreign Secretary during the formal signing of some obscurely discreditable treaty.

Olivia did at least abandon this tiresome person as soon as she had been given a cup of tea – crossing the room to sit down close by Clout on a small sofa. 'Colin,' she murmured, 'who's the Yank?'

'Chap called Milder. He wants to put Joscelyn into a corner of a book on genteel theft.'

'And the one made of putty?'

'That's Gingrass, my boss. He brought Milder and me along.'

'What does Sir John think of all this academic interest?'

'I don't know that he thinks much at all. His feeling seems to be that Joscelyn was learned, and that this sort of thing was to be expected sooner or later. He seems to think that your George Lumb is going to make some kind of announcement.'

'He's not my George Lumb. I suppose he's your Miss Sackett's George Lumb – if he's anybody's. And I think I know what he's up to.' Olivia's tone was grim. 'He's definitely going over to those Jorys.'

'What do you mean by *those* Jorys?'

'Our host and hostess, of course – and the dim one I came in with.'

Clout's heart gave a bound. 'Jerry Jory? Is he nice?'

'Oh, he's quite all right.' Olivia spoke indifferently. 'But I'd like to do him down, all the same.'

Clout could only vastly admire this pertinacity, 'In the name of family justice?'

'Of course. Joscelyn Jory *was* a thief, all right, and your American colleague is welcome to him. But his chief theft was from his brother.'

'What does your father think, Olivia, about this Caucasian treasure business?'

For a moment Olivia hesitated. 'As a matter of fact, I haven't discussed it with him. I wanted to find out more first, so that there wouldn't be any doubt about the facts.'

'Do you think Lumb's found out more – and that that's what this is about?'

Olivia nodded gloomily. 'Yes. He's got hold of something. And his announcement, as you call it, is to be made to everybody, so that we all start square. George Lumb has no idea of fair play. Don't you agree, Colin?'

As she asked this question, Olivia Jory had with a beautiful impulsiveness and adequate unobtrusiveness laid one of her hands on Clout's. 'Yes, of course,' he said. He was only dimly aware that, if the interest of the finest precision was to be observed, these words stood in need of a little qualification.

'These Jorys know absolutely nothing at all. So giving them the slightest hint is nothing but horrid favouritism on George Lumb's part. He's probably infatuated with one of the daughters – and you should see *them*. Yes – he's goggled adoringly at both of them, ever since his nose could show above the vicarage pew.'

Clout, although he knew that there was a wild fallaciousness in this conjecture, had no difficulty in admiring the *élan* with which it had been expressed. 'Are you sure', he asked, 'that the New Hall Jorys don't know the family tradition you do – the wager, and the swap, and your great-great-grandfather never getting his due?'

'If they do, they never think of it. I'm the first person who saw the plain implication: that the whole discreditable business almost certainly resulted in that enormously valuable stuff being hastily hidden away – and never brought to light again.'

'How do you know it wasn't?'

'I don't – not positively. But, if it had been, the fact would almost certainly be remembered. I don't say we're on a certainty, Colin darling. But I do say we're on a good thing.'

To this, not unnaturally, Clout contrived absolutely no reply. He was wondering whether his ears could possibly have deceived him, and no astounding term of endearment in fact been added to his name. If uttered, it had certainly been casually, and with nothing demonstrative accompanying it. It had been only for a moment that Olivia's hand had touched his. And she had now contrived to make the little sofa seem much bigger. She was sitting, one might say, at the other end of it, and had suddenly contrived an air of listening with respectful attention to Gingrass.

Gingrass had for some time been rather in eclipse. It wasn't any good his preserving an air of exhibiting Professor Milder as a refined comedy turn for the sophisticated. The Jorys weren't sophisticated – or certainly not in that way – and they wouldn't have accepted a guest as a comic turn anyway. Nor was it any good Gingrass bringing out Hilary and Lytton and Virginia and Willie and Bertie and Tom. The Jorys, although they might have heard of some of these persons, would not have been specially impressed by even the largest claims to their acquaintance. But it wasn't for nothing that Gingrass prided himself on being a man of many facets other than the merely academic. He was now producing, for Sir John's benefit, what was in fact a companion piece to the Lake Garda episode. Only this time, it was not a career as a novelist that Gingrass had renounced; it was the life of a landed proprietor. His father's small estate had been heavily burdened; and he himself, after a solitary week spent tramping the adjoining moors, had decided that in the interests of the tenantry he must sell to a new man, able to plough in his rents for a period of years. Gingrass had kept nothing but a patch of land, where there was not a bad stretch of trout stream and a little rough shooting.

Both Sir John and his son received these confidences with proper civility. Only the recumbent spaniel behaved with some lack of propriety – raising his head for a moment, gently swaying his great ears in a gesture that couldn't be construed as at all acceptive or affirmative, and then relapsing into slumber or abstraction. Professor Milder had now got hold of Dr Jory, and appeared to be offering him a brief factual history of the National Health Service in these islands. Clout wondered whether anything was going to happen after all. The New Hall Jorys were a very nice study in themselves, and they would work up at least into a satiric sketch of the gentler sort. Moreover to be in the same room with Olivia was a happiness that set all other considerations aside. All the same, he couldn't help feeling that there had been in the air a promise of drama that hadn't fulfilled itself. Nor was much headway being made in the purely learned way. If the widow of the late Alderman Shufflebotham had – what wasn't likely – the entrée here, and should wander in now, she wouldn't be likely to feel that he, Clout, had done much as yet to justify his having entered upon the enjoyment of her husband's benefaction.

Clout had got so far in his reflections when the drawing-room door opened and George Lumb came in. He was carrying a portfolio. And he was accompanied by Sadie Sackett.

Sadie, rather to Clout's surprise, appeared to have been here before. Lumb must have brought her in to help him on the strength of her professional qualifications as a librarian. And she was clearly in favour with Sir John. He was giving her tea with great politeness. But he had also taken up with her what appeared to be some familiar vein of banter, for Sadie was blushing and laughing aloud. He hadn't shown any tendency to a similar relationship with Olivia. Perhaps it was really true that two opposed parties were building themselves up in this room.

But now Sir John was serious again. Sadie had said something that made him turn to Lumb inquiringly. 'George,' he asked, 'what's this about letters?'

'I've f-f-found some, Sir John.'

'Are they any good? I mean, could one get anything out of them?' Sir John went with admirable simplicity to what he plainly conceived to be the relevant point. 'Penfold – fellow who told me you can get the deuce of a lot out of books – said nothing about letters.'

'It may be autographs, John.' Lady Jory supplied this. 'They are sometimes quite valuable, I believe. When I was a girl I once had a letter from Mr Arthur Balfour. He had been lunching with Papa and Mama, and had spoken a few words to me in the garden, and afterwards been told that it was, in fact, my birthday. So, of course, he wrote this little letter to explain why he had not congratulated me. And one of my brothers gave me five shillings for it, simply because of the signature.'

'Is that so, m'dear?' Sir John was much struck by this anecdote, which it appeared his wife had not previously communicated to him. 'George – is that what you've got on to? Letters from big-wigs – eh? Five shillings is always something, if you ask me. I can remember Jerry here saving nearly a tenner out of his weekly five bob. Pleased me very much. I put something to it, and there he was with his own gun.'

'It was a new saddle. The gun was a present from my grandfather.' Jerry Jory offered this correction in a well-bred way, with no suggestion that it was of the slightest importance to anybody. But Clout at once decided that he was a thoroughly dull man.

'Quite so.' Sir John nodded cheerfully. 'Well, George – is that it?'

'N-n-no. The writer of these letters' – and Lumb held up the portfolio – 'was quite obscure. She was a m-m-member of your own f-f-family, sir.'

'The deuce she was!' Sir John, although disappointed by this news, saw no offence in the manner in which it had been intimated. 'Then, why, my dear boy – '

'There are references to something that should be known to you – and to D-D-Dr Jory as well.' Lumb was for some reason very serious. 'M-m-my idea is, sir, that Sadie should read them to us.'

'Certainly, George. A capital plan!' Sir John was so enthusiastic about this that Clout had to conclude him quite gone on Sadie Sackett. That, of course, was all right in its way. Sadie was a good sort of kid, and not without the looks that might prompt an old buffer to begin feeling fatherly. But considering that Olivia too was in the room, one really had to conclude that Sir John was as stupid as his agreeable but vacuous wife.

Lumb had handed the portfolio to Sadie. He now came over and stood beside Clout. He glanced quickly at Olivia – so unhappily that it was impossible not to feel sorry for him – and then spoke in a low voice. 'I s-s-say, Clout – of c-c-course you're in on this. And I suppose Gingrass c-c-can't be turned out. But who's that other chap?'

'Name of Milder. You needn't worry about him. Harmless bore. Wants to write a bit about Sir Joscelyn's collecting methods in a general history of the subject. But even if he does, nobody will ever read it. It seems agreed he should just be let tag around.'

Lumb nodded. 'M-m-may Sadie begin?' he asked Sir John.

'Certainly, certainly. But you haven't told us who the letter-writer is.'

'Sophia Jory.' It was Sadie who answered. 'A younger sister of Joscelyn and Edward. The letters are to her old governess, it seems. They're not the actual letters, or of course they wouldn't have turned up here. They're Sophia's own copies. She'd been taught to keep a letter book.'

'And p-p-perhaps she thought she could m-m-make use of them. I think Sophia Jory enjoyed writing.' Lumb added this with a note of respect.

'Sophia Jory.' Sir John repeated the name thoughtfully. 'I don't think I ever heard of her. Jerry, did you?'

Jerry shook his head. 'I know Joscelyn and Edward had sisters. But I'm sure I never heard of Sophia by name. I can't think she did anything much.'

'She d-d-didn't. She c-c-c – ' For a moment Lumb was in more difficulty than usual. But he overcame it. 'Sophia didn't *do*,' he said firmly. 'She chronicled. Sadie, begin.'

4

'Dear Miss Bird, – Your last letter (which has remained unanswered longer, I fear, than you would at all have sanctioned while you yet had some control of a sadly negligent pupil) is full of interest. But then am I not perpetually astonished, as often as I hear from you, by the inexhaustible variety of incident and observation that Harrogate seems to yield? But diversion is all in the eye; and to most I am persuaded that your remarkable town would seem a dull place enough!

From your account of your present state of health, although you give it so lightly, I cannot derive other than anxious thoughts. I am particularly disturbed that your physician should have prescribed *porter*. No doubt it is, as you say, less repulsive than the *waters*; yet I cannot believe that anything of the sort is (to speak plainly) a drink for gentlefolk. Mr Charles Dickens, the new novelist, is, you have remarked, extremely entertaining; but let us not choose our beverages on the recommendation of his coarser female creation! It was often observed by my dear papa that there is no constitution which a sound burgundy will not fortify. The axiom is one which I have never seen reason to question, and I am therefore happy to say that my brother has eagerly concurred in my suggestion that he should dispatch a dozen of this excellent *specific* to you forthwith. *Only don't let her mix it,* he said to me as he gave the instruction to his butler, *with the damned stuff from the pump.* You will forgive Joscelyn this profanity, will you not, and religiously take a glass when you dine? It is to be *Clos de Tart*, assuredly a strange name for a wine, but highly to be commended (it seems) nevertheless.

But, I hear you exclaim, *what is this of Sir Joscelyn, and how comes he to be at home?* And thus, dear Miss Bird, I enter upon my own news!

My visits to the Hall are commonly made, as you know, in the absence of *both* my brothers. My sister, Lady Jory, is a very good sort of woman, in whose company I can pass a fortnight, or even a month, with a placid sort of satisfaction that is well enough. But Joscelyn I had rather avoid. Although you never, of course, had the charge of one so much older than myself, it will be within your recollection that his interests were seldom enlivening. They might be described, indeed, as precisely the opposite, although I am sadly out for the right antonym, if there be one. (However, it is something to remember the word *antonym* itself, is it not? Doubtless I once writ it out for you.) I may fairly say that my first recollection of Joscelyn is of his burying a dead puppy; and my second of his exhuming it a few weeks later. For some years now he has ridden his hobby at the gallop and on the loosest rein; there is this great *mausoleum* a-building; and vastly ridiculous, to my mind, it makes the family seem.

So my visits to my old home are commonly made while its master is on his travels. Indeed, if I have not totally forgotten the *Use of the Globes*, it has been from the frequent occasions I have taken to consult the terrestrial one in order to assure myself that Joscelyn was yet at a comfortable remove upon the surface of the planet. And for different reasons I have not much, of recent years, cultivated the society of Edward – who, while in England, seems to be as frequently at the Hall (and this despite his ill terms with Joscelyn) as in his own house and amid his own family. It is, perhaps, the fact of Edward's *having* a family that displeases me. A sailor, they say, may have a wife in every port. But ought a husband and a soldier, wearing (now and then) the uniform of a young and virtuous Queen, to have a mistress on every island between the Peloponnese and Asia Minor? Edward's is undoubtedly an extravagant course of life, repugnant to the principles of religion and (what is more) laughable in one of his more than mature years. But all this you know. I come to the Hall when both these tiresome men are about their wanderings. On this occasion, however, my calculations have been upset. My brothers are in the house as I write. And that's not all. There are strange matters, it seems, between them – for they have been brewing up some folly that might pass among lads lately breeched, but which it is excessively mortifying to have to chronicle of fathers of families.

Near a year ago, it seems, Sir James Dangerfield (did I tell you he was like to be made a peer, a thing extravagantly absurd?) persuaded my brothers to a wager – and this upon an occasion so public that the whole country was presently in possession of it. Joscelyn was to overgo all his previous wormy triumphs and acquire a trophy transcendently of the dead; Edward was to achieve a like predatory triumph among the living; the contestants were to confront each other with their spoils in the presence of Sir James and a few others of like character; and the monstrous wager was to be solemnly adjudged. Patience, dear Miss Bird, almost deserts my pen as I recount such a *bêtise*. A freak of this sort is not only immoral; it is also – what makes it much more humiliating to contemplate – no longer the *ton*. But let me press forward with what has become, I see, a narrative.

Each of my brothers appears to have judged it in his interest to conceal his true movements from the other – and so necessarily from our family and its connexions at large. From concealment, moreover, they proceeded to deception; and it is as a consequence of this that I find myself under one roof with them now. Joscelyn I had supposed to be yet at Ordzhonikidze (which I cannot doubt you unhesitatingly recall as standing midway between the Black Sea and the Caspian) and Edward to be staying with old friends (pirates by profession)on the island of Skyros. But – lo and behold! – each appeared at the Hall within twenty-four hours of the other. Joscelyn was first. Let me tell you something of the occasion, and of my own part in it.

Thursday last, the autumn weather continuing mild, I had taken the privilege of my more than forty years to walk solitary by our navigation canal. You will recall that it skirts for a space the eastern verge of the park; and that a short arm, indeed, extends to a small wharf belonging to the Hall. It is thus that we have for long got our sea coal and other bulky commodities – as we shall no doubt continue to do, despite talk of the Messrs Stephenson bringing their steam locomotives into the region. By the canal, then, was I walking on Thursday afternoon – not wholly idly, indeed, since it was my intention to visit several families of the good poor in Bardley – the parish in which is situated, as you will remember, our family's dower house, New Hall.

Do you, my dear Miss Bird, visit the good poor? It is a course recommended by Dr Arnold of Rugby School as instructive and useful. I am bound to add that I myself find the frequentation of this virtuous minority a little dull, and have a suspicion that there might be more entertainment in that almost infinitely larger body known to be wholly undeserving. This is not entirely by the way, for while I lack courage positively to enter the portals of the latter class, I like to keep an eye open for them as I move abroad. Perhaps I am enough of Edward's sister to conjecture that ruffians and desperadoes may be highly amusing. Well, upon such a one I presently came.

He was seated – I had rather say sprawled – upon the hatch of a barge which a wretched nag, urged by a tatterdemalion boy, was painfully hauling in a westerly direction. The cargo involved appeared to be coals: a man, boy, and nag together attested this by the black dust and grime, which smothered them. Perhaps the dust had got, too, painfully into the man's throat; in this there might be some excuse for the large and continual potations (could it have been of porter, dear Miss Bird?) in which he was indulging. A firkin was set up on the deck beside him, and if he paused in drawing from it into a cannikin as grimy as himself, it was only in order to bawl the most horrid curses and objurgations alike at his human and his equine assistant. I stopped to watch him with some interest, and was surprised to discover that his shouts were directed at bringing the barge to a standstill by our wharf. It was presently plain that he intended to tie up there for the night. This is something which I knew not to be permitted to the bargemen unless they have business at the

Hall. The matter was not, strictly, any concern of mine. But the lower classes, even when amusing, must not be insubordinate. I approached with the idea of asking the man if he had any proper occasion there.

The fellow appeared to resent my interest. With some notion, I supposed, of exploiting my modesty in order to drive me away, he now rose uncertainly to his feet, staggered the length of the barge while waving his cannikin above his head, and broke into most profane and dreadful song. I was not, however, to be thus put off! Advancing to the edge of the towing-path, I regarded the grimy monster fixedly. Scarcely had I done so when a strange suspicion assailed me; a moment more, and it had become conviction. *Joscelyn,* I said sternly, *what folly is this?*

For it was indeed my brother – a person, dear Miss Bird, occupying a respectable eminence in the Baronetage of this Kingdom! You will not, I conjecture, judge my question to have been intemperately phrased, and I waited in some indignation for an answer. But no intelligible answer came. Joscelyn gave me a swift look, let his glance travel first to the boy and then to a couple of idle labourers who had strolled up to stare at us, and finally expressed himself merely by spitting rudely into the canal. I turned and walked away. Whatever impropriety was afoot would not be mended by being brought to public notice. Several times of late years have I been advised of a growing *bizarrerie* in my elder brother. Now it had come directly within the scope of my own observation! I said nothing of the incident upon my return to the Hall. On the following day – yesterday, that is – Joscelyn appeared, without explanation, at the dinner-table. He was scrubbed very clean; his manner showed its customary melancholy reserve, although he spoke affectionately to his family and affably to the servants. Once or twice as he looked at me I caught a gleam in his eye. I suppose it to have been of triumph, and sincerely trust it was not of lurking madness! At least he appeared disposed to pay a proper attention to the duties of his station – and I must not omit to mention, dear Miss Bird, that he inquired of you with respect, and instantly arranged for the dispatch of the small present which I have taken earlier occasion to mention.

Let me add that after dinner, and before we assembled again in the drawing-room, I slipped through the park and to the canal. The barge had gone. But there were the marks of a wain in the lane hard by. I had no doubt of there having been some nocturnal operation, the object of which was the covert conveyance into the Hall of something which could not openly be brought there without indiscretion. Without doubt it was the foolish wager that was in question.

I had not long returned to the house when this persuasion was confirmed. Joscelyn was restless as we drank tea, and it occurred to me that he was in some apprehension lest I should divulge the circumstances of our encounter of the day before. Several times he addressed me, his topic being the slow progress made during his absence towards completing his mausoleum in the park. He has, as you know, large collections ready to move into it. I spoke soothingly about this, the more particularly as I have reason to believe that a growing financial stringency in part is accountable for the delay. Eventually he beckoned me from the room. We proceeded to the old coach-house, where Joscelyn's treasures have their temporary home.

Man's mortality, dear Miss Bird, is surely a respectable as well as a solemn topic, and may properly take its place among the subjects to which a gentleman should give regular attention. Joscelyn's activities have done much – as his museum, if it is completed, will do more – to bring it back into polite notice; and I am far from wishing to be a severe critic of my brother's interests. Yet a coach-house approximated to a catacomb, in which *storied urn and animated bust* jostle with the uncouth memorials of Hottentots and South Sea Islanders, and in which the refined mortuary conceptions of the late lamented Mr Nollekens the younger stand at gaze with the monstrous mummies of Egypt and funerary urns of Etruria, is surely very little to the taste of a Christian gentlewoman. I own that I averted my mind from my poor brother's laboriously accumulated morbidities until the moment at which his latest – and certainly most startling – acquisition was obtruded with some urgency upon my notice. I was in the receipt of a confidence. It was incumbent upon me to be reasonably attentive.

Several packing-cases stood in the very centre of the coach-house. Their exterior was besmirched with coal-dust; and I could not doubt that it was these that had been smuggled into Old Hall with the grotesque precautions of the day before. The lid of one had been prised hastily open, and straw and sawdust had been scattered about the floor. My brother bade me advance. I did so, although with some hesitation. The packing-case I found to be divided into two compartments. In the first was what I would fain spare your feelings by describing as a skeleton – but in fact it was a desiccated female body, from which the flesh appeared to have dried away, leaving the skin as a sort of shrunken integument, clinging to and defining the bony structure beneath. The colour was that of mud. And this made the more startling the contents of the adjoining compartment. What there greeted my startled eyes was a blaze of gold and gems!

I believe that I fell back with a cry. On the one hand putrefaction and corruption long ago arrested in dust; on the other the incorruptible splendour of fine metals and precious stones – themselves, in a sad sense, the most *corrupting* substances known to man! Dimly I became aware that my brother was explaining to me the source and nature of his latest prize. The loathsome cadaver was a Caucasian queen – and along with the body he had acquired the queen's ransom which had been buried with her.

Two perceptions presently came to me; and each with very tolerable clarity. The first was obvious. Here was a treasure of enormous value; and if it could be supposed to have had an owner, there was no possibility that Joscelyn could have made him any just recompense for its removal. I have only an uncertain notion of the value of our family estates, and an unhappy suspicion that their present owner's earlier vagaries have placed heavy burdens upon them. But it is very certain that the Jorys, lock, stock and barrel (to use a vulgar phrase), are by no means worth what this single smuggled packing-case of my brother's contains.

My second perception was of another order. Joscelyn had triumphed – for it seemed impossible that Edward could overgo this astounding *coup*. Nevertheless, even as we gazed at his prize, there was that in his manner which suggested discontent or *ennui*. He has always been moody, and much of his life has been conducted by fits and starts. Yet his mortuary studies and the forming of his collection have constituted hitherto an unintermitted vein of almost passionate interest, and have brought him a measure of distinction which may yet lay some claim upon posterity. Could it be possible, I asked myself, that his old obsession was failing my brother at the portals of old age, and that he was not experiencing from his latest and most splendid possession the large satisfaction which he might have anticipated?

But I saw that there was another explanation. This time, Joscelyn might have gone too far – and been aware of it. The grotesque course which he had adopted for bringing the Caucasian treasure covertly home suggested, to say the least, an uneasy conscience. An English gentleman cannot, of course, *steal*. But it seemed to me only too likely that Joscelyn's acquiring of these costly objects had been not unattended by some measure of *legal irregularity*. This was a thought of some weight. Joscelyn's mausoleum has already put him under an imputation of singularity in the country; and the respectability which the family of Jory of Old Hall has long enjoyed would be sadly impaired if to this there were now a super-addition of positive scandal. The alarming prospect is still with me as I write. But it at least is no longer my sole anxiety. Did not I inform you at the outset of this letter that my brother Edward, too, is returned? And no more than Joscelyn has he returned in a manner befitting a person of property and consideration in the neighbourhood. The rest of this letter, dear Miss Bird, must be painful and short!

I lingered not long with Joscelyn in the coach-house, for it was soon clear to me that he was disinclined to be truly communicative. A display of his treasure to some member of the family he had been unable to resist, and he did indeed talk freely of the foolish wager and the confidence he now had of winning it. But on the *provenance* (as collectors call it) of his crowning acquisition he would not speak, and questioning rendered him uneasy. I wonder, is Joscelyn a courageous man? I almost had the sense of his being a little frightened!

I went back, then, to the Hall, intending to make my way to the drawing-room, where my sister (her tranquility quite undisturbed by the abrupt return of her husband from unknown wildernesses) would be attending our nightly encounter at bezique. But on the very threshold I was encountered by Mrs Jennings, the housekeeper. The good woman had plainly been waiting for me, eager to impart a further piece of news. *Mr Edward too was arrived*, she said. *He was not alone. And he had gone to the Temple of Diana.*

You know enough of Old Hall to realize that this had an ominous sound! Edward has retained for him here a small set of apartments high in the oldest part of the house. That he should have made his way not to these but to a retired building in a corner of the park, was a circumstance the least propitious that one could conceive. The Temple was *never* a place of good repute. The interests of Sir Arthur Jory, who built it, were vain and amatorious; and it was for long understood that much transacted itself in the structure (so jocosely dedicated to the goddess of chastity) that it would have been injudicious to obtrude upon the notice of society. It had from the first the character of a dwelling – although upon somewhat sketchy and uncomfortable lines – and various Jorys have from time to time, upon one occasion or another, taken up a temporary residence there. The last was my dear Aunt Elizabeth, during those periods in which she believed herself to be a barouche-landau. The place is secluded. It was only too obvious why Edward had repaired to it.

At that moment the subject of my anxious thoughts came into the house behind me, and Mrs Jennings withdrew. Edward greeted me affectionately, as is his habit. He had arrived early in the afternoon, he said, together with his friend Kent. They had taken up their quarters in the Temple.

I forget whether Mr Kent is known to you. He is a familiar of Edward's, his companion (I imagine) in many unedifying escapades, and, although a gentleman, not one whose acquaintance a lady would wish to cultivate. I asked Edward drily whether he and his friend were to be alone in the quarters they had taken up. *Aha!* he said. *So you have heard the gossip? We have smuggled in a monstrous fine wench in a covered wagon. Jim Dangerfield is to judge of her, over against anything that Joscelyn can summon. There's a fortune in her, my dear –* mark my word.

I confess that I was in some uncertainty as to how to reply. Had Edward been thirty years younger, I believe I should have laughed – although no doubt it would have been a culpable thing to do. But conduct thus sadly disordered has no charm in the elderly. I said at once that I could view his behaviour only with severe disapprobation. *Why,* he said, *a spinster should surely commend a fellow for bringing Aphrodite to do homage at the shrine of Diana.* To this I thought it reasonable to reply that he had at least done well to take his wench to the Temple, and not venture to march with her into his sister's house. *Wench,* says he, *is no name for my charmer.* I rejoined that he had presumably found her among the lower orders of society. *Lower orders?* Edward said. *All that begins to change, my dear Sophia, as soon as you step off the packet at Calais. And it's devilish different by the time you get to Kythera or Naxos.*

And at this I suddenly saw Edward's conduct not as scandalous and immoral (as it undoubtedly is) but simply as heartless. The mention of those far places brought vividly before me, I suppose, the unkindness of dragging some girl – God knows with what delusive promises – across the whole extent of Europe in order to fulfil a nonsensical undertaking entered upon in some moment of recklessness and inebriety. I said firmly that the Ministry was to blame – that the Governments of the several countries necessarily traversed were to blame – for permitting a traffic so disreputable. Such matters should be inquired into, I said, upon the quays and in the customs-houses. It seemed to me that for a moment Edward looked startled at this, as if I had succeeded in introducing him to a new view of the matter. And although he was quickly at his jesting once more, there was now revealed to me something uneasy in his demeanour. Precisely as in Joscelyn's case, I wondered whether he did not suspect himself to have gone too far. And of the second brother as of the first I was suddenly asking myself: *Is this a courageous man?*

Edward, however, continued with his banter; and it was clear to me that he was bent upon mystification. I asked him if the unhappy girl was a peasant. He replied that he believed her to come, on the contrary, *of maritime stock*; and that although he had found her *in a very lowly situation*, there was good reason to suppose her connected with *the highest circles*. He then recurred to the theme that she was going to be *too much for Joscelyn by a long way.* It was apparent that Edward believed himself to have accomplished some stroke of extraordinary adroitness. I asked whether the poor creature was provided with any friend or attendant of her own sex; and whether, if not, some discreet woman from among the cottagers might not be employed in this office. Edward seemed to think little of this. I therefore begged him – such was my distress as I felt with increasing poignancy the misery that must attend the girl in her isolation – to let me go to her myself. At this, Edward was silent for a while. I was happy, and at the same time touched, to observe that my offer had, for the moment, made him unmistakably ashamed of himself. He took a turn about the hall, muttered something to the effect that I was a good sort of soul enough – and then, with a sudden change of mood, burst into laughter. *She wasn't yet,* he said, *fit for the company of ladies. He must first take soap and water to her, and then we should see.* To this Edward added something further in bad French. I caught the words *tetons* and *fesses*. This grossness I was unprepared to suffer. I bade Edward good night, and left him.

It is now Saturday, and I have entertained myself (not, I hope, to any effect of tedium in yourself) for the greater part of the day in the composition of this epistle. We await, I suppose, the arrival of Sir James Dangerfield and others of his set, whereupon our gentlemen will no doubt divert themselves with playing out the last act of their comedy. From something let drop by Lady Jory's maid (who is good enough to attend on me for a few minutes when I rise) I gather that not only the servants' hall but the whole country (and our neighbourhood, as you know, is extensive) is very well aware of the state of the case, and that the Duke himself has declared he is minded to ride over from Nesfield Court *to have a few words with Ned Jory's Maid of Athens.*

All this is most distasteful, as you may imagine, to my sister and myself. At breakfast (which, according to the sound old custom of this house, we partake of at a set hour and together) we were none of us in spirits. If Joscelyn had experienced any triumph in bringing his Caucasian queen and her treasure safe to Old Hall, he appeared now to be experiencing some dismal reflex of feeling. He delivered himself of a sort of jeremiad on the insufficiencies of his whole collection. *If the mausoleum were never finished,* he said, *it would be no matter. He had, indeed, variety enough of funerary exhibits to deploy in it. But the great things had always eluded him.*

I was much struck by the revelation of this vein of the highest connoisseurship in my brother; it somehow made his hobby-horse appear to me of greater interest than hitherto. I asked him what in all the world he most coveted. He replied gloomily that the Medici Tombs of Michelangelo would be something; that he had treated at one time for the Lorenzo II, which he judged to be the finest; but that the damned Florentines refused to part with as much as the Dawn or Twilight on the sarcophagus beneath it. He added that in Toledo he had come across something yet more to his liking – the burial of a certain Count Orgaz depicted by a painter named (if I remember rightly) Theotocopuli and popularly styled El Greco. He had again made a handsome offer. *But,* he concluded, *there's nothing so proud as your damned penniless Spaniard.*

I own that I was diverted by these confessions of Joscelyn's unsuccessful designs. There is quite as much of the artist in him, surely, as there is of the savant or the philosopher. His collection has fallen short of its possible perfections, and the consciousness of this makes him melancholy. Is it conceivable that Edward is in similar case – tormented that he has not been able to do as Faust did, and add Helen of Troy to the number of his conquests? But this is an idle speculation, and indeed you may judge it not a delicate one. I can only plead something sadly corrupting in the present air of Old Hall. Certainly I have been drawn on into writing at most inordinate length on the present perplexing posture of our family affairs. But then are you not one of that family's oldest friends? Once more, then, I subscribe myself, dear Miss Bird,

Your affectionate pupil,

SOPHIA JORY.'

5

There was a short silence when Sadie Sackett concluded reading this letter. The spaniel, which had earlier retreated to a secluded corner, now advanced across the floor, stood on the hearth-rug, and gazed upward in a sort of melancholy dubiety at the portrait of Sir Joscelyn.

'Berkeley', Jerry Jory said, 'is a most intelligent dog. He wonders. He wonders whether Mr Clout ought not perhaps to devote his learned energies to somebody else. It sounds to me as if the family could stand up to a little of Joscelyn in a footnote of Professor Milder's but might find a full-length biography rather too much of a good thing.'

'My dear boy – I don't see that at all.' Sir John Jory was unexpectedly emphatic. 'Joscelyn appears to have been an interesting fellow. Went all over the place collecting things, you see. Mind you, I don't say a wager of that sort would be quite the thing today. Still, Joscelyn's side of it was perfectly decent and so forth. Edward's enterprise is another matter. But then it's always been known that Edward was a bit of a bad hat. Eh, Jory?'

Dr Jory, thus appealed to, vigorously shook his head. 'No Jory – I don't see that. Edward, I take it, had simply picked up somewhere or other a particularly beautiful mercenary girl, hoping she would win him his bet. Not very moral, perhaps – but decidedly not criminal.'

'I agree with Daddy.' Olivia had sat down with some informality on the floor and was stroking Berkeley's muzzle. 'So far as Sophia's letter goes, we don't even know that Edward's relations with his exhibit weren't entirely virtuous. Whereas Joscelyn – '

'Whereas Joscelyn', Dr Jory said, 'had plainly involved himself in large-scale loot or robbery. His turning up on that barge and so forth is very amusing. But he was obliged to it simply because he had been engaged in theft.'

'Depredation, Dr Jory.' It was Professor Milder who came forward soothingly with this. 'Depredation, I guess, is the proper word. I find Miss Sophia Jory's letter most interesting – most interesting, indeed. But it's unfortunate about Mr Edward Jory. Yes, all that is very much to be regretted –! very much to be regretted. I was struck by what Miss Sophia writes about the duties of governments in the matter. In my country, right now, you just can't take a girl across a state boundary that way. American womanhood makes a stand against anything of that sort. I need hardly say that my own work will make no reference to Mr Edward Jory. All that is quite aside from my field of research. But I do find Sir Joscelyn's Caucasian treasure very interesting – very interesting, indeed.'

Jerry Jory nodded. 'So, I imagine, do several of us. What happened to it? All this makes me feel that I know shamefully little of the family's history. But if this treasure entered prominently into it, I supposed one would have heard. Perhaps George knows.'

'There's m-m-more, you know, to c-c-come.' George Lumb pointed towards Sadie's portfolio. 'B-b-but it's indefinite. The t-t-treasure may be hidden away. That's what Olivia thinks.'

Olivia nodded. Clout could see that this public hammering out of the situation wasn't to her taste. But she appeared to be taking it in good part. 'Yes,' she said. 'My first guess when I heard of it – and it does, you see, exist as a sort of hazy tradition in our branch of the family – was that it might be buried in the mausoleum. But of course it might be buried anywhere else – anywhere in that whole great park.'

'Buried?' Olivia's father shook his head. 'That would be just too bad, eh?' He seemed to take a humorous view of his daughter's involvement in the mystery. 'You know that, if it were found under the soil, it would undoubtedly belong to the Crown?'

'Treasure trove!' Lady Jory, who had not hitherto participated in the debate, brought this out triumphantly. 'I had a very interesting book about it from the circulating library not long ago. The illustrations were good – which is always the great thing.'

'But suppose', Olivia asked, 'it was found not buried, but tucked away in a secret chamber – '

Jerry Jory interrupted with laughter that Clout didn't think at all polite. 'My dear Miss Jory, Georgian houses don't have secret chambers.'

'Well, something of the sort.' Olivia was unperturbed. 'Whose would it be then?'

'The University's.' Gingrass, who had been fidgeting on his chair while seeking an entry into the conversation, brought this out perhaps with more absoluteness than he had intended. It was not well received.

'The University?' Sir John demanded. 'Stuff and nonsense – eh, Jory?'

'Certainly not the University, Jory. I regard the Professor's suggestion as absurd.' Dr Jory turned to Gingrass. 'Quite absurd, sir. Olivia here could scarcely get a sillier notion into her head – and that says a lot.'

Gingrass was somewhat abashed by this onslaught. 'A share,' he said – apparently by way of hedging. 'I think it likely that the University would be legally entitled to a share. If the stuff were not in fact buried, that is to say.'

'Most improbable.' Jerry Jory was preremptory in his turn. 'The University owns what it bought – or what its predecessor, the College, bought before it. And it certainly didn't buy a treasure that nobody had ever heard of. If I sell my house, you know, and leave my wrist-watch on a mantel-piece, it doesn't become the property of the chap who moves in. If he pockets it, I can jolly well have him put in quod.'

Dr Jory laughed. 'Isn't that where somebody might have had Joscelyn put? Even if this treasure turned up in England in such a way that it was not technically treasure trove now, it was almost certainly treasure trove, or the equivalent thing in the lingo of the Caucasus, when your enterprising ancestor, my dear Jory, first nabbed it. A very reasonable claim, I imagine, would vest in whatever is the legal government of those parts now. The Russian Government, would it be?'

'The Russians!' Lady Jory was disturbed. 'Surely it wouldn't be right to give a valuable treasure to them? John, dear – you would certainly have to consult the Prime Minister first.'

For a moment Sir John made no reply to this. It was to be conjectured that a new and startling idea was forming in his mind. 'There might be a lot in this treasure? More to be got out of it by a long way than out of books and so forth? Jory, you've a head on your shoulders. What would you say?'

'If the treasure was valuable when Miss Sophia saw it, you may be sure it's more valuable today. Pearls and enamels and the like might deteriorate. But not diamonds and rubies. And gold doesn't corrupt – or not if one sticks to the intransitive use of the verb.'

'Is that so?' Sir John was a shade baffled by this grammatical subtlety. But he clearly had a high regard for his kinsman's sagacity. 'I'll be glad of your advice my dear fellow, I need hardly say. If you care to give it, that is. Of course I realize the affair's no concern of yours.'

Olivia, who had grown bored with Berkeley and returned to her sofa, reacted violently. 'No concern of ours, Sir John? You mean we're butting in?'

'Not at all, my dear – not at all.' As he made this hasty and courteous disclaimer Sir John eyed Olivia with some shrewdness. 'I merely mean that, if this treasure can be thought of as legally Joscelyn's – and not belonging to some fellows in the Kremlin, as your father seems to suppose – then, of course, it would come down in the senior line. Full of interest for you, and all that. But, regarded as *property –* '

'You haven't heard the whole story, Sir John. You haven't heard about the swap. It's true that it too has only been a vague tradition, so far. But I think we'll find Sophia has something to say about it. Has she, Miss Sackett?'

Sadie had been turning over her papers. At this question she nodded curtly. 'Yes,' she said. 'There's something.'

'There's something f-f-fairly d-d-definite,' George Lumb put in. 'And there's something *n-n-not* definite as well – and rather sinister, I'm afraid.'

'Sinister?' Jerry Jory asked sharply.

Sadie nodded seriously. 'There's something that certainly puts Dr Jory – or all the junior Jorys – into the picture. And there's something rather grim, as well. But of course George and I don't know either what force those wagers and bargains and so on have, or how much Sophia Jory may have taken to imagining things. Shall I read the next letter?'

Lady Jory, to whom this question had been addressed, nodded with her customary placidity. The somewhat sombre tone of both Lumb and Sadie by no means disturbed her. 'Yes, my dear,' she said. 'When I was a girl, we always had reading aloud after tea. It is a very nice sort of thing to have, just at that time of day. Particularly in winter, and with candles.'

6

'Dear Miss Bird, – Do not be unduly alarmed when I say that I write this letter (so soon after my last) in an endeavour to calm an agitation of spirits! We are of a sudden surrounded at Old Hall by perturbations and *suspicions* – and I have been the more distressed in that one of these last concerns *myself*. It is not unknown to me that unmarried members of our sex may become subject, at a certain age, to disorders of the imagination, and these, too, in the most intimate departments of life. My Aunt Elizabeth (whose sad history you will recall) was a case in point. On those occasions when she believed herself to be a conveyance, her concern was embarrassingly with attracting the notice of gentlemen whom she judged *likely to be skilled with the reins*. I have had to ask myself whether it be merely by some like aberration of intellect that I have come to suppose my elder brother suddenly overthrown by a violent erotical distemper.

You will not find it difficult to believe that I shudder as I pen these appalling words. Yet I persuade myself that I am in my senses, and that the events upon which I must now touch are not in fact the product of my fancy. Women of no, or inconsiderable, station have wrought havoc in our family before. Arthur Jory, having successively and without unseemly enthusiasm enjoyed the favours of several ladies of rank, hanged himself for a milkmaid. And there have been other painful instances of this inflammable propensity in our menfolk, which it would be idle here to recall. Yet that Joscelyn, whose course of life hitherto, although in some particulars singular and perverse, has been distinguished, to my almost certain knowledge, by an entire probity in this so often fatal sphere of feeling and action – that Joscelyn, I say, in the very evening of his life, should be suddenly subjected to a libidinous and concupiscent frenzy, is surely a circumstance conducing, dear Miss Bird, to the most solemn reflections on the hazardousness of the earthly condition. Dr Samuel Johnson, selections from whose Moral Prose we used to read with such profit and pleasure together, has, I think, some serious and edifying observations on this subject in his *Rambler*. But let me not procrastinate telling what I must tell!

This morning early, being Sunday, my brother Edward, together with his reprehensible friend Mr Kent, presented themselves at the Hall. Breakfast indeed being not yet concluded, they sat down with us and proceeded to make good the large deficiencies doubtless characterizing their temporary housekeeping in the Temple. Edward, with a familiarity to which he must, I suppose, be held entitled at his brother's board, called loudly for broiled bones; and Mr Kent, with what was certainly unpardonable insolence, rudely demanded to know whether there was no salmi of game? Lady Jory and I, you will readily believe, rose to withdraw at the earliest moment compatible with unflawed civility. But I was not allowed to pass behind Edward's chair without his catching me round the hips – a frolick gesture permissible to a brother in strict family privacy, but intolerable in the presence of such a *low blackguard* fellow as his Mr Kent – and jocosely whispering that *the soap and scrubbing-brush had done wonders, and her flanks were now gleaming like a thoroughbred's.* And at this Kent gave a loud guffaw. I disengaged myself with what dignity I could. Mr Kent, upon the pretext of politely anticipating the servant who was preoccupied with the chafing-dishes, moved to the door and held it open – this for the sole purpose, I am persuaded, of favouring me with a final vulgar smirk. Such was the displeasing prelude to a melancholy day.

Shortly afterwards the gentlemen repaired together to the coach-house, and I concluded that the two parties to the fatal wager had made a compact each to be permitted a glimpse of the other's *bid*. It was known to me that Sir James Dangerfield and several other gentlemen had been engaged to a supper which Lady Jory and I were not expected to attend; and I had accounted it a token of grace in Joscelyn that he had by this arrangement mitigated the gross impropriety that would have marked our exclusion, when resident in the country, from the more formal occasion of *dinner*. There was something a little unexpected, it seemed to me, in this preliminary inspection. Since the whole sorry affair appeared conceived in terms of theatrical effect, it would have been natural to suppose that an element of absolute surprise would have been treasured to the last. But about both my brothers there has been – as I believe myself to have remarked in my last letter – an odd air of uneasiness. Neither seemed very confident of what he was about. It almost seemed as if each was seeking some reassurance from the other.

I next saw Edward at about noon. Going out to take a turn in the shrubbery (for I am convinced of the value of vigorous exercise at that time of day) I observed him standing moodily at the far end of the terrace. I resolved at once to take advantage of Mr Kent's absence to expostulate with him on both his own behaviour at the breakfast-table and that of the companion whom he had thought proper to introduce to it. He heard me, I fear, without attention – and then burst into inconsequent speech of surprising vehemence. It seemed, he said, that I had been admitted to the coach-house; did I realize what it was that Joscelyn had brought home? And was Joscelyn demented? Did he really propose, for the sake of their paltry wager, to divulge to Jim Dangerfield and half the riff-raff of the country a prize that, rightly disposed of, would set us above all but the Duke himself?

Although I had no doubt that this was a grossly exaggerated estimate of the worth of the Caucasian treasure, I was yet rendered very uneasy by Edward's speech and manner. I replied that Joscelyn was scarcely a practical man of affairs, and that his ambitions had ever been aside from the ordinary. The intrinsic value of what he had brought home with him he had probably given little thought to. Had he done so in the first instance, indeed, he might have felt a wholesome hesitation in possessing himself of it.

At this, Edward asked me if I supposed Joscelyn made no distinction between the treasure and all the loathsome rubbish he had been collecting these past thirty years? I replied that I believed Joscelyn to regard this as by far his most notable acquisition; but that yet he appeared not contented, and that I was inclined to suspect his long mortuary mania to be at last burning out in him.

Edward heard me broodingly, took a turn on the terrace, and then fell into a long complaint of what he chose to term his beggarly condition. He was ashamed of his stables; he had not a sound wine in his cellar to set before a guest; when he travelled abroad it was in the condition of a parson or a governess; and things were at such a pass that, were he minded to make a small gift to a lady, he must first sell the gown off his own wife's back.

To a speech ending in so offensive a turn I could make no other reply than to walk away; but Edward pursued me, talking still. From his present condition (as he chose to depict it) he passed to a sort of diabolical essay on the right use of riches. With any account of this I shall not distress you. Suffice it to say that I was reminded of Sir Epicure Mammon in the old play, entertaining himself to the most wicked imaginations of a more than *Neronian* licence. At length he looked at his watch and was recollected. The hour had come, it seemed, at which he was to conduct Joscelyn to the Temple. I returned to the house and endeavoured to compose myself by reading one of Dr South's sermons.

It was with some relief that I found only Joscelyn and his wife at the dinner-table. Edward's presence would have distressed me, and Mr Kent I should now have found intolerable. Joscelyn was quite silent, and I noticed that he was very pale. Although conversation, even within the family circle at its narrowest, is surely essential to good-breeding, I myself judged that on this occasion we had better dine as quietly as Joscelyn chose. But it will be within your recollection, dear Miss Bird, that Lady Jory, although placid, is not perceptive. No doubt her husband's appearance caused her some anxiety; and this she endeavoured to dissipate in chatter. It appeared that she had not been privileged to visit the coach-house, but she was aware that Joscelyn had brought some notable accession home with him. She must have known too, in a general way, about the wager. Now she asked for particulars – a request very reasonable in a wife – and Joscelyn, although his manner was constrained, replied with civility. Gathering that something very valuable was in question, and in an endeavour to see her husband in better spirits, Lady Jory professed herself to be highly pleased at his good fortune, and happy in the prospect of presently being permitted to view objects so splendid. And at this Joscelyn suddenly cried out in a high, strange voice, such as I had assuredly never heard from him before, that *it was all nought but barbarous rubbish, such as might adorn some savage orgy, but was of no consonance with the dignity and absoluteness of death.*

I need scarcely say that this speech was incomprehensible to my poor sister, and that I had myself no confidence of discerning from what state of mind it issued. But if I felt alarm, I felt at least curiosity too. With some boldness therefore I asked my brother whether he had been this morning at the Temple; and, if so, had he there seen anything that it was fit to tell us of?

He eyed me askance. It is no habit of Joscelyn's; and it was in this moment, I believe, that I first conceived the shocking thought that all was not well with his reason. His reply was enigmatical. *He had indeed been at the Temple. And it had lived up to its name as a place of revelation.* Pray what was that, my dear? asked Lady Jory. *That Edward*, he answered, *had made the better bargain with Fortune, and commanded the only true felicity he could now conceive.*

Here was something more that my good sister could make nothing of, and I chose not myself to probe the matter further. For the truth, I think, had begun to dawn on me, and I judged that we should be better separated while Joscelyn remained minded to such rash and unbecoming utterance. If it was a mere vagary, a freak of fancy roused by the unashamed vice of Edward and the lewd suggestions which one can well imagine emanating from Mr Kent, then the arrival of Sir James Dangerfield and his friends, although little likely to conduce to edification in any positive sense, might divert his mind from the fond and dangerous channel in which it had begun to run. Meanwhile Joscelyn had fortunately fallen into an abstraction, and said no more. So sunk in sombre thought, indeed, did he become, that when my sister and I rose to withdraw, he remained inert and regardless in his chair – an action (or *lack* of action) unparalleled in my recollection.

That Sunday afternoon may with a peculiar appropriateness be dedicated to charitable exertion is a lesson which, my dear Miss Bird, I have never forgotten your impressing upon me; and, when at Old Hall, I am the more exigent with myself in the discharge of such duties upon those alternate Sundays on which we are unhappily without a morning service in our parish church. It was my intention, then, on this occasion, to go a round of the cottages, making such inquiries, and distributing such small gifts, as seemed proper. I was to be back, you see, with the *good poor*; and if the employment was not likely to be entertaining, it might at least distract me from those anxious thoughts to which the whole trend of events around me was irresistably prompting.

Providing myself, then, through the kindness of my sister, with a stout serving-maid fit to carry a well-filled basket of soups and preserves, I set out on this unexciting occasion. You may wonder, indeed, why I pause to record it. Another moment will enlighten you!

The third on my list was Mrs Grindell, the widow of a stone-breaker, necessarily very poorly left, and with but one young son (whom I supposed I had never seen) to afford her some support. I had been told that the boy was now entered upon casual labour on the waterways, and unlikely to be at home; it was therefore no surprise to me to find Mrs Grindell in solitude. Our conversation did not very well sustain itself, for the good woman's cottage was clean and orderly, so that I found little upon which to admonish her; moreover she appeared neither to suffer from any of the ailments common to her station nor to nourish any persuasion that she did so. This, you will admit, was a hard case for the visitor! I was about to bid her return to her employments, and myself proceed in search of less stony ground, when there was a sound of running feet in the lane outside, mingled with what could only be a dismal blubbering. A moment later there burst in upon us a panic-stricken lad who could be no other than Tom, Mrs Grindell's son. He was not, after all, unknown to me. I had last seen him, not in his present decently-patched attire, but in wretched rags – and in receipt of the curses and objurgations of my own grotesquely disguised brother. Here, in a word, was Joscelyn's assistant smuggler!

I was so confounded by this unexpected irruption that it was some moments before I became aware of what had reduced young Tom to so unmanly a condition. It was likely, I confusedly thought, that some other lad had bested him in a bout of fisticuffs, or that he had been swinged by one of our farmers for robbing an orchard. Presently however I caught a reference to *the Squire*, and realized that Joscelyn was involved in the boy's story. I therefore bade him with some severity address himself to me, and begin his narrative again. The effect of my interposition was sobering; Tom made some rude effort after coherence and lucidity; and presently I was in possession of new and perplexing intelligence.

The Squire (Tom said) had lately employed him about some private business, wholly without sense to it, such as only the gentry could engage in. There was a wager to it, he supposed; much of the madness of the gentry was over wagers. What the Squire had required of him was no concern of his; he had done what he was told, been rewarded generously, and instructed to say nothing to anybody. Nor had he – not even to his own mother. But now the outlandish men had got it out of him. Not much – for it was not much that he knew. But what he did know, he had been frightened into telling.

Tom Grindell had now stopped his blubbering. I could see that he was ashamed alike of it and of his failure to keep my brother's confidence. I could see too that he was a lad not without some natural quickness of wit. Thus when I asked him whether by outlandish men he meant simply persons not of this part of the country, he replied, *begging my pardon, that he meant those they called foreigners.* Foreigners! I exclaimed in surprise. *Yes and if it pleased me,* Tom said, *those that dragged him to the inn were out of Muscovy.* And at this Mrs Grindell, sensible woman though she be, fell to blubbering in her turn, declaring *it was but a Providence her boy's throat had not been slit from ear to ear.* Bidding the woman be silent, I questioned Tom with all the diligence (and discretion) that his astonishing statement required. And presently I satisfied myself that there could scarcely be any doubt of the alarming fact. The boy had been waylaid by a stranger and in some manner enticed to the inn, where he had been interviewed by another stranger in a private room. When, by means of threats and promises, these men had extracted from him something of his late services for Joscelyn, they commanded him to stay where he was, and both hurried out to the yard. Tom, although vastly terrified, had ventured on a peep through the window. What he had seen was a carriage with drawn blinds, and his captors reporting, cap in hand, to some person (whom he judged to be of great consequence) invisible within. Almost immediately, the carriage drove away. The two men returned to the inn, commanded Tom to say nothing to anyone, and dismissed him. At this the boy (although already on the verge of tears) had the spirit to demand who they were, that had so treated him? Whereat one of the men, laughing contemptuously, had replied *that it would mean little to an English peasant lad to be told that he was in the presence of those who served the Tsar of all the Russias.*

All this, although surprising, was scarcely *Greek* to me. I assured the Grindells, mother and son, that nothing of moment had occurred; that the interview at the inn was but a trivial matter consequent upon the wager which Tom had so sagely suspected; and that it would now be best to forget the matter, and in particular to say nothing of it to the neighbours. I then gave Tom his own jar of our housekeeper's special strawberry conserve, and came away (I trust) in what a soldier would call good order – although with grave and serious thoughts, as you may imagine.

But the afternoon's revelations were not over! I had scarcely determined upon the truth of our situation (namely, that Joscelyn's possessing himself of so inordinately valuable a treasure as he had, must have roused the concern – perhaps *the just indignation* – of a powerful and arbitrary Ruler), when, upon turning into the park, I encountered once more the objectionable Mr Kent. He appeared to be hurrying from the Hall to the Temple, and was at first disposed to pass me by with a bare civility. Then he paused, in an odd irresolution, and I observed that he was agitated. He asked me, *had I heard any untoward news abroad?* I replied instantly that I had not. *Nothing of foreigners come into the neighbourhood?* This put me rather at a stand. But I presently replied that had I intelligence of anything of the sort, it would be with my brother, Sir Joscelyn, that I should think proper to discuss it. *Sir Joscelyn!* he cried violently. *The devil and nothing it had to do with him, the covert, cunning dog. It was poor Edward that would take the knock, did it come to a bruising-match.*

I was about to bow and pass on (for I had no wish to bandy riddles with a *low* person) when he burst out with information that made me pause. The Duke of Nesfield, it appeared, had that morning sent his steward (a man he would occasionally employ upon the most highly confidential business) post-haste to the Hall, with the message *that Mr Edward Jory had better know the jest was gone too far. His Grace had news there had been interest made at Court; that a certain Chancellery was incensed; and that it would be well that the Grecian tune be transposed swiftly from the Lydian to the Dorian mode.* Mr Kent repeated this last expression with the utmost contempt, clearly regarding it as little better than gibberish. But his uneasiness was not to be mistaken. I think I must myself have betrayed evidence of some dismay, and certainly I cried out that we were all like to be involved in the just retribution presently to be visited, it seemed, upon Edward's latest base amour. Mr Kent stared at me and then burst into his harshest laughter. *It was too bad*, he said, *to be a virtuous Christian gentlewoman, and at the same time sister to one who had abducted the mistress of the Sublime Porte.* He then turned from me with a flourish of his hat and hurried on to the Temple.

I confess myself to have been in such agitation by this time (my dear Miss Bird) that only after an interval did the element of unashamed nonsense in Mr Kent's last asseveration become apparent to me. The Sublime Porte is *not* a person. But I have no doubt that it is an institution scandalously prolific, if not in *mistresses*, at least in *concubines*. It seemed only too assured that Edward's prize was not the unregarded peasant girl I had imagined. And here were we, an English family of honourable, if private, station, subjected, through the folly of my brothers, to the unfavourable notice – perhaps to the *unscrupulous enmity* – of *two* formidable Foreign Powers!

It has been my intention, so soon as I should arrive back at the Hall, to seek out Joscelyn, give him my disturbing news, and endeavour to draw him to a course of rational conduct, which should include immediate reparation of the luckless treasure. I have been the more hopeful of success, since he expressed himself at dinner as so violently discontented with it. Unfortunately I have not been able to put this plan into execution. Joscelyn is invisible; and to a note that I sent him (with a brief, and, as I hoped, *arresting* account of my experience) there has been returned only the very formal answer *that he hopes to have the honour of attending on me later*. Meanwhile the evening wears away; and I have endeavoured to beguile its anxieties by penning you these few rude and hasty pages. But now I must break off! At an earlier hour than I have apprehended, the sound of a curricle on the sweep informs me that either Sir James Dangerfield or one of the other expected guests has presented himself.

What, then, are we to suppose should issue from the crowning folly planned as this night's diversion? That my next communication will give other than a melancholy reply is something, dear Miss Bird, for which I devoutly hope, but which I by no means find myself able to expect!

Your affectionate pupil,

SOPHIA JORY.'

7

'That is very nice.' Lady Jory – who seemed to Clout to have all the placidity attributed to her predecessor of a century before – was absently fondling one of Berkeley's large ears. 'There is nothing more pleasant, after tea, than a good long read. And you read very well.' Lady Jory paused, and some echo of Sadie Sackett's honest regional accent seemed to strike her ear. 'Unaffectedly, that is to say. My dear father used commonly to remark that he always loved an unaffected girl. There was frequent evidence that he did.' Lady Jory looked round her drawing-room, as if a little puzzled by the direction her own remarks were taking. 'George, don't you agree?'

George Lumb hesitated. 'About your f-f-father, Lady Jory?'

'About that being a very nice piece of reading – very informative and entertaining.'

'I l-l-like Sophia Jory's m-m-majestic and m-m-monotonous prose. A b-b-bomb couldn't alter its tempo, one feels.' Lumb delivered this professional appreciation with some enthusiasm.

'*Was* there a bomb – or what used to be called a bomb-shell?' Jerry Jory asked. 'Are we going to know? Is there more?'

Sadie nodded. 'There's one more letter. It was written on the following morning. And Sophia certainly felt there was a bomb-shell. Several.'

Olivia Jory leaned forward. 'The swap, for instance? There's something about that?'

'You needn't worry, Miss Jory. You'll get your swap. It's on record, all right – for what it's worth.'

'It sounds to me', Dr Jory said, 'as if it was worth the deuce of a lot. Jory, what do you make of all this?'

Sir John Jory, thus appealed to, walked slowly to the hearth-rug, as if feeling that a more authoritative pronouncement might be made from this point of vantage. 'It doesn't seem to me', he presented offered, 'that they were all quite playing the game, you know. Travelling and collecting and so forth is all very well, and if a fellow carries off a tomb or two from niggers or savages, I don't say there's any great harm done. As for Edward Jory's girl – well, it was quite the thing at that time, as I believe I've said before. But, of course, bringing her along was another matter, particularly if she was the sort of girl that the people in some embassy or legation were going to get worked up about. I'm sure Jerry, with his experience of that sort of thing, agrees.' Sir John stopped. Like his wife, he was inclined to become rather bewildered about the tenor of his own utterance. 'I mean, that is, Jerry's experience of diplomatic folk, not of girls – or at least of *that* sort of girl.'

'Thank you very much,' Jerry Jory said. Clout remarked, with strong disapproval, that the young man had permitted himself a cautious grin at Olivia.

'In fact,' Sir John pursued, 'it looks to me as if it was all rather a poor show. Joscelyn after Edward's girl, and Edward after this stuff Joscelyn had brought from the Caucasus. And the women-folk worried by it all, and having to put up with bounders about the place, and a lot of talk about mistresses and concubines. Concubines, in particular, is very offensive, I'd say. Wouldn't you agree?'

Professor Milder felt it proper to offer his support at this point. 'I guess I certainly agree with that, Sir John,' he said. 'Yes, that is very correct – very correct, indeed. We must omit all consideration of this Mr Edward Jory, and what he chose to install in the Temple of Diana. I take no interest in that, myself – no interest whatever. But Sir Joscelyn is another matter – discreetly handled, of course.'

'I can't say I'm very clear that he is.' Sir John shook his head doubtfully. 'For one thing, the two brothers seem to have got themselves awkwardly mixed up together. I'm inclined to think we should drop it all. Honour of the family, and so forth. Not a thing one jaws about. Still, you know what I mean.'

Dr Jory nodded. 'I'm bound to say, Jory, that I have a good deal of sympathy with that point of view. Edward looks like being rather an embarrassing great-grandfather. But isn't it a little late in the day just to knock off these investigations? Here's Miss Sackett waiting to read another letter. And here are all these academic gentlemen, marshalled for you, it seems, by Professor Gingrass, eager for the ardours of research, the diffusion of knowledge, and all the rest of it. And somewhere, too, there may be that treasure. Have you weighed that? There's no occasion to believe it a mere legend any longer. It's taken on some solidity, if you ask me. Well, where is it?'

'And *whose* is it?' Olivia Jory asked this. 'Aren't we going to try to find out?'

At this point something happened that Clout had been expecting for some time. Sir John Jory did really chew the tip of his moustache. 'Ah, yes,' he said. 'We must consider that. If property is involved – family property, that is – the matter becomes very important. We were talking of treasure trove. Goes to the Crown, eh? But of course the Crown is only a manner of speaking. Doesn't mean the Sovereign. Merely means the bally Government. Difficult to see why those blighters should get the whole of Joscelyn's find.'

'You mean, don't you,' Olivia asked, 'the proceeds of Edward's exchange with Joscelyn? On those terms, I quite agree.'

Dr Jory frowned. 'Don't mind my girl,' he said to his kinsman. 'She does, you know, sometimes speak out of turn. Still, if there was a gentleman's agreement between our respective great-grandfathers, I've no doubt, Jory, you'd recognize it.'

Sir John gave some appearance of being cornered by this. Then inspiration came to him. 'It's all a bit deep, isn't it?' he asked. 'George Lumb here is the man to settle it, if you ask me.'

'I don't know much about Mr Lumb.' Dr Jory, to the satisfaction of Clout, was unimpressed by this proposal to call upon the authority of the Great Brain. 'I'd say one wants a lawyer, not a librarian.'

'What do you mean – a librarian?' Sir John was for a moment incensed, as if this description of the parson's boy was grossly opprobrious. 'Very old friend of ours, George Lumb – very old friend, indeed. Great reliance on him. Lad with judgement. George, I'll thank you for your views on all this.'

Thus formally appealed to, Lumb blushed in what Clout felt to be a foolish and pitiful fashion. It looked as if his stammer would be at its most uncontrollable. But in fact, when he spoke, it was without any difficulty at all. 'Of course there was a lot of deception going on. One saw that – didn't one? – as soon as one came to those M-M-Muscovites. So it's very confused, and the truth is hard to arrive at. There's one critical point, at which you'll find that one brother is said to have been drunk, and the other sober. But it was a queer sort of sobriety. I mean, you know, that he was clearly in an odd state.'

'Ah!' Sir John was impressed. 'Not responsible – eh?'

'It's arguable that Sir Joscelyn must have been a bit touched. And a gentleman's agreement entered into by a madman is scarcely a thing another gentleman would insist on the honouring of.' Lumb propounded this with much seriousness. 'Drink, I think, is different. A gentleman is expected to stand by any commitment he makes while in liquor. Although it might depend, I suppose, on the extent to which other people's interests were involved.'

'Quite right.' Sir John continued to receive this high doctrine with gravity. 'Still, this doesn't quite tell us where we are, my dear boy.'

'We shan't know that, sir, until we f-f-find the treasure. And Miss Sophia's next letter doesn't make it very clear that we ever shall.'

'You see, Sophia cleared out.' Sadie intervened with this explanation. 'She got it into her head that something very dreadful might have happened – '

Lumb nodded. 'N-n-not surprisingly, considering that her brothers had bolted.'

'And so, you see, the record just breaks off. Shall I go on to the last letter now?'

Sir John nodded. 'Yes, my dear. Please do.'

8

'Dear Miss Bird, – It is scarce twelve hours since I closed my last; yet all is now confusion at Old Hall! This very day must see the end of my visit to this the *hitherto* honoured home of my ancestors. And when I leave, I shall not be the first to go. For my brothers – such is the incredible truth – are both fled! Did I not express doubts as to their being courageous men? Alas and alas!

But already (as I address myself to one who has so often calmed my *childish* perturbations) a proper resolution begins to return to me. I can at least review, and perhaps order, the final horrid events which have now taken place; and I can at least endeavour to compose my mind before the *dread probability* that there has been a *dire* termination to the affair!

I resume, then, the broken thread of my narrative. It was indeed Sir James Dangerfield who had presented himself. There were several more arrivals, within the hour, and by dusk the supper-party was formed. My sister and I were, of course, resolved to hold ourselves invisible. But presently, as we sat together in the small drawing-room, we were entertained to an unexpected glimpse of the company. It must have been resolved that at a very early stage of the proposed convivialities there should be a solemn inspection of these *exhibits* upon which Sir James was to adjudicate; and to this end a procession formed, and passed along the terrace within our view. Sir James himself walked in front, with my brothers on either side of him; and it was patent that he took more satisfaction on the occasion than they did. A brief glance told me that Edward was both uneasy and sullen;

no doubt he had received Mr Kent's disturbing news – and was moreover in a continued displeasure that the wager should go forward at all, with its consequence of announcing to a large circle the potential accession of great wealth to Old Hall. Joscelyn for his part was silent and absorbed. Indeed, I almost persuaded myself that he was grown wasted and haggard, like a man consumed by fever. My note, it was to be supposed, had contributed to his unease.

This distressing spectacle was with us only for a moment, and then the company disappeared round the corner of the terrace. They must have spent some twenty minutes in the coach-house. After that interval, we heard distant voices, and conjectured that they were moving on to the Temple of Diana. I do not think my sister at all fully understood what was going forward. It was my own endeavour to remove my mind from any contemplation of it. There was no reason alas! – to suppose that much *regard for decency* would attend the next of the necessary preliminaries to a settling of the wager.

They were all back in the Hall more quickly than I should have expected; and from the dining-room there soon began to issue the common hubbub of gentlemen at their wine. It would have been reasonable that both my sister and I should now retire for the night. But we doubted whether sleep would be easy to gain amid a clamour which only *a bachelor establishment* could have excused; and wakefulness seemed less insupportable in each other's company than alone. It thus came about that we continued to sit together until near midnight. Sometimes the gentlemen entertained themselves with loud conversation, and sometimes with song. Once or twice we thought we detected high words, or even the beginnings of a brawl; and frequently, of course, there were shouted oaths, the crash or tinkle of breaking glass, and those *view-halloos, tally-hos, gone-aways,* and *come-up-my-beauties* by which the guests on such occasions endeavour to persuade themselves that they are about the most blissful of all human activities. There were, indeed, rare intervals of quiet, during which it might be possible to imagine the going forward of reasoned speech or serious debate. But on the whole it appeared a festivity conducting itself quite after the common fashion.

It was already after midnight when I thought I twice heard the peal of a bell. Whether servants were yet in attendance I knew not; it was very possible that they had been dismissed – although, if so, they were like to be shouted from their beds later to carry one or another of the guests to his carriage. The second peal had been peremptory, as if some belated boon-companion of my brother's were clamouring for admission at the closed front-door of the Hall. I was certainly not minded myself to act as porter to such a one; and a moment later the circumstance was erased from my mind by a fresh, and altogether disagreeable (indeed alarming) turn to the events of the night. The drawing-room doors burst open, and the greater part of the gentlemen tumbled in on us.

It was an act, assuredly, of high impropriety; and I was glad to find even the complacent Lady Jory instantly sensible of the fact. She rose at once, and I saw her glance seeking for her husband in the crush; it was plain that she was going to make a peremptory request that he and his friends withdraw. But before my sister could speak, Sir James Dangerfield advanced, raised both arms for a silence which was instantly accorded him, and commenced a speech with drunken solemnity. Witnesses, he said, were wanted – sober witnesses, whose subsequent testimony could be relied on. It was for this reason that he and his friends had ventured, even at this late hour, to pay their respects to the ladies. A bargain – an unexpected bargain – had been struck between their host and his truly amiable and gallant brother. As to the wager, it could be taken no further. Sir James professed himself unable to come to a determination on that point, and the brothers had shaken hands and agreed that it be void. Instead, there was this bargain; to wit, that there be an irrevocable exchange. What had been Joscelyn's was now Edward's and what had been Edward's was now Joscelyn's – this vastly to the content of either party. He, Sir James, did not profess to determine which of the Jorys came the winner from that market. He had no skill in what Joscelyn had brought home – and very little in what Edward had brought home, either. (Need I add, my dear Miss Bird, that at this sally all the gentlemen laughed uproariously?) But this he would say: that the exchange was boundlessly to the credit of each, as a sportsman and a gentleman. Here was the sort of conduct that showed the English country interest sound as a bell – and let any Whig dog there deny it! (Here, naturally, the applause redoubled itself.)

To all this nonsense – indisputably the vain and empty product, I supposed, of hopeless inebriety – I had paid small attention, so far; for it was rather my concern to determine whether some of the gentlemen were so flown in wine that my sister and I might possibly be at the hazard of absolute insult. But now there was a disquieting development. My brothers were summoned by Sir James each in turn to advance and solemnly endorse the exchange that had been announced. Edward did so first, and I saw, with mortification but without surprise, that he was sadly intoxicated. He made the statement required of him. It then became Joscelyn's turn – and he at once stepped forward and solemnly declared himself in the same sense. But, whereas Edward had been as drunk as a lord, Joscelyn was as sober as a judge! I was horrified – for only liquor, surely, could excuse any man's engagement in all this low levity and open wickedness. Joscelyn, indeed, was not himself; he had the appearance of one at once alarmed and resolute; he spoke in the same high, strained voice that he had used at table earlier in the day.

It seemed now to be agreed that the bargain had been ratified in high legal form, with Lady Jory and myself the court that had registered it. Some of the gentlemen began to bring in bottles, swearing that we should drink a toast to the amity of the brothers. Others, slightly recollected, endeavoured to restrain their companions from this crowning impertinence. Several sang senselessly in chorus. And one fell to shouting *that they should now fetch in the other brace of ladies.* I realized with contempt and loathing that he meant thus to designate Edward's (now Joscelyn's) hapless *Paphian* girl, and Joscelyn's (now Edward's) mummy (if that be the word for it) so sacrilegiously haled across Europe from the Caucasus. And at this some blackguard at the back, thinking to gain the credit of overgoing all in outrageous jesting, cried out, *Yes, and let the four of them play a rubber together.* There was a moment's silence, followed by a blow, a crash, and an ugly curse – the last speaker having been felled instantly to the floor by one of the party whose breeding had not wholly deserted him. Upon this there might have succeeded a general *mêlée*, had a surprising diversion not at the very moment occurred. Once more the house bell pealed – and was this time accompanied by such a thunderous knocking that all were startled into a sudden silence. And upon this, again, no more than a questioning murmur had succeeded when a frightened man-servant ran into the room, looked wildly round for his master, and in a trembling voice announced, *His Grace the Duke of Nesfield.*

I had not recovered from my own astonishment before I was aware that the Duke was among us, and bowing with his customary *polite ease* over the hand of Lady Jory. He did the same by myself – and I observed that he by no means forgot that additional shade of cordiality and respect so agreeable to an inconsiderable female of the family. He then turned to face the gentlemen. They stood dumbly at gaze before him. Neither Sir James Dangerfield nor any of the others thought (I remarked) to call into notice that here was the largest *Whig dog* in the country come to bark at them.

Joscelyn's sobriety now stood him in a moment's good stead. He said a word to the servant, and with great dispatch a glass of wine was offered to the Duke on a salver. He took a quick sip and then thrust it impatiently aside – but a civility had been offered and accepted. I breathed a shade more easily for the credit of our house!

It now became clear to most of the company – a little *disintoxicated* as they were by the appearance among them of so august a personage – that the Duke's presenting himself at an hour so late had some motive other than courtesy. They therefore withdrew in tolerable order to the dining-room from which they had so unbecomingly issued in the first instance, leaving the Jorys as a family to discharge whatever business should be proposed to them. I judged, however, from certain snatches of talk that I caught from the retreating gentlemen, that they were not without a shrewd suspicion that the late luckless wager was about to unload some legacy of trouble upon Old Hall.

And of this the Duke presently left us in no doubt. He had sent a message to Edward Jory, he declared; but his errand was now alike to one brother and the other – and it was one he was glad to carry through, even at the cost of this nocturnal exertion, out of old regard and friendship for our family. First, let us know that what he had bade his steward communicate earlier that day had been most seriously intended. There was a new tone at Court, to which Cabinet intended that respect should be paid, and a gentleman flying in the face of decorum might find himself repenting it. He himself had been brought up in other ways, and he had no thought of turning parson now. But he had been constrained thus to present himself out of the certain knowledge, gained only a few hours since, that there were those with the Queen's commission making post-haste for Old Hall at this moment. Edward had better forthwith disburden himself *of that which he wot of,* or he might find himself in the county gaol by dawn. What was worse, his name would infallibly go in the new Black Book – with what consequences he could guess at.

At this dire prognostication I saw Edward go pale and tremble! That this same new Black Book is other than a legend – albeit a wholesome one – I am unconvinced. I have met no one that professes to know precisely who keeps it, or where. Nevertheless belief in it has of late gained notable currency among our country gentlemen, and the penalties attending incorporation in its pages appear to be all the more daunting for being decidedly vague. For some time (as I have already remarked) it has been observable that my brother Edward was not easy about his late exploit – and indeed, soberly considered, it has been an act of wild profligacy to which it is to be suspected that his friend Mr Kent had urged him against a certain caution and timidity which (despite his sadly unprincipled course of life) is indubitably inherent in his character. And now I could discern a cold sweat on Edward's brow! He muttered *that the Duke's advice was kindly taken; that all these fools had best be sent packing ere the night was an hour older; and that he would reserve but Kent and one other, to help him do that which must be done.*

I was relieved by this speech of Edward's, although I could not, indeed, admire it. It was rational, but it was scarcely spirited. Against all my better judgement, I would fain have heard something more befitting – if not the friend of corsairs and pirates – at least a Jory of Old Hall! And a like mingling of relief and humiliation now awaited me. Joscelyn in his turn became the subject of the Duke's serious admonition, and he too was left in little doubt that the new Black Book yawned for him (if books, indeed, may be said to yawn as well as to occasion yawning). It seemed to me that of my two brothers the Duke of Nesfield preferred the younger. There was something dry in his manner as he remarked *that, in the common judgement, there would be some distinction made between one who was led into irregular courses by beauty, and one who was led into these same courses by gems and gold.* This was very fine. And yet (my dear Miss Bird) I could not altogether approve it. The distinction was unjust to Joscelyn, who had certainly possessed himself of his Caucasian treasure *not* for its intrinsic value, but because of its *mortuary* interest. Moreover I recalled, that, before this Court disfavour and the like was threatening, the Duke himself was known to have spoken of the whole wretched affair in terms of the most tolerant amusement!

However this might be, there was no doubt that for Joscelyn too the Duke had the most alarming intelligence. I was myself, as you know, a little prepared for it, on the score of what I had learned from young Tom Grindell. But the Duke had further news – and such as one might have expected to hear from *the melodramatists of Drury Lane* rather than from a great English nobleman! Being concerned by what he had heard of the ill odour into which Edward's freak was leading him, he had caused discreet inquiries to be made elsewhere. And Joscelyn's pillage, he found, was strongly conjectured, although perhaps not positively known in a quarter which, *although exalted, was accustomed to the exercise of absolute power, and took small account of law. Moreover the theft that had been perpetrated was like to be regarded, in that same circle, less as a misdemeanour than an insult; and the punishment visited upon it might well be arbitary, violent, and much in disregard of the Queen's peace. It would be, perhaps, the black eye first, and the Black Book thereafter!*

It was at this point that I began – and that with some indignation – to *smoke* the Duke of Nesfield. His concern for us was perhaps genuine, and his proposals rational. But – incurably – he was a jester, and it was now his amusement to appal and dismay his foolish neighbours! That confidential inquiries were already being made after the treasure I believed to be true; that the accredited agents of a friendly Power, even if not of the most civilized, would venture to offer personal violence to an English *Baronet*, I judged absolutely not possible. But Joscelyn (I am ashamed to say) appeared otherwise persuaded; something of Edward's unworthy panic appeared to be communicated to him; although *sober*, he was not *collected*; and a judgement which *bad conscience* rendered infirm, *excessive trepidation* now quite overthrew! He began to cry out in ignoble agitation, and to no reasonable purpose!

All this, I verily believe, was highly diverting to the Duke of Nesfield. But a nobleman always remembers the proprieties requisite in the society of ladies. Now, glancing at Lady Jory and myself, he seemed conscious that at any moment the night's absurdities might take a turn so extravagant as to be wholly unfit for our notice. And at this he advanced upon my sister with gravity; announced that he now proposed, together with Sir Joscelyn and Mr Edward, to join once more the gentlemen in the other room; and expressed his wish that Lady Jory's high sense of the duties of hospitality should not longer detain her, or her charming sister, from repose.

On this sufficient hint, we bade the Duke goodnight, and he bowed himself from the drawing-room, taking my brothers with him. It was now necessary that I should endeavour to calm Lady Jory, whose distress at his Grace's alarming communications was not lessened by the fact of her making very little of them. For this purpose I sat down beside her, and it thus happened that we remained for a little time, downstairs and together, before finally parting for the night. I said what I could, and without great effort as to the choice of words. On such occasions, after all, it is the *tone* and *demeanour* that are of account.

Meanwhile my ear was less attentive to such remarks (and they were very little to the purpose) as my sister offered than to the sounds yet coming from the dining-room. It was to be supposed that the Duke's endeavours would be directed to a quiet and expeditious dispersal of the party still gathered there. Once the gentlemen were climbed into their carriages (or tumbled into them) and away, he would then address himself to the task of extricating my brothers as quickly as possible from the impending consequences of their folly.

What I presently heard, however, was peculiar. The whole company appeared to be yet present – and to be now at a violent debate. There were many cries of indignation, and a few of alarm. Gradually the proportions of these changed, and I had the shocked impression of an entire besotted gathering in mounting panic! How could this come about? Were the high personages from Court, or were the unprincipled emissaries of the Czar already present and declaring themselves? I had only to ask myself such questions for the large truth to dawn upon me! I recalled what I had heard from time to time of previous *sportive* exploits of the Duke of Nesfield. The element of irresponsible levity in his attitude was much larger than I had suspected. He was in fact, subjecting my brothers and their guests to an elaborate and terrifying imposture! It was even conceivable that I had myself been the first of his victims, or *butts*, in crediting the extraordinary story of Tom Grindell!

My first impulse, when this humiliating perception came to me, was to pass at once into the dining-room and challenge the Duke to give his word that the alarms he had brought among us were authentic. But several circumstances restrained me. Of these the simplest was the fact that my sister, terrified by the clamour now arising, was clinging to my arm. The next was my realization that truth and falsehood were probably inextricably mingled in the affair; and that the Duke's conduct, although fantastic and reprehensible, was yet directed, like some similar stratagem in a stage comedy, to the mirthful *reproving of vice and reforming of manners*. And finally, I had to acknowledge that the situation was grown suddenly beyond any hope of my controlling – for the hubbub was now frantic, and included indeed a great crashing of glass, as if some of the more frenetic of the company were blindly escaping out of window. But at least there was one duty that I could perform. I encouraged Lady Jory to rise, conducted her firmly out of the room and to the quietness of the service staircase, by which we then made our way to her own chamber. There her maid, a faithful creature enough, awaited her, so that presently I was blessedly able to withdraw to my own quarters. I was unfeignedly sorry for my sister. Yet in such extraordinary casualties as we were confronted with a stupid woman is but a tiresome companion. So soon as I was alone, I fell to considering what my next course of conduct should be.

There was still noise in the house; and there appeared to be further uproar both in the remoter offices and in the park. Several times I heard what I took to be a hunting-horn (an instrument which gentlemen delight to have recourse to when upon a frolic) but presently determined to be a bugle; and this was soon followed by what could only be a roll of drums! Was it conceivable that the Militia had been called out? It appeared to be much more likely that these *loud alarums* merely attested the further extravagance of the Duke's jest.

I felt some commiseration for my brothers, and particularly for Joscelyn, at whom the whole country was likely to be laughing for a twelvemonth. Yet there was nothing that I could do to assist him, since his condition would be all the more humiliating were it to be added to the story *that his maiden sister had been running demented about the park, whether fearing for her virtue at the hands of the invader, or endeavouring to recall her craven brothers to some sense of manliness and reason.* It would be best, then, that I should remain invisible, until all this career of folly was run through and over. So much had I determined, when I remembered that which instantly called me to an imperative duty. There was the girl! Isolated from her sex in the abominable Temple of Diana, utterly bewildered (one might be sure) by the pandemonium now unloosed around her, was the unfortunate creature whom the caprice (and, it was to be feared, *vice*) of Edward had lured so far from the security of her home. It was intolerable that – even for the making of a *ducal* holiday – this hapless young person should be exposed, unattended, to such terrors. I caught up my cloak and passed rapidly downstairs.

Once in the open air, my route took me past the stables; and there I beheld an extraordinary scene. Outside the coach-house, and by the light of several uncertainly waving lanterns, a small group of gentlemen, still very drunk, were endeavouring to harness a pair of our carriage-horses to some species of cart or wagon. Others, it seemed, were hammering and banging within; and I could just detect through the din the voice of my brother Joscelyn urging his friends to a better speed. The Caucasian treasure, I supposed, was to be hurried away from Old Hall. But to this it appeared that there would be opposition – and that of the most bizarre kind. From somewhere not far off in the park there came a sound of trampling feet, and of commands shouted in a sort of gibberish which might, to persons who had lost all command of themselves, have passed as a foreign tongue! I was much disgusted, alike by this further evidence of the *tasteless elaboration* of the Duke's jest, and by the wretched imbecility to which it had reduced my brother and his companions. But now the uproar, combined with the incompetence of the gentlemen at their task, had a further effect. First one, and then instantly the other, horse broke free and disappeared at a terrified gallop into the darkness. Ineffective curses and cries of dismay followed them. I tarried no longer. Snatching up from the ground an abandoned lantern that was yet alight, I made my way rapidly to the Temple.

Quite suddenly, and so that they barred my way, I found myself in the presence of three men – outlandishly dressed, and with ludicrous beards such as one might employ in a charade! I was in no mood to be again one of the *duped or gulled*, and I ordered them sternly to stand back. They hesitated. I added that it was to be presumed no part of their master's frolic *to affront one of the ladies of Old Hall*. And at this they made me a sort of sheepish bow and moved aside. Another hundred yards and the Temple was before me. I had expected to find it perhaps yet deserted, and disturbed only by the general uproar pervading the air of our demesne. But here too there was a confusedly animated spectacle! Setting down my lantern, I moved into the shadow of a tree in order to take my bearings as I might.

At the door a further group of the *mummers* (as they must be called) was pounding with their fists, and at the same time crying for admittance (one supposed) in the same sort of ridiculous gibberish I had already heard. Even as I looked, the round window in the pediment above them opened, and I could see my brother Edward peering down with a pale and frightened face. He seemed then to call out directions to friends behind him; one of the mummers looked up and shouted; Edward hastily drew back his head and clapped the window to. At the same moment I thought I heard, from the back of the building, the creak of some light vehicle being moved softly over grass. You may remember that immediately behind the Temple the ground drops sharply to a narrow, concealed lane, and that upon this there look out several windows, modern in form, belonging to the upper living-rooms in this *spuriously antique* structure. It seemed to me likely that Edward and his companions – all as fuddled and bemused as himself – were proposing to make their escape through one of these. And no doubt the wretched girl would be obliged to accompany them.

So far, my resolution had not notably failed me; but I was now conscious of a nervous agitation possessing me to an ominous degree! Determined to master this if I could, I moved forward, skirting the side of the Temple, until I found myself at its farther end and leaning over the low stone parapet which there gives protection against the sharp declivity ending in the lane which I have just mentioned. I had neglected to resume possession of my lantern, and all was shadowy and obscure around me. Glancing sideways along the back of the building, I caught a gleam of candlelight at a window, and had the impression of a sash cautiously raised. I peered down into the darkness below. There was certainly a conveyance in the lane, but I was totally unable to determine its character. Then I heard whispers;

a second sash had been thrown up; the candlelight, however, had disappeared, as if those within were persuaded that their safety called for absolute darkness. I could only listen. And presently I heard Edward's voice, slurred but distinguishable, declare *that they must trust her, by G—d, to the ropes.* Instantly I guessed what was afoot – and I endeavoured (although it would have been of small avail) to cry out against this criminal folly. But no sound would come from my throat; my limbs trembled; a sensation of horrid vertigo overcame me!

For some moments (apart from the pounding and shouting that was yet going on at the front) there was no sound except further unintelligible whispers and heavy breathing, intermingled with here and there a smothered curse. Then I heard my brother call *to lower away, for the b—ch was secure.* I opened my eyes (which without my own awareness I must have closed in an effort to fight off my giddiness) and saw with horror a faint white blur descending through the darkness from the farthest window. It was unmistakably a woman's form, with arms held out as if in protection against the rough stone down the face of which she was being lowered. But, even as I looked, it vanished! There was a crash, a cry, and then my brother's voice raised briefly in a single abominable imprecation. I looked below, and supposed for a second *that the world was spinning round me.* Then I saw that what I faintly discerned was a wheel slowly turning in air. The vehicle below had been overset in the course of the appalling accident I had just witnessed. I glanced beyond and saw the glimmer of a pale figure, prostrate on the lane. My spirits could sustain no more. For what must have been a matter of some minutes, I fainted away!

Voices recalled me to myself – although not, it was to prove, for long. They came from below, and I realized that Edward and his companions had themselves, by one means or another, gained the lane. They were speaking now in hoarse undertones, and (I thought) upon a new note of terror. I distinguished the tones of Mr Kent, declaring *that she had come down on the cart, and that bottom upwards;* an unknown voice rejoining angrily *that it was no occasion for jesting;* and then Edward crying out suddenly *that by G—d, he would be hanged.* At this a deadly premonition came upon me; horror could no further go; it was without further access of emotion that I next heard Mr Kent call out roughly *that there was nothing for it but to get her under ground.*

Dear Miss Bird – does it surprise you that I knew no more? This time my state of insensibility, moreover, must have been of longer duration. When I came to, there was no further sound from the lane beneath. And I was not alone. Bending over me was none other than the Duke of Nesfield himself! I was assisted to rise; the Duke offered me a brandy-flask, from which I was glad to sip; he then handed me into a carriage which had been summoned, and himself accompanied me back to the Hall. He was very subdued, saying only *that it had been something too much; that he hoped my brothers would get off to bed and forget their discomfiture; and that he would do his best to ensure that the bruit of the matter got very little about the country.* I made him only the briefest replies, and finally bade him goodnight with the utmost reserve. He no doubt judges me offended, as I am very willing that he should do. But *shock and horror* were the actual occasion of my reticence!

I went immediately to my room, and for I know not how long lay, without undressing, on my bed. There was still some stir about the house, but it quickly died away. I fell into a light slumber, from which I was awakened by a sound of galloping hooves. It was not yet dawn, but at once I rose, unaccountably filled with a fresh access of uneasiness. I resolved to seek out Joscelyn, were he to be found, and attempt with him the sort of serious conference that his, and Edward's, situation seemed to demand. Taking a candle, therefore, I made my way to his private apartments. There was a light in a dressing-room; I knocked, entered, and found only his personal servant, himself but half-dressed, composedly ordering the tumbled contents of a number of open drawers. I asked, *where was his master?* He answered me, impassively yet with a strange look, *that Sir Joscelyn was ridden away, he believed to port and the packet-boat.* I was much staggered, and inquired after Edward. *Mr Jory,* the man replied (now with the ghost of a grin), *was also departed – he believed on foot and with Mr Kent, there having been a misfortune with the only horses available.*

Such, then, is the fallen condition of this house! Both my brothers exposed, ridiculed, and ignominiously fled; and a young life, I too strongly fear, lost as the price of the younger's folly! My poor sister is wholly bewildered; and it is my intention to take her, this very afternoon, to her brother's in Yorkshire. She will be kindly received there, until our unfortunate situation is *better understood, and if possible to some extent retrieved.* I shall write no more at present. But you may be assured, dear Miss Bird, that I shall continue our correspondence, commonly so pleasing; and that, even in periods of such perturbation as this, you shall not fail at least of *the fugitive and hurried confidences* of your old pupil and devoted friend,

SOPHIA JORY.'

PART THREE

OLD HALL

1

'You see?' Olivia Jory asked. She was driving Clout away from New Hall in a small car of dangerous antiquity. 'He's gone right over – as I said he had.'

'Lumb?'

'Yes – and your girl.'

Sadie's not my girl. I don't know why you should say such a thing.'

'Very well – his girl. They're one hundred per cent behind Sir John. It's disgusting.'

'Nobody could be precisely *behind* Sir John.' Clout was feeling gloomy and disputatious. 'Except in the sense that you can get behind a wheelbarrow. Sir John might be shoved one way or another, but I can't imagine him taking an initiative, or giving a lead.'

'Can't you? I don't think you know much about that sort of person.' Olivia too was not in good humour.

'I don't claim to. That's just what I think. And I think that Jerry Jory is another matter. He seems detached and ineffective. But he might take quite a vigorous hand in the affair. If there really *is* an affair.'

'You think that of Jerry, do you?' Olivia was silent for some moments, as if she had just been given matter for serious reflection. And when she spoke again it was impatiently. 'Look here, Colin – can't *you* discover something?'

'What do you mean – discover something?' Clout had meant to speak gruffly. But the magic of his own Christian name on Olivia's lips was too much for him. 'You know that I'd discover anything for you that I could.'

She took her left hand from the steering-wheel and laid it for a moment on his knee. 'And you do believe that the swap ought to be honoured? After all, it was absolutely agreed to in the presence of those two women.'

Clout hesitated. He was making what he knew was a feeble effort to cling to common sense. 'Certainly it was. But, even so, it wasn't much more than an agreement to exchange stolen goods. And you were wrong, you see, in the notion that Joscelyn somehow went back on his bargain and cheated his brother. There was that panic, and the effect seems to have been that the whole thing just lapsed. Or rather, it was something more than that. The folly of Edward and his pals resulted in the girl's death. But that wasn't anything they intended. And there hadn't been any proposal that the bargain should go through whether she was alive or dead. Joscelyn didn't want a corpse. Come to think of it, he *precisely* didn't want a corpse. All that sort of thing was just what he felt he was through with. It's arguable that even if he retained control of the treasure – which is something we don't know – there was no call on him to hand it over.' Clout paused. 'And, of course,' he added rather desperately, 'the whole thing wasn't a bit nice. It would have been absolutely disgusting, even if it hadn't ended in a fatality. I think we ought to consider that.'

'You talk like that idiotic American professor. I suppose you're all the same in universities and places.' Olivia tossed her head, and the car swerved ominously towards the ditch. 'Well, you can consider all those proprieties and decencies and delicacies when writing your idiotic Shufflebotham thing. But it's just not the way the minds of my sort of person work.'

'Then it would be a damned sight better if it was.'

Clout had snapped this out in a manner that surprised himself. And Olivia seemed less offended than impressed. 'Colin, darling,' she said, 'I suppose you may be right. But – really – do we know enough about the whole story to say positively that we ought to drop it? That's all I'm saying, you see. There's more to find out. More that *you* could find out. I know George is tremendously clever. But I don't see why it should be he who finds out everything.'

Clout rose to this challenge. 'Well,' he demanded, 'just what is it you want me to find out?'

'First, whether there really was a serious element of theft. I can't see it in Edward's case. One can't believe that he really forcibly abducted that girl and carried her across Europe. It was just an ordinary – well, episode of that time. Not a bit nice, as you say. But gentlemen did take young persons under their protection – wasn't that the term? – and nobody thought much about it. Even Professor Milder must know that, if he's any sort of scholar. And we don't actually know the truth about Joscelyn either. We have only a lot of surmises to go on – chiefly the interminable gabble of Sophia Jory to her old governess. I see no real evidence that anywhere in the world there was anybody who had taken the slightest exception to Joscelyn's proprietorship of the treasure.'

'You're quite wrong.' Clout shook his head decidedly. 'I admit that the business of agents from Muscovy and so forth was probably sheer invention by the Duke of Nesfield. But it can only have worked as it did, producing all that wild confusion, because Joscelyn had a thoroughly guilty conscience. And then there's the way he brought the stuff to Old Hall. That wasn't a mere taste for play-acting. He must have been seriously concerned to elude observation. Incidentally, Edward must have had a guilty conscience too, or he wouldn't have been so easily taken in by what the Duke put across *him*. But I agree there's still a lot waiting to be found out.'

'What happened afterwards.'

'Exactly. I don't think there's much doubt about Edward. He did bolt from the country and never returned.'

'He didn't have much chance to, Colin. He died about a year afterwards.'

'Yes, I know. And he wouldn't be in a hurry to return to England, if he and his drunken companions that night actually buried the poor girl in hugger-mugger.'

'And what about Joscelyn? You could easily find out, couldn't you, whether he too really did leave England in a hurry, and whether he came back again?'

Clout laughed. 'Dash it all, Olivia, I do know *something*. I've been beginning, after all, to earn the Shufflebotham dole. Joscelyn died at Old Hall in a perfectly respectable way, several years later. He travelled such a lot that the record isn't easy to work out. But if he went abroad immediately after the catastrophe we've now uncovered, it wasn't for particularly long. The impression I get is, I think, the one you already have: that Joscelyn simply went a bit dim in his last years, and then faded out. But one thing is certain. He can't himself have sold up the treasure and enjoyed the proceeds. Money was clearly pretty tight. And it continued tight. George, the next baronet, held on for about thirty years, making various economies. Then he sold up and went off to New Hall. And if nobody on that side of the family cashed in on the treasure, it's certain, I suppose, that nobody on your side did, either.'

Olivia nodded. 'Quite certain. So there we are. Don't you see? Unless Joscelyn was so scared by the Duke's joke that he privately made some sort of restitution of the treasure soon after, it simply *must* be about Old Hall still.'

'Do you think so?' Clout shook his head. 'At the most, it's a probability. After all, if Joscelyn lost his nerve about it, he might have found it a relief to hide it somewhere much farther away. He was trying to get it away, you remember, that night.'

'And didn't – because the horses bolted. Can't you guess what these people would do, there and then? Precisely what Edward and his friends were doing. Get their compromising possession straight under the soil.'

Quite suddenly, Clout realized that he was in the grip of a growing excitement. It wasn't simply the excitement that had been with him ever since he first saw Olivia Jory, and that could still make him quite dizzy when he so much as thought of her. It was the quite distinct excitement of the hunter. Buried treasure – it came to him – must be one of those deeply emotive notions that can really get you. There was probably an interesting subject of research in it – indeed, the fascination of research itself was related to it. Probably it had exercised a great pull on Joscelyn. There might be an appendix to the Shufflebotham – like one of Milder's appendices – on buried treasure as an archetypal image. Not that there would ever be a Shufflebotham – or not with Sir Joscelyn Jory as its subject. Clout had an obscure certainty of that. However all this business ended it would be in a fashion that entirely knocked a biography of Sir Joscelyn on the head. The University would have to shunt him on to something else.

'And now you're not even listening to me, Colin Clout.'

'I'm sorry.' Clout realized that, amazing enough, Olivia's reproach was justified. Pursuing his own speculations, he had actually been for some seconds heedless of that marvellous voice.

'I was saying that there's another thing we want to know about. I mean that Temple of Diana. I've read what I could about Old Hall. One can find out quite a lot – as you've probably done yourself by now – about Joscelyn's mausoleum, for instance. But I haven't come across anything about a temple.'

'I have, as a matter of fact.' Clout was rather pleased at having got ahead of Olivia here. 'Not that it seems important. You're not proposing, I take it, to do any digging for that girl's skeleton.'

'No I'm not. And I'm not convinced that there is, or ever was, a skeleton. We only know that the girl fell, and that those terrified drunks believed she was dead. They may have been quite wrong – and let's hope they were. Anyway, I'd like to know about that queer building – it sounds quite as queer as the mausoleum – even if it's not particularly relevant.'

'Then I'll tell you what I found out about it – Olivia, darling.' Clout paused on this. He had a feeling that he hadn't brought it off particularly well. It certainly didn't draw a glance from the girl. But then, she was having to keep her eye on the road. They were coming to a bend. 'The Temple of Diana was a high-class early eighteenth-century folly, built – as you remember Sophia Jory knew – by Sir Arthur Jory. It was a temple in front and a small house behind. He used it for meeting women, and that sort of thing.'

'So I gathered.'

'And then it was used, off and on, for various purposes. But quite often it was empty; and so it fell more or less into decay. Finally, Sir George – the last Jory to live at Old Hall – knocked it down, as one of his economies.'

'Is it economical to knock things down?'

'I suppose he used the stone for walls and cottages and cow-houses and so forth. Anyway, there's nothing left now but some traces of foundations in the grass. The steep drop into a lane or track is still there, of course. I recognized the place in Sophia Jory's description.'

'I see.' Olivia was silent for some time. She appeared to have lost interest in the Temple of Diana. 'Colin,' she asked presently, 'what do you think they'll all do now?'

'All those people we were having tea with? How should I know? They're not my sort of person, as you've said. I mustn't presume to guess about them.'

'How funny you are.' This time Olivia did glance at him – and in her very most dazzling way. 'At least you can tell me about the professors.'

'Gingrass will be wondering if he can't track down the treasure himself. Not to nobble it. He hasn't the guts for that. But just to get in on it in a learned archaeological way – doing a special article for *The Times*, and generally gaining merit with the local notabilities who boss the University. As for the frightful bore of a Yank, he'll want permission to copy out as much of Sophia's stuff as doesn't infringe his moral code: all about Joscelyn's loot, but nothing about Edward's trollop.'

'And George Lumb and *his* trollop?'

'You mustn't speak of Sadie like that.' Clout found himself seriously shocked. 'Sadie's a very decent kid.'

'Of course she is – and it was disgusting of me.' Olivia's penitence was charming. 'But what will *they* do?'

'Just what you've suggested, I'm afraid. They'll do all they can for the New Hall Jorys. Lumb's view will be that we must presume the treasure to have been Joscelyn's legal property until we positively know otherwise; and that the swap involved far too valuable a consideration to be held valid out of hand. You remember his suggestion that Joscelyn might well have been mentally deranged.'

The ancient car was labouring up a mild incline. Olivia changed gear viciously. 'You could trust George Lumb to think up something like that,' she said. 'I think he's a beastly little man. You'd never think he'd been at a decent public school.'

'You can talk the most awful rubbish, Olivia Jory!' Clout, although he knew himself to be suddenly enraged, listened with amazement to his own voice. 'It goes terribly against Lumb's wishes to embrace Sir John's side. He's absolutely cracked on you, as you know.'

'Cracked?' Olivia's voice was cold. 'Just what do you mean by that vulgar expression?'

'Don't be silly. Lumb's devoted to you. He's as much devoted to you as I am.'

'How absolutely absurd.' Olivia had spoken so quickly that Clout's final words were drowned. 'George Lumb! Me! I never heard such nonsense.'

In strict logic, Clout ought to have found these words comforting. But there was something in their tone, on the contrary, that would have made them sound ominous even to a much less intelligent young man. He managed, however, to repress too vivid a consciousness of this. 'What about your father?' he asked abruptly. 'Will he back you in all this? Or will he take a slipper to you?'

Olivia laughed. 'You must come from a *very* funny world,' she said – and this time, astoundingly, she spoke in a way that made Clout's heart pound as it had never pounded before. It suggested what precisely they hadn't had: achieved months of steadily growing affection, of progressively confident approaches to the condition of confessed lovers. 'I suppose', she went on, 'you'd enjoy beating me savagely if there was something not quite to your liking about the tripe and onions or the beans on toast?'

'I don't know what we're talking about.' Clout was aware that this was a singularly feeble response to Olivia's swift change of mood. He now felt that he had said something outrageous to her, and its having prompted her only to this intoxicating raillery was confusing.

'Talking about!' She turned her head – at hazard of imminent disaster on the Queen's highway – in sudden, vivid challenge. 'We're talking – aren't we? – about an enormous treasure, dead in front of our noses! Think, Colin! Grub about, if you can, in any further records you can find. But – above all – think! I know you can. But I know George Lumb can too. You're the ablest people that your absurd University has turned out for ages, I expect. And you're rivals! Aren't you?'

'Well, yes – I suppose we are.' Clout's confusion continued. He wasn't at all sure in what sphere it was that Olivia envisaged this rivalry as operating.

'Then, you must beat him. *We* must beat him.' Olivia Jory seemed all on fire. 'We *must* beat him – do you hear? *And* that perfectly nice Miss Sackett. *And* that tiresome young F.O. type.'

'Jerry?'

'Yes.' Olivia's laughter rang out. 'Jerry, or Terry, or Berry, or whatever he calls himself. We must whack the whole lot. Mustn't we?'

'Yes!' Overwhelmingly, two distinct streams of excitement had met and were mingling in Clout. 'We must, Olivia. And we shall.'

2

A couple of mornings later, Sadie Sackett visited Clout in his attic. As she didn't much trouble herself with the formality of pausing after she had knocked on the door, she entered just in time to see the Shufflebotham Student diving into what appeared to be a cupboard. 'All right, all right,' she said dryly. '*All* young women aren't pathologically predatory, you know. You needn't bolt from *me*.'

Clout turned back into the room with as much dignity as he could manage. 'I can't think what you're talking about,' he said. 'If you mean Miss Jory, you're being thoroughly stupid. She's not in the least predatory.'

'Miss Jory?' Very tiresomely, Sadie affected to be momentarily at a loss. 'Oh – I see. I'm to refer to your grand friends in a respectful way. Thanks for reminding me.'

'Don't be an idiot, Sadie.' Clout was really exasperated. Hadn't he, quite lately, pulled up Olivia for speaking disrespectfully of Sadie? And this was all the thanks he got! 'If you want to know what *I* call predatory,' he said, 'it's dancing before George Lumb, in the name of studying Eng. Lang. and Lit. Lawrence, indeed! It would have made Lawrence sick.'

'I think that's absolutely the most childish thing I ever heard said.'

'So it is.' Clout sat suddenly down on his table and looked at Sadie in dismay. 'I'm sorry. I must be catching something.'

Sadie smiled cheerfully. 'All right, all right. If you're sorry, then I take back what I said about Olivia Jory being predatory. At least, she's not predatory in relation to *you*, Colin Clout. *You're* not her quarry.' And without pausing on this ambiguous remark, Sadie went on: 'Why were you diving in there, anyway?'

'Milder.' Remembering the duties of hospitality, Clout pointed to a chair at the other end of the table. 'Sit down.'

'Is that where all those girls sit to read you their absurd essays on epics and lyrics and things?'

'Yes.'

'Then I don't think I will.' Still very cheerful, Sadie swung herself on to the table too. 'Milder badgers you?'

'He's a complete blight – convinced I know far more about Sir Joscelyn than I do, and determined that we should get on the track of the treasure together. He sees Joscelyn as taking a rather more prominent place in his idiotic book than he had intended for him. And he thinks that a big photograph of this purloined Caucasian stuff would make a swell frontispiece for the whole thing. And he's very disturbed, conversely, because some workmen have appeared in the park, and are laying a drain or a cable or something right down that lane where the Temple of Diana used to be.'

'Why ever should that worry Milder?'

'He feels they may come on the skeleton of Edward's unfortunate girl, and that that would be a highly indelicate thing to do.'

Sadie laughed. 'What about Joscelyn's mummy, or whatever it was called? If the treasure really is buried somewhere about the place, presumably that's buried along with it.'

'Of course. But the Caucasian lady was already an old-established corpse before Joscelyn began trapesing her across Europe. So Milder's moral sense isn't offended. I suppose that in America you can take corpses across state boundaries with impunity.'

'Do you know, Colin, I don't quite believe in Milder?' Sadie stared thoughtfully at the rows of Clout's books on one side of the room. She might have been noticing that the works of Kafka had been moved down to an unobtrusive corner.

'You'd believe in him, all right, if he had constituted himself a sort of incubus on *you*.'

'I'm sure Milder would consider being an incubus highly indelicate.'

'Well, he's been up here once already this morning. Mostly talking and asking questions about Joscelyn. But he managed to get in a short history of this University, and – more briefly – a sketch of the English educational system as a whole. When that man's about, one's only wish is not to attend to him.'

'Of course, all professors are awful.' Sadie offered this generalization with careless confidence. 'Have you heard about Gingrass? It's what I came up to tell you about. He's had himself elected Patron of the Junior Archaeological Society. He says it needs waking up. And he's just taken delivery of a young lorry-load of picks and shovels.'

'Good lord!'

'And he gave a short talk at the Society's business meeting last night. All about his dear old friends, Arthur and Flinders.'

'Arthur and Flinders?'

'Arthur Evans and Flinders Petrie, I suppose.'

Clout groaned. 'How absolutely revolting!'

'Oh, no – just the usual Gingrass line. As a young man, he was much tempted, it seems, to become an archaeologist. All the big-wigs in the business urged him to it.'

'But he took a short, meditative holiday, and decided – '

'Just that. But he'd already virtually made his name at the job. The Junior Archaeological – or some of it – was impressed. Gingrass was particularly hot on the gold helmet of Mes-kalam-dug.' Sadie laughed. 'That's something you can read about in the appropriate Pelican book. I suppose Gingrass did. However, it's plain he's after the credit – even if he can't go after the profit – of digging up Joscelyn's hoard.'

'And what about you and Lumb?'

'Yes, we're after it. But I doubt whether it's for profit. Sir John, if you ask me, has a much better chance of getting his puddings and pies and a few dozen of claret and so forth out of his library than out of the Caucasus. We could dig up no end of gold and jewels, and it would be claimed absolutely by the Crown.'

'Olivia points out it mayn't be buried – just hidden.'

Sadie shook her head. 'Would it really make much difference? At least, if the stuff exists at all, burial is overwhelmingly probable. I can't think why the girl doesn't face up to that, and that there's nothing in it in the way of cash. Unless her idea is to dig it up quietly on a dark night and decamp with it.'

'I haven't discussed it with her.' Clout was cautious. 'But I suspect Sir John is thinking of something of the sort himself. And I'm sure his son Jerry is.'

Sadie jumped off the table. 'In fact we're all hoping, first for the vital clue, and second for a quiet, dark night?'

Considering this for a moment, Clout decided on evasion. 'Well – not Gingrass, at least. He want to make a big find amid circumstances of the largest publicity. Professor Gingrass standing beside his remarkable discovery: a picture by our staff photographer. That sort of thing.'

'And if you and your Olivia get there first?' Sadie was persistent. 'It seems a shame there shouldn't be a photograph in *The Times* of so handsome a couple. But you'll simply – ' She suddenly broke off in this banter. 'Listen, Colin. There's somebody coming up your staircase.'

'It's him.' Clout sounded resigned. 'I know that tread now. I'll recognize it – and cower in my shroud – if it ever passes over my grave.'

Sadie was amused. 'Your mind's coming to work just like Joscelyn's. I suppose that's as it should be. But is it really Milder?'

'Infallibly.'

'Then let's hide – as you were doing. If there's room, that is, for two in your cupboard.'

'Come on, then.' Clout grabbed Sadie's hand. 'There's lots of room. It's not as much a cupboard as another attic, running close by the eaves.'

In another moment they were in darkness. 'It seems a waste,' Sadie murmured in Clout's ear.

'What do you mean – a waste?'

'It's being only me, Colin dear.'

'Shut up, you idiot – or he'll hear.'

There had been a knock, and then the sound of a door opening. Professor Milder was undoubtedly in Clout's room.

'That's funny! He's poking about.' It was a couple of minutes later, and the words came from Sadie in a cautious whisper. Clout could feel her breath on the side of his face. And – what was quite unnecessary even amid the crowded junk around them – her whole body was pressed close against his side. He knew that there was nothing even faintly lecherous about Sadie, and that she wasn't attempting any covert return to their first and almost infantile relationship. She was just being mildly malicious. She knew that she was making him slightly uncomfortable; and she knew that, at the same time, he would have felt he was being very offensive if he edged away. And now she proceeded to travesty this situation. 'I'm terrified,' she breathed – and suddenly hugged his arm. 'Oh, how thankful I am for a protector!'

'For goodness sake, be quiet. If he finds us, we'll look absolute fools. Why doesn't he go away? He's no business, hanging round my empty room.'

'Milder's of an inquiring mind. Perhaps he's making a mental inventory of your books. For conversational purposes, you know, when he gets home.' Sadie, who had the merit (unlike a certain Duke of Nesfield, Clout thought) of never overdoing a joke, had withdrawn into the darkness of their long triangular tunnel. 'What a mass of rubbish,' she whispered.

'It's been lying here for centuries, I imagine. Now, whatever can that chap want, hanging around?' Clout stiffened suddenly. 'Ssh! There's somebody else.'

There was certainly a sound of voices from Clout's room. Sadie felt her way cautiously back to the door. 'It's Gingrass,' she whispered.

Clout was annoyed. This was a ridiculous situation. Their dive into hiding had been thoroughly childish in itself: and if by some accident they now gave themselves away it would be most humiliating. Gingrass would be hugely and tiresomely amused. Or – equally conceivably – he would turn highly censorious and moral, and hurry off to the Vice-Chancellor for the purpose of unmasking this guilty relationship. Gingrass was always unpredictable. It was chiefly what made him such a nuisance about the place. And, in a way, Sadie Sackett was unpredictable too. She might take it into her head to startle the two professors with an enormous synthetic sneeze. Clout peered into the gloom. Here and there chinks of light appeared in the sloping roof – this part must have slates, not lead – and now he could just see Sadie stretching out an arm to him. She took him by the sleeve and drew him gently towards the door by which she was crouching. The murmur of voices was a little louder. He realized that she had heard something which was prompting her to eavesdrop upon Milder and Gingrass. He wasn't going to be more fastidious than she was. He listened too. Gingrass, he supposed, had come up to pester him with some instructions about the Higher Literary Forms – and finding Milder in the room instead of his assistant, had stopped to gossip. And now Milder appeared to have said something that excited him.

'No doubt of it?' Gingrass was saying

'...whatever...your young man...fresh document...' Milder, because of the monotonous drooling which served him for articulate speech, was harder to follow than Gingrass.

'Right on the spot?' Gingrass' voice was eager. 'Of course, it's what might be expected. There they were.'

'Sure...sure...' The gently soporific tones of Milder flowed relentlessly on. '...your young man...to a solicitor...seeking advice... but just before death...never even mailed.'

'Mailed?' Gingrass – who could be enormously stupid – was perplexed.

'Posted. Never even posted, you would say. So I reckon no action would have been taken...certainly...not more than a day's work.'

'And you were going to discuss it with my young man?'

Milder's reply was long and indistinguishable. Probably he had done one of those neat switches of his – like relay-racers transferring a baton – and was giving Gingrass some statistics about the English climate, or the principal exports of the Gold Coast. And then, rather suddenly, there was silence. The two professors had departed.

'Too much dust and cobweb here. Let's get out.' Sadie thrust open the door and they emerged into Clout's room. Then she looked back. 'I don't see', she said, 'how a university ever came by the sort of junk they've shoved in here.'

Clout shook his head. 'It goes back further, I suppose. Just never cleared out.'

'Goes back to Jorys?'

'I suppose it very well may. I've sometimes thought I'd have a rummage there.' Clout was glancing round his room. Milder's mysterious hovering in it had made him obscurely uneasy.

'Would you mind if I had – one day?'

'Go ahead, any time.' Not much attending to Sadie, Clout walked over to his table. 'Milder's left me a note.' He picked up an envelope. 'That's queer. And I wonder if he writes as he talks.'

'Then open it, you ass, and see.'

'Yes, of course.' Clout tore open the envelope. The communication inside was quite substantial, but it stopped short of being actually a treatise or an essay. 'How very odd,' Clout said presently. 'He's asking me to lunch.'

'Why should it be odd?' Sadie was rather impatient. 'You're colleagues, each with this interest in Sir Joscelyn; and Milder's the senior man. He *ought* to ask you to lunch. When's it for?'

'It's for today – and in about an hour's time.'

'Refectory?'

'No. In town – the Metropole. He must have plenty of money. But then all Yanks do.'

Sadie nodded. 'Well, it's very decent of him – although it's at rather shorter notice than seems quite polite. You'll have to be off almost at once.'

'I don't see why I should be bothered with him. I've already suffered a great deal, as I've said.' Clout scowled at the letter. 'But wait a minute. There's quite a lot more.' He read on – and suddenly startled Sadie with a shout of excitement. 'I've wronged him!' he cried. 'I've wronged that admirable man!'

'Do you mean he's offering you something?' Sadie looked excited. She had a trick of tumbling to things.

'Yes – he is! A couple of years at his own college. They have a Fellowship in Creative Writing. He says a young novelist is just what they want.'

'And he's found out that that's what you are, Colin?' Sadie seemed rather more amused than was wholly tactful. At the same time she had a puzzled frown. 'I wonder why he doesn't choose George.'

Clout felt no need to resent this. He was reading the letter again. 'It's not an absolute offer. But he thinks I've an excellent chance. And he wants to discuss it at once, so that he can write off to America this afternoon. I say! I'd better be off. Do you mind?'

'Certainly you'd better be off.' Sadie was staring at him thoughtfully. 'Lucky, lucky Clout! And perhaps poor old George can have the Shufflebotham, after all.'

'I hope so – tremendously.' Clout felt he could be magnanimous.

'I suppose you'll be across the Atlantic in no time. But you won't forget to find Olivia Jory her treasure first? Just another one in the eye for George as you go.'

'Shut up, Sadie. I won't have it put across me that I'm doing a gloat over George Lumb. He's not a bad chap, and I expect he'll wish me luck. If I do really get the thing, that is. And now, let's go.'

'All right – let's go. Or rather, you go. I'll follow you down in a few minutes, if that's all right.' Sadie resumed her seat on the table.

'Quite all right – of course.' Clout supposed that, for some reason, Sadie hadn't a fancy for being seen tagging round with him. It was because of Olivia, no doubt. 'Shall you still be at the University after tea?' he asked. 'I'd like to come and tell you how it went.'

Sadie nodded. 'I'll be in the Library,' she said. Ever so faintly in her tone there was an acknowledgement that she had liked his saying that. 'So long, Colin. And good luck.'

Clout gave her rather a sheepish grin – he knew very well that he was sufficiently excited to seem mildly ridiculous – and departed. For some seconds Sadie sat quite still. Then she got up and walked to the window. She stood there, looking thoughtfully out, for quite a long time.

3

It was an hour or more after any normal lunch-time that Olivia Jory, in her turn, knocked on Clout's door. As she got no reply, she waited for a few seconds and then knocked again. This time a voice called to her to enter. It was a girl's voice. Olivia opened the door and walked in.

Sadie Sackett was the only person in the room. She was sitting on the table in the middle, with an oddly obtrusive air of doing nothing at all. This struck Olivia so powerfully, indeed, that she at once suspected the room's owner of having bolted into hiding. Probably she had interrupted a disgusting petting-party. She pointed at the only other door she could see. 'I suppose Colin's in there?' she asked coldly.

'In there? Colin?' Miss Sackett was certainly startled. At the same time, she looked rather threatening. For a moment Olivia couldn't decide quite why. Then she saw that it was because the girl was casually swinging what might be called a blunt instrument. It was, in fact, a crowbar. 'Colin?' Sadie repeated. 'No, he's not here. He's gone to lunch with that American professor – Milder.' And she added: 'I've been doing a bit of cleaning up for him. The old women on the job are no good.'

'Somebody might do a bit of cleaning up for *you*.' Olivia had now noticed that Sadie was quite fantastically begrimed. 'You look like somebody going to a fancy-dress ball as a cobweb.'

Sadie laughed at this as if she heard nothing offensive in it. 'I'll bet I do. I've been having a go at that cupboard. It's full of junk.' She tossed the crowbar carelessly into a corner, where it fell with a bang that made Olivia jump. 'Did you want Colin? I don't know when he'll be back. By the way, you look scared.'

'Scared?' Olivia was indignant.

'Well, agitated.'

'I'm not agitated. But something's happened, and I do want Colin. Why should that Professor Milder invite him to lunch?'

Sadie grinned. 'That', she said, 'turns out to be a very great puzzle. What do *you* think of Milder?'

'I don't think of him all.' Olivia spoke impatiently. 'He's somebody one would positively try *not* to think of, I'd say.'

'Exactly.'

Olivia frowned. 'I don't think Professor Milder's of any importance, anyway. But Professor Gingrass is.' She hesitated. 'Look here – we're on different sides, I know. But I'd better tell you what I came to tell Colin. Gingrass has got ahead of us. He's doing a tremendous dig.'

'For the Caucasian treasure?'

'Yes, of course. He's got together a big party of your scruffy students –'

Sadie Sackett got off the table. ' Your manners are awful,' she said.

Olivia flushed. 'All right – I apologize. But it's objectively true, you know. They wear their hair too long, and have spotty complexions, and ridiculous ties. I don't say they're not very decent chaps.'

'But a great gulf yawns?' Sadie laughed. 'Still, I don't suppose *they're* planning to make off with valuable property on the quiet.'

For a moment Olivia Jory seemed at a loss. 'Look here,' she said. 'There's no point, is there, in our starting a slanging match? Gingrass has mobilized some sort of archaeological society, and is digging away behind the old coach-house. Come to think of it, that's quite an intelligent guess. That's what would have happened when those horses ran away. The sots would have buried the stuff there and then.'

Sadie shook her head. 'No,' she said slowly. 'As a matter of fact, it hasn't been, with Gingrass, just an intelligent guess. Somebody's spun him a yarn. There's something mysterious about it.'

'Well, the yarn must have made him pretty confident. He's blowing great guns. Turned out the guard. You positively feel the absence of a great brass band. It's infuriating.'

'Is it?' Sadie, on the contrary, seemed to find amusement in Gingrass' proceedings. 'There's a crowd?'

'Everybody.' Olivia made a gesture round the attic of the Shufflebotham Student. 'Every Tom, Dick, and Harry belonging to this venerable place of learning is on the spot. From your Vice-Chancellor downwards.'

'The V-C?' Sadie was delighted. 'Let's go and look.'

Olivia nodded. 'Very well – we'll go and look. But, considering that you and George Lumb have been all out to get this stuff for Sir John, I think you take it very lightly. Why were those miserable professors allowed to come to New Hall, anyway? They had no business there at all.'

'Displaced persons, you feel?' Sadie moved to the door. 'Well, your great-great-grandfather's Grecian girl-friend was that. Not to speak of Sir Joscelyn's mummy. In fact, there's a lot that's got displaced in this affair. But come along.'

Gingrass' dig was already a spectacular event, and everybody was delighted with it. Or everybody except the young ladies and gentlemen of the Riding Club. These – they were the hard core of the University's smart set – had been granted the use of the old coach-house, and of part of a range of stabling beyond. On turning up after luncheon, nicely dressed, for an afternoon's equitation under the admiring eyes of their simpler fellows, they were naturally annoyed at finding the greater part of the stable-yard a chaos of pits and trenches. They mounted and rode away, but nobody attended to them. This had the effect of bringing most of them back, from time to time, to the fringes of the crowd. Their opinion of the Junior Archaeological Society was, in any case, low; and they watched these grubbing and grovelling proceedings with disdain. Nevertheless their presence suggested a mounted escort called out to lend consequence to Gingrass' endeavours. And these could scarcely have conducted themselves amid a more dazzling publicity. The Vice-Chancellor was presiding as if over some formal academic occasion; grouped around him, the greater part of the Staff lent amiable and instructed countenance to these learned proceedings in their midst; and, in a wide ring beyond these, virtually the entire student body speculated, gossiped, and wondered – with now and then a little skylarking thrown in to help pass the time.

Gingrass was directing operations with a great appearance of science – or might have been described as doing this had any of the members of the Junior Archaeological Society been paying any attention to him. But these young people were only aware that they were engaged in some species of treasure hunt; many obscurely supposed that it was being conducted upon competitive principles; and all were convinced that the deeper and farther they got with pick and shovel the better.

All this laudable zeal had already yielded striking results. One vigorously wielded implement had pierced a water-main, and as a consequence a substantial corner of the yard was now occupied by an elaborate *jet d'eau*. Just as Olivia and Sadie came upon the scene it was blindingly lit for a second by a lurid green flash; the air in the yard seemed to snap and crackle; girls screamed, horses reared, the Vice-Chancellor with discernible difficulty maintained a philosopher's proper calm, Gingrass bawled commands, prohibitions, and exhortations, and old Professor Harlock was heard to declare in her high, clear voice that, to her certain knowledge, ants or beetles would put up a better show even after the majority of their reflexes had been carefully destroyed in a laboratory. Meantime somebody ran to turn off the electric current which had been so rashly tapped; two dazed young men who had been chiefly involved were haled away forcibly to undergo the horrors of First Aid; and the dig went on.

It went on for a long time. Large excavations were achieved more or less in terms of some plan which Gingrass had devised. As these, however, yielded absolutely no result, the plan had to be modified and extended impromptu. This involved digging in sundry places where the surface had unfortunately been piled high with the earth from previous trenches and chasms. The junior archaeologists, conscious that the eyes of the whole University were upon them, laboured mindlessly and heroically on. Occasionally from one or another of them there would come an excited shout; Gingrass – like a referee in some lunatic game – would blow a whistle; all the diggers would pause in their labour; and amid a breathless hush the possible significance of some ambiguous find would be investigated. Tiles and bricks and sundry scraps of rusty iron or rotted timber were solemnly pronounced upon. And then the digging would go on more frantically than ever.

'It doesn't make sense.' Olivia, pausing with Sadie at a little remove, viewed the confusion with disgust. 'You realize that, as soon as you actually see them at it. They've dug up nearly the whole of this yard. But Joscelyn and his friends may just as well have buried the stuff in front of the building as at the back.'

Sadie shook her head. 'You forget that Gingrass has received a tip straight from the horse's mouth – or believes he has. That's why he's backed himself so heavily. And now he's worried. He sees he's going to look an awful ass if nothing turns up.'

Olivia looked round the crowd. 'I think people are getting a bit restless already. Some of your young friends are drifting off. And the Vice-Chancellor is tapping with his foot in an irritated way.'

'And you can see that the Staff are edging towards an attitude of sceptical amusement. That's so as to save themselves from feeling asses too, if nothing does turn up. Hullo!' – Sadie broke off as Gingrass' whistle sounded. 'There he goes again.'

This time there was a longer pause. A small group of diggers had gathered round Gingrass, but it was possible to see that he was stooping to examine several small objects – dull yellow and dirty grey – that had just been turned up and were now placed before him. Suddenly his voice was heard, sharp with excitement. He was calling for a stretcher-like contrivance, constructed of wood, which was waiting on the fringe of the excavations. This was brought forward in what was now a tense silence, and the newly discovered objects were set upon it. The Vice-Chancellor called out something in a tone of majestic calm; this apparently was a summons, since the discoveries were now borne solemnly towards him by two sweating students. Everybody stood on tiptoe or craned their necks. It was a highly dramatic moment.

Olivia gave an exclamation of horror and dismay. 'It's bones!'

Sadie nodded. 'A macabre scene – but funny, all the same.'

'Funny?' Olivia was indignant. 'It must be the Caucasian queen, or whatever she was – Joscelyn's mummy! It means they'll be on to the treasure in no time.'

'That's what Gingrass thinks. He's expounding it all to the V-C now. And the Staff's making haste to look impressed and serious again. And reverent. A respectful bearing in the presence of the dead – particularly royal dead.' Sadie appeared quite unsuitably amused. 'Now Professor Harlock's having a look. She's the elderly woman with the white hair. I wonder – '

Sadie had lowered her voice, because of the complete hush in the stable-yard. Now she broke off. Miss Harlock had been examining the bones with care. She turned to Gingrass – and her clear tones had never carried to the back of a lecture theatre with more deadly effect. 'Equine,' she said.

Gingrass gaped at her. 'What do you mean – equine?'

'My dear man, I see no occasion to goggle. What is more natural than to find a few horse's bones buried behind a coach-house?' Miss Harlock looked round the silent crowd with withering scorn. 'I'm going to get some tea,' she announced; and moved off.

A few other people began to move off too. But most stayed behind. The Vice-Chancellor appeared to be reasoning or expostulating with Gingrass. This in itself was an entertaining spectacle. But better was to follow.

Gingrass was annoyed. Partly because of this – and partly, perhaps, because of his efforts with the whistle – his usually pallid face was flushed a deep red. As he was now, for some reason, revolving slowly on his axis, the effect was rather as of some small lighthouse that a careless keeper had forgotten to switch off at dawn.

Presently this beam suddenly paused, transformed into a searchlight. It had come to rest upon a solitary figure, at present advancing through an archway on the farther side of the yard. 'Hi – you!' Gingrass shouted rudely. 'Come here at once.'

The figure halted for a moment. It was that of the Shufflebotham Student – returning, presumably, from his luncheon with Professor Milder at the Metropole. Clout was already staring in astonishment at the scene before him; now he halted and regarded his discourteous chief with amazement and disfavour. As a consequence, the succeeding exchange took place across a considerable empty space. And this lent it a theatrical flavour highly to the taste of the audience. 'Where have you been?' bawled Gingrass. 'Where the devil have you been?'

Thus assaulted in the presence of the entire University, Clout allowed his own indignation to mount. Gingrass was impossible, and this must be the end of him. 'I've been lunching with Professor Milder,' he replied with dignity. 'And I'm resigning the Shufflebotham. I've accepted a Fellowship in Creative Literature in America.'

'Oh, you have – have you?' Gingrass spoke with difficulty. 'And perhaps you've been doing a little in a creative way already – eh?'

'I don't know what you're talking about.'

'Perhaps you'll deny telling Professor Milder you have found an important document – a letter from Sir Joscelyn Jory to his solicitor, never posted, saying that he had been obliged to bury some extremely valuable property in this yard?'

'Milder says I said that?' Clout now spoke in consternation. He was aware that the Vice-Chancellor was regarding him with distinct disfavour. And somewhere in the crowd an idiotic girl had begun to titter. 'It's entirely untrue. He must have gone off his rocker. Or perhaps' – and Clout glanced rather wildly round the chaos of the stable-yard – 'perhaps he goes in for jokes…practical jokes.' Clout paused, aware that this was both a feeble and a tactless line to take.

'If he does, his joking extends to offering non-existent Fellowships in Creative Twaddle to imbecile students.' Gingrass looked about him. The circle of gaping faces apparently brought home to him more vividly the fiasco in which he had involved himself. He uttered a surprising noise that might have been categorized, roughly, as a howl of humiliation and rage. 'To *unemployed* students, I should add,' he bawled across the yard. 'Now, go away!'

'But he couldn't!' To Clout too the full realization of a horrid position was coming with force. 'An American professor! It's not possible.'

'Listen, Colin – it's no good.' Clout turned and found that Sadie Sackett had come up beside him. 'Gingrass has been had, and you've been had too. Milder may be an American. But he's certainly not a professor.'

'Not a professor!'

Sadie looked at his dismayed expression and laughed. But her laughter held a contrite note which somehow comforted him. 'It's only dawned on me today. It never entered my head before. But – don't you see? – as soon as the suspicion comes to you, you know it's true. No *real* American professor could be *quite* like that – not outside the Light Programme.'

Clout felt that he ought to make the sort of gesture conventionally described as dazed – perhaps clutch his hair, or pass his hand slowly across his forehead. But all he managed was to stand quite still. For the first time, he spied Olivia, standing rather aloof in the crowd. It was all getting worse and worse. 'I can't believe it,' he said feebly. 'Why did he ask me out to lunch?'

'To get you out of the way – so that you wouldn't blow the gaff on all this nonsense.' Sadie pointed to the dig.

'And all this?'

'Just a distraction, I think. He wanted the whole University out of the way.'

It was at this point this the Vice-Chancellor moved augustly forward. He ignored the unfortunate Clout. 'Out of the way, Miss Sackett?' he asked. 'Pray, out of the way of what?'

Sadie shook her head. She seemed genuinely puzzled. 'I'm afraid I just don't know, sir. But out of the way of some operation of his own.'

'It's astounding...incredible!' The Vice-Chancellor was outraged. 'A perfectly well-accredited man. He lunched with me. Thoroughly scholarly, to judge from his conversation. Although a little on the dry side. In fact, a bore.'

'That's his technique, I think.' Sadie offered this explanation with confidence. 'He puts on such a turn as a bore that the mind simply revolts from him. And so nobody gets curious and questioning.'

'I see.' The Vice-Chancellor looked at Sadie with respect. He might have been acknowledging that, contrary to reasonable expectation, this large gathering contained one other individual with some claim to intellectual competence. 'Do you suppose, Miss Sackett, that this Mr Milder's aim had been to possess himself of the treasure which has led Professor Gingrass to – to such fantastic courses?'

But before Sadie could answer this question, or Gingrass protest against the terms in which it had been framed, a further diversion occurred. Through the same archway by which Clout had made his hapless appearance on the scene, there advanced, in hurried dignity behind his large brass buttons, the head porter, Gedge.

4

'Mr Vice-Chancellor, sir!' Gedge, having located the University's fountain-head of authority, was propelled, as by a natural affinity, straight towards it. 'All that there digging, Mr Vice-Chancellor, sir, turns out to be unauthorized and pretentious. I've just had it on the telephone from the Company.'

'Unauthorized, Gedge? I don't know what you can mean. Can't you see that I have been present myself? That it may have been pretentious is another matter.' The Vice-Chancellor glanced balefully at Gingrass. 'There I am disposed to agree with you.'

'No authority was given, Mr Vice-Chancellor, sir. And no gas pipes is, in fact, to be put down there. Pretenders they are, Mr Vice-Chancellor, sir, engaged upon unknown felonious purposes.' Gedge paused on this – clearly because he had struck out a turn of phrase that gratified him. In this pause he became aware – seemingly for the first time – of the extraordinary scene around him. His jaw dropped. 'What's this here? It ain't going on here too?'

The Vice-Chancellor stared at Gedge in perplexity. Then he remembered that there was one other person of appreciable intelligence present besides himself. 'Miss Sackett,' he asked, 'can you make anything of what the man is talking about?'

'I think I can, sir.' Sadie turned to Gedge. 'Do you mean that people have turned up, pretending to be from the Gas Company, and have been digging pits and trenches like this in the old sunk lane?'

'Just that, Miss Sackett, miss.' Gedge's brow cleared a little. 'And entirely pretentious, it turns out to be. Noticed it was, chance-like on account of my thinking to ring up the Company and ask if there would be a night-watchman, or if we was to be responsible. Never heard of this pipe, they hadn't. I've sent down my assistant, Spokes, to warn them off now.'

Suddenly Gingrass produced one of his odd, multi-purpose noises. This one compendiously indicated states of enlightenment, despair, and fury. 'That's it!' he yelled. 'It's by the foundations of the Temple of Diana. They must have taken the treasure there, and buried it at the same time as – ' He stopped suddenly. 'And that wretched impostor, Milder, has found out. And while he's kept us all digging and sweating here – ' Again he broke off. But this time it was because sheer inspiration had visited him. Clout, who had always admitted a covert vein of admiration for his unspeakable professor, was conscious of it now. Gingrass' eye had fallen upon the young ladies and gentlemen of the Riding Club, mounted and wondering at the back of the crowd. It was a crisis in which they could be of far more use than the Junior Archaeological Society. 'Ride!' he bawled at them. 'Ride to the lane! Canter! Gallop! Stop the villains! Intercept them! Apprehend them!' He waved his arms frantically above his head.

Not unnaturally, this exhortation was immediately effective. The young equestrians, delighted at thus unexpectedly coming to dominate the scene, departed as spectacularly as possible, followed by shouts and cheers that were partly encouraging and partly facetious or ironical. The Vice-Chancellor, after a moment's hesitation, moved off after them. Gedge, as the person of next greatest consequence present, strode beside him. The Staff, whether out of curiosity or habit, formed themselves into a characteristically shambling academic procession and followed. The body of the students, rapidly spreading out on either side, completed a large sickle-like movement which was presently sweeping across the park towards the site of Sir Arthur Jory's long-vanished temple.

Sadie somehow disappeared. The discomfiture of Clout was enhanced by an obscure feeling that she had been ill at ease. But at least he could now join Olivia, whom he distinguished hurrying forward with the crowd. Olivia – perhaps because she was actually running – hardly glanced at him as he came up to her. It wasn't easy, he found, to hit on the right remark to make. 'I say,' he tried, 'this is a pretty queer situation, isn't it?'

'It certainly isn't one that you seem much in command of.' Olivia snapped this out rather breathlessly. 'Although you've contrived a bit of an achievement, one must admit.'

'An achievement?'

'Getting the sack before your whole assembled University. Rather like the bad boy being expelled in some ghastly Victorian school-story.'

'Oh, that!' Clout felt genuinely untroubled. 'I doubt if the V-C would back Gingrass up. Not that it matters. I shan't stop for the absurd Shufflebotham thing in any case.'

'Because you're going to America to be creative?' As soon as she had uttered this gibe, Olivia appeared to have the grace to be sorry for it. 'Probably you shouldn't have come back here, Colin. I don't believe you should have left Cambridge.'

'Oxford.'

'It's the same thing. I'm sure you'll get something better. Are we nearly there?'

'Just across the east drive and round a clump of trees.'

Olivia dropped to a walking pace. 'It's sure to be too late, anyway. And, even if the treasure's still there, it will be in all the headlines tomorrow morning. And what good will that be?'

'What indeed?' Clout realized that he was tired of the beastly treasure. He wished that Olivia's mind didn't so constantly brood on it.

'I can't understand how Milder found out.'

Clout nodded gloomily. 'Nor can I. And I don't understand *what* he's found out. How did Joscelyn and Edward join up again that night? And why ever should they lug the treasure all the way to the temple for the arbitrary and ghastly purpose of burying it beside the unfortunate girl?'

'Economy of labour. One pit.'

'I suppose so.' But Clout seemed unconvinced. 'It's queer psychology, if you ask me... Look out!'

They had drawn rather to the side of the hurrying crowd, and were about to cross a narrow, subsidiary drive that ran from Old Hall to the north gate of the park. Round a bend, and coming from the direction of the Hall, an estate-car had just appeared, so that they had to pull up to let it pass. It was going on its way without haste; and there was plenty of time to notice that the driver was Jerry Jory, and that beside him sat George Lumb. Neither appeared to be in the least interested in the extraordinary procession across the park. Jerry, who was wearing what Clout considered to be a highly affected deerstalker hat, took this object off gravely, and bowed with what seemed a merely distant courtesy to Olivia. Lumb stared at her with his usual asinine devotion. He also gave Clout a wave – rather a queer wave. And then they were gone.

Olivia laughed. 'What would that solemn Terry be doing here?'

'Not Terry. Jerry.'

'Yes, of course... Oh, look!'

They had rounded the trees, and the lane above which the Temple of Diana had once stood was now before them. It exhibited a remarkable spectacle. For almost half its length it was ploughed and furrowed in a far more drastically effective fashion than the Junior Archaeological Society had achieved in the stable-yard. And the explanation of this was apparent. On the farther side of the excavations – which had held up for the moment their pursuers whether on horseback or on foot – several heavy vehicles, laden with uncouth mechanical contrivances, were making off down the lane. Gingrass screamed, Gedge bellowed, the Vice-Chancellor himself emitted calm but powerful noises. But nothing of this had any effect. The heavy vehicles vanished round a bend, and nothing was left except a single, powerful-looking car. It was empty. Even as they looked, however, a figure sprang up apparently out of the ground. It was Milder, and he was covered in dust and mud. He ran to the car – he must have been essaying a last desperate delve into the unrewarding earth – jumped into it, and started the engine. As it sprang into life he turned round for a second and shook his fist. Those at the front of the crowd declared afterwards that his features were contorted with fury. Having achieved this very sufficient melodramatic effect, Milder let in the clutch and drove rapidly and efficiently out of the picture. Nobody ever saw him again.

Gingrass now produced what was perhaps his most surprising effect of the afternoon. This time, no conflicting emotions were mingled in it. It was a howl of triumph – and of such a volume that the Vice-Chancellor jumped. 'He's been baffled – thwarted!' he yelled. 'We're in time! Where's the Society? Call up the Society! Picks! Spades!'

There was a disconcerted silence. The Vice-Chancellor and Miss Harlock – who had appeared again, presumably fortified by tea – could be seen hastily conferring, as if some horrid doubt as to their colleague's sanity had sprung up simultaneously in the mind of each. But such was the effectiveness of Gingrass' frenzy that several of the young people turned and hurried off to retrieve their implements. It looked as if the digging might really begin all over again. This time, certainly, it would be without the countenance of the Vice-Chancellor, who had turned and was walking firmly away, followed by Gedge. Clout, watching in sombre fascination, became aware of Olivia speaking urgently beside him. 'Surely this awful Gingrass is right really? Milder didn't look like a man who is getting away with anything. His people must actually have been interrupted before they had any success. Don't you think?'

Clout hesitated. He was at least clear-headed enough to be extremely puzzled. 'It's difficult to know what to think,' he said. 'I agree that Milder hasn't got the treasure – if it was the treasure he was really looking for. But I doubt whether Gingrass will get it either.'

'He won't.'

The words had been murmured in Clout's ear, and he swung round towards the speaker. It was Sadie. And she was looking at him strangely. 'He won't?' Clout repeated. 'And how do you know?'

'He won't – and you won't.' Sadie glanced swiftly at Olivia as she said this. But she spoke only to Clout. 'If you want to know why – go to your room.'

'My room?' He stared at Sadie stupidly.

'I've left a note there – explaining.' Suddenly, and very unexpectedly, Sadie put out her hand and touched his. It was the sort of thing Olivia sometimes did – and yet, somehow, it was quite different. 'Sorry,' she said. 'So long.' And she turned and walked quickly away.

Olivia watched her go. 'Was she serious?' she presently asked. 'Did she mean anything?'

Clout nodded. 'She meant something. I'd better go.'

'I'll come too.'

He nodded, and they walked away together. Even with things all going extremely badly, there was comfort in walking side by side with Olivia. But they didn't talk. And after only a few paces, something made Clout halt for a moment and turn. One or two people, who must have carried their spades as they ran, were already digging again, and others were hurrying up. The folly that the notion of buried treasure could let loose – he realized – was something appalling to contemplate!

And then Clout saw something else. It was George Lumb. He couldn't have accompanied Jerry Jory further than to the park gates. Now he was standing, high above the diggers, on the very spot where the Temple of Diana must have been reared. He was standing quite still. And – more powerfully than ever before – Clout had his nasty feeling about the formidableness of Lumb. And there was no doubt about Lumb's state now. He was sunk in profound thought.

Clout turned away. Together, he and Olivia walked quickly to Old Hall.

5

'What a funny place.' Olivia looked round Clout's room. 'Is this where you give instruction to Miss Sackett?'

'You know very well I don't teach Sadie. We were contemporaries.' For the moment, Clout didn't bother to feel annoyed by this deliberate silliness of Olivia's. There was an envelope on his table, with 'CC' scrawled across it and 'Private' in a corner. He picked it up and tore it open. Sadie had written quite a lot – and evidently at top speed.

DEAR COLIN, – Olivia Jory was right. She is evidently clever as well as the possessor of a beautiful nature. So how lucky you are. But we (call it George and me) are lucky too, because we have found the treasure. It wasn't buried – that's what I mean by that girl being right – but simply stuffed away in that queer tunnel off your attic. You gave me permission to explore, you know, and I did. I'm sorry. At least I think I'm sorry. But all's fair in this sort of thing. Or is it? Ask *her*. She's an acknowledged authority, George says, on fair play.

It was in a packing-case, well nailed down, and with a label:

> *Bound sermons*
> *Bibles*   } *effects of*
> *Religious Tracts, etc.*   *E Jory, dec.*

Pretty smart of Joscelyn? And you can see why the stuff was just
abandoned when the Jorys left Old Hall. Who'd want to lug
away that, if they could leave it quietly staying put?

I rang up New Hall to see if I could get George. I got Jerry.
He said what he said he had said before: that it was just
like leaving your wrist-watch when you sold a house,
and recoverable. He said he and George would come across and
collect. This will have happened by the time you get this.

'*Effects of E Jory, dec.*' I give you that, although I think
perhaps Jerry J wd. like it kept quiet. It can be read as an
acknowledgement by Joscelyn of the validity of the swap. On
the other hand, it can be read as just part of a blind. Jerry says
that we'd better get the stuff out of the clutches of the
University and fight about it afterwards. Possession nine-tenths
of the law. Of course it must all come out. I expect I'll be
sacked. That's *something* we shall still have in common, Colin
old chap.

Love,

S.

When he had read this, Clout handed it to Olivia without a word.
She read it through. 'Well?' she asked. She didn't seem to be
experiencing much emotion.

'Women.'

Olivia stared at him. 'What do you mean – women?'

'Something somebody once said.' Clout took the letter, tore it in
two, and tossed it into a semi-disintegrated waste-paper basket. 'I
don't appear to have been terribly smart.'

'Well, no – you don't.' Olivia was affording him a sort of casual
commiseration that he didn't like. 'To have been quartered next door
to a lot of Jory junk and not to have taken a look at it. I think you're
right. Not smart. Dim.'

'Yes, dim.' Clout was frowning. 'You realize it leaves some puzzles?'

Olivia was slightly impatient. 'It's certainly true that just what happened is still a bit obscure.'

Clout shook his head. 'One can take a guess, as far as the Caucasian stuff is concerned. We don't know what Joscelyn did with the treasure that night. But he did return to Old Hall from abroad, and I suppose he never really found out whether there had been any substance behind the Duke of Nesfield's joke. And Edward was dead – without even having begun to recover from *his* fright. So Joscelyn adopted this means of stowing the stuff unobtrusively away for the time being. And then he went a bit ga-ga and died. There's not much difficulty about all that.'

'Then what do you mean by there being puzzles still?'

'I mean that crook Milder, chiefly. He knew pretty well everything that we knew. But that was just nothing at all, so far as any certain notion of the whereabouts of the treasure was concerned. Why did he set Gingrass digging behind the coach-house, which was quite a likely place on the basis of the knowledge we had, and then himself perpetrate that elaborate dig below the Temple of Diana, where there was likely to be nothing but the skeleton of an unfortunate Greek girl?'

'I haven't a clue.' Olivia shrugged her shoulders. It was an unbeautiful gesture to which she contrived to lend all her old, heady charm. It came back to Clout – what, of course, he had always absolutely known – that she was a quite dazzlingly superior person. They had lost – at least for the time being they had lost – the game. And it was a game upon which Olivia had been desperately keen. Yet, now, she was being quite astoundingly philosophic about it. 'Probably', she said, 'that chap Milder is just mad.'

Clout considered this. 'No,' he said.

'How can you be sure?'

'Lumb doesn't think so.' Clout felt his mind groping after some important truth. 'When I say there's still a puzzle I really chiefly mean that Lumb feels there's still a puzzle.'

'How very odd! You seem to have become uncommonly dependent on the opinions of Lumb.'

'Lumb has a brain.' Clout uttered this with sober and humble conviction. 'He and Sadie and that detestable Jerry have got the treasure. And yet Lumb feels there's still something to think out.'

'However do you know that?'

'Just from the last glimpse I had of him, Olivia. He was standing above all that mess – below the site of the Temple of Diana, I mean – watching Gingrass getting his idiotic dig going again. And he was thinking something out.'

'Well, if there's something to think out, you can think it out too.'

'That's perfectly true. I'm not quite a moron, after all.' Clout felt himself to be announcing this as a surprising discovery. 'But the business of thought is to prompt and guide action. I wonder who said that?'

'You'd better ask your pupils.' Olivia pointed, with something of her old, objectionable scorn, to the row of empty chairs along one wall. Suddenly she laughed. 'No wonder your Sadie was covered in dust and cobwebs. And no wonder she was waving a crowbar. But how did she know about this place off your attic?'

'We hid in it together – from Milder.' Clout stared at the door behind which he and Sadie had taken refuge such a short time before. 'It goes on and on. And it's absolutely crammed with junk. Sadie must have been lucky to come so quickly on what she was after. A thorough search would take ages.' Rather to his own astonishment, Clout banged his fist on the table. 'God lord! If I was a fool not to make a thorough search before, surely I'm still a fool not to make it now? For there's still a puzzle, as I've said.'

'Then, search away.' Olivia's voice expressed not the slightest interest in his proposal. For a moment Clout thought that she was going to take herself off. But she hesitated , and as she did so her eyes travelled over him. 'I'll wait and watch,' she said.

'Good!' Her words ought to have filled him with joy – but somehow they made him feel slightly uncomfortable. He must be very tired, he thought – for he was having to repress a shocking sense that Olivia's interest in him had become, in some indefinable way, wanton. 'Sit down,' he said, 'and I'll have a go. If there's anything that looks interesting, I'll bring it out.'

6

Dusk was falling, and Clout had got himself far more smothered in grime than Sadie had done. On the table in front of him lay a mouldering, leather-bound manuscript volume, the pages of which he was slowly turning over. 'Interesting,' he said. 'I mean, interesting in itself. But too late to interest *us*. It's Sir George's – the last Jory to live here.'

'What's it about?' Olivia, who had thrown the window open and was leaning on the sill staring idly out, allowed her attention to be held for the moment. 'Don't say it's copies of letters, like Sophia's.'

'Nothing like that. I think it would be called the day-book of the estate. Records jobs doing, and to be done, about the place. Materials needed, their likely cost, and so on. Sir George certainly made a big effort to get the place economically on its feet again, before he was forced to quit. I don't think there's much point in raking through – ' He broke off, and read silently for some moments. 'But this *is* interesting. It's notes on the demolishing of the Temple of Diana.'

'Bother the Temple of Diana! I'm tired of hearing about it.'

Clout made no response to this, but turned over a page. 'Sir George', he said presently, 'employed a couple of masons of his own. And it's as we thought. He got no end of minor building and repairing done with the material that became available.' He turned over another page. Olivia had gone back to gazing through the window. A minute went by. Then she wheeled quickly – for Clout had uttered a very odd sort of gasp. 'Asses!' he said. 'Utter asses that we've been!' he laughed wildly, and then with a great effort controlled himself. 'It wasn't a woman, Olivia. It was a statue.'

'A statue?' For the first time in their acquaintance – Clout dimly noticed – his marvellous girl looked merely stupid.

'Sir George's men came on a marble statue – the statue of a goddess. Sir George doesn't make any ado about it. A statue was of no particular use to him. He just notes that it can be stuck up somewhere…' Clout paused, and then gave a cry of mingled triumph and mortification that would have done credit to Gingrass himself. 'Oh, what asses! Olivia, don't you *see?*' He pushed the book away, and buried his head in his arms, as if feeling that he might thereby be assisted to a clearer inward vision himself. 'Would it be – well, just any old statue?' He looked up again. 'No! That wouldn't fit.'

If Olivia had looked stupid, she now asked a question which showed a very tolerably swift intelligence. 'Why did Edward say he was likely to be hanged? Surely that meant he'd as good as committed murder?'

'He said nothing of the sort. He said, if Sophia got it right, "By God, I'll be hanged." It was a mere profane exclamation. No, there's only one solution to the puzzle – and you'll see it all fits. What Edward brought home was a bit of Greek statuary – and it must have been superb of its kind.'

'Why?'

'Because of the extent to which Joscelyn was bowled over by it, for one thing. He was quite an aesthete, remember; and he had become disheartened because all his mortuary stuff contained nothing absolutely first-rate – a Medici tomb, or something like that.'

'*This* must have been something like that?' Again Olivia's intelligence flashed out. 'Something mortuary, as you call it? That *does* make sense of the whole business of the swap.'

Clout laughed – this time at a relaxed pressure. 'It makes it a good deal more decent too. But there's another reason, you see, why the statue must have been pretty tremendous. There's not merely the fact that Joscelyn was willing to swap his own top-notch Caucasian treasure for it. There's the fact that Edward had quite as guilty a conscience as Joscelyn had.'

Olivia's eyes suddenly rounded. 'You mean that this statue would itself be enormously valuable?'

'Of course. Think what the Venus de Milo would fetch, if the Louvre shoved it on the market today. Edward's statue might conceivably be in that class. But Sir George, who was clearly just a sound, practical landowner, had no notion that his men had tumbled on anything other than a common-or-garden ornament.'

Olivia in her turn produced an inarticulate cry. 'That's it, Colin!' Her eyes sparkled with excitement. 'A *garden* ornament! That's what Sir George would do with it.'

They tumbled downstairs and out of the building. Beyond the terrace, the grounds of Old Hall were already shadowy. 'One doesn't know where to begin,' Olivia said.

'No.' Clout walked forward to the balustrade. 'Do you see the significance of the fact that Milder knew about both the treasure and the statue – and was determined to get the statue? *That* gives you a pointer to their comparative value! He must either be a genuine scholar, you know, or in contact with one. What we've been up against is a chap – or an organization – concerned to track down some very celebrated vanished work of ancient art. It's really rather a thrill.' Clout's voice was excited – but the excitement was of a fresh sort. He had glimpsed something that really touched the imagination.

'To hell with your thrill.' Olivia's voice was harsh. '*Where's the statue?*'

Clout looked at her without replying, and in a sudden desolation he couldn't begin to explain. Only he was falteringly aware of the discovery that they weren't – Olivia and himself – at all the same sort of person. He had felt tired in his attic; now he felt quite exhausted. He took another step forward and leaned his arm on an empty pedestal. Something queer happened in his stomach. He looked up.

Close by, and a mere silhouette in the gathering dusk, loomed a large, obese Hercules. Beyond that was a gigantic boar. But here…*here* – '

'Are you l-l-looking f-f-for – ' The voice of George Lumb, gentle and struggling, was in his ear. 'Are you looking, C-C-Clout, for the Aphrodite Epitumbia? I'm s-s-sorry. B-b-but we've got that too.'

'*You* have?' It was Olivia who had swung round on Lumb.

'Well, the J-J-Jorys. We've t-t-taken it to New Hall.'

'And it's called *what*? I never heard of it.' Olivia seemed quite calm.

'The Aphrodite of the Tomb.' Lumb's stammer had taken one of its dives to earth. 'It's known to have been at Delphi. The dead were summoned to it to receive libations. One of the really great things. You can imagine what Joscelyn Jory felt he would give for it.'

'And what people would give now?'

Lumb nodded, but didn't speak. There was a long silence. Clout found it oppressive. He knew there was something he had to say. And he managed it. 'I'm sorry, Olivia, I've let you down. Lumb has got in first again. I can't think how.' He turned to his rival. 'You see, *I've* found something of Sir George Jory's that puts one on the track of this. But I don't see – '

'J-j-just thinking it out, C-C-Clout.' Lumb didn't speak with the least trace of triumph. His eyes were on Olivia, and he was looking very sad. 'Milder wanted to dig up what Edward Jory had b-b-buried. But, whatever it was, he f-f-failed. It was gone. One had to make sense of that. And of the p-p-precise expressions and p-p-possible ambiguities in Sophia Jory's letters. Only a great statue fitted. And it's certainly the Epitumbia. You see, there is an extant Graeco-Roman c-c-copy, and I've just looked that up in a b-b-book.'

There was another long silence. Again it was Clout who had to break it. 'I'm terribly sorry, Olivia. That's all I can say.'

'It doesn't matter a bit.'

He looked at her in wonder, for she had never appeared to him so marvellous. 'You mean you don't really care about who gets all this potential wealth?'

'Well, I don't care which branch of the Jorys gets it. That's irrelevant now. You see' – and she smiled dazzlingly – 'Jerry Jory and I got engaged yesterday.'

This time there wasn't a second's pause. 'I congratulate him,' Clout said.

'And s-s-so d-d – '

It was still light enough to see that Olivia had achieved something quite new. She had blushed deeply. Then, before Lumb had finished his sentence, she turned and walked away.

The two young men looked at each other in sombre silence. It was something they had done before, and for an instant there was complete understanding between them. Perhaps it was this close communion that made them both turn simultaneously. Sadie Sackett had emerged from Old Hall. Presumably she hadn't noticed them, for she was walking off down the long avenue to the main gates. Sadie was going home.

Still as if entirely of one mind, the young men hurried after her. Instinctively, they kept in step. Mostly, their eyes were on Sadie. But they glowered at each other from time to time as they walked.

MICHAEL INNES

APPLEBY AT ALLINGTON

Sir John Appleby dines one evening at Allington Park, the Georgian home of his acquaintance, Owain Allington, who is new to the area. His curiosity is aroused when Allington mentions his nephew and heir to the estate, Martin Allington, whose name Appleby recognises. The evening comes to an end but, just as Appleby is leaving, they find a dead man – electrocuted in the *son et lumière* box that had been installed in the grounds.

APPLEBY ON ARARAT

Inspector Appleby is stranded on a very strange island, with a rather odd bunch of people – too many men, too few women (and one of them too attractive) cause a deal of trouble. But that is nothing compared to later developments, including the body afloat in the water and the attack by local inhabitants.

'Every sentence he writes has flavour, every incident flamboyance'
– *The Times Literary Supplement*

MICHAEL INNES

THE DAFFODIL AFFAIR

Inspector Appleby's aunt is most distressed when her horse, Daffodil – a somewhat half-witted animal with exceptional numerical skills – goes missing from her stable in Harrogate. Meanwhile, Hudspith is hot on the trail of Lucy Rideout, an enigmatic young girl who has been whisked away to an unknown isle by a mysterious gentleman. And when a house in Bloomsbury, supposedly haunted, also goes missing, the baffled policemen search for a connection. As Appleby and Hudspith trace Daffodil and Lucy, the fragments begin to come together and an extravagant project is uncovered, leading them to a South American jungle.

'Yet another surprising firework display of wit and erudition and ingenious invention' – *The Guardian*

DEATH AT THE PRESIDENT'S LODGING

Inspector Appleby is called to St Anthony's College, where the President has been murdered in his Lodging. Scandal abounds when it becomes clear that the only people with any motive to murder him are the only people who had the opportunity – because the President's Lodging opens off Orchard Ground, which is locked at night, and only the Fellows of the College have keys...

'It is quite the most accomplished first crime novel that I have read...all first-rate entertainment' – Cecil Day Lewis, *The Daily Telegraph*

Michael Innes

Hamlet, Revenge!

At Seamnum Court, seat of the Duke of Horton, The Lord Chancellor of England is murdered at the climax of a private presentation of *Hamlet*, in which he plays Polonius. Inspector Appleby pursues some of the most famous names in the country, unearthing dreadful suspicion.

'Michael Innes is in a class by himself among writers of detective fiction' – *The Times Literary Supplement*

The Long Farewell

Lewis Packford, the great Shakespearean scholar, was thought to have discovered a book annotated by the Bard – but there is no trace of this valuable object when Packford apparently commits suicide. Sir John Appleby finds a mixed bag of suspects at the dead man's house, who might all have a good motive for murder. The scholars and bibliophiles who were present might have been tempted by the precious document in Packford's possession. And Appleby discovers that Packford had two secret marriages, and that both of these women were at the house at the time of his death.

TITLES BY MICHAEL INNES AVAILABLE DIRECT
FROM HOUSE OF STRATUS

Quantity		£	$(US)	€
☐	THE AMPERSAND PAPERS	6.99	9.95	13.50
☐	APPLEBY AND HONEYBATH	6.99	9.95	13.50
☐	APPLEBY AND THE OSPREYS	6.99	9.95	13.50
☐	APPLEBY AT ALLINGTON	6.99	9.95	13.50
☐	THE APPLEBY FILE	6.99	9.95	13.50
☐	APPLEBY ON ARARAT	6.99	9.95	13.50
☐	APPLEBY PLAYS CHICKEN	6.99	9.95	13.50
☐	APPLEBY TALKING	6.99	9.95	13.50
☐	APPLEBY TALKS AGAIN	6.99	9.95	13.50
☐	APPLEBY'S ANSWER	6.99	9.95	13.50
☐	APPLEBY'S END	6.99	9.95	13.50
☐	APPLEBY'S OTHER STORY	6.99	9.95	13.50
☐	AN AWKWARD LIE	6.99	9.95	13.50
☐	THE BLOODY WOOD	6.99	9.95	13.50
☐	CARSON'S CONSPIRACY	6.99	9.95	13.50
☐	A CHANGE OF HEIR	6.99	9.95	13.50
☐	CHRISTMAS AT CANDLESHOE	6.99	9.95	13.50
☐	A CONNOISSEUR'S CASE	6.99	9.95	13.50
☐	THE DAFFODIL AFFAIR	6.99	9.95	13.50
☐	DEATH AT THE CHASE	6.99	9.95	13.50
☐	DEATH AT THE PRESIDENT'S LODGING	6.99	9.95	13.50
☐	A FAMILY AFFAIR	6.99	9.95	13.50
☐	FROM LONDON FAR	6.99	9.95	13.50
☐	THE GAY PHOENIX	6.99	9.95	13.50

ALL HOUSE OF STRATUS BOOKS ARE AVAILABLE FROM GOOD BOOKSHOPS
OR DIRECT FROM THE PUBLISHER:

Internet: www.houseofstratus.com including synopses and features.

Email: sales@houseofstratus.com
info@houseofstratus.com
(please quote author, title and credit card details.)

TITLES BY MICHAEL INNES AVAILABLE DIRECT
FROM HOUSE OF STRATUS

Quantity		£	$(US)	€
	GOING IT ALONE	6.99	9.95	13.50
	HAMLET, REVENGE!	6.99	9.95	13.50
	HARE SITTING UP	6.99	9.95	13.50
	HONEYBATH'S HAVEN	6.99	9.95	13.50
	THE JOURNEYING BOY	6.99	9.95	13.50
	LAMENT FOR A MAKER	6.99	9.95	13.50
	THE LONG FAREWELL	6.99	9.95	13.50
	LORD MULLION'S SECRET	6.99	9.95	13.50
	THE MAN FROM THE SEA	6.99	9.95	13.50
	MONEY FROM HOLME	6.99	9.95	13.50
	THE MYSTERIOUS COMMISSION	6.99	9.95	13.50
	THE NEW SONIA WAYWARD	6.99	9.95	13.50
	A NIGHT OF ERRORS	6.99	9.95	13.50
	THE OPEN HOUSE	6.99	9.95	13.50
	OPERATION PAX	6.99	9.95	13.50
	A PRIVATE VIEW	6.99	9.95	13.50
	THE SECRET VANGUARD	6.99	9.95	13.50
	SHEIKS AND ADDERS	6.99	9.95	13.50
	SILENCE OBSERVED	6.99	9.95	13.50
	STOP PRESS	6.99	9.95	13.50
	THERE CAME BOTH MIST AND SNOW	6.99	9.95	13.50
	THE WEIGHT OF THE EVIDENCE	6.99	9.95	13.50
	WHAT HAPPENED AT HAZELWOOD	6.99	9.95	13.50

ALL HOUSE OF STRATUS BOOKS ARE AVAILABLE FROM GOOD BOOKSHOPS
OR DIRECT FROM THE PUBLISHER:

Tel: **Order Line**
0800 169 1780 (UK)
International
+44 (0) 1845 527700 (UK)

Fax: **+44 (0) 1845 527711 (UK)**
(please quote author, title and credit card details.)

Send to: **House of Stratus Sales Department**
Thirsk Industrial Park
York Road, Thirsk
North Yorkshire, YO7 3BX
UK

PAYMENT

Please tick currency you wish to use:

☐ £ (Sterling) ☐ $ (US) ☐ € (Euros)

Allow for shipping costs charged per order plus an amount per book as set out in the tables below:

CURRENCY/DESTINATION

	£(Sterling)	$(US)	€ (Euros)
Cost per order			
UK	1.50	2.25	2.50
Europe	3.00	4.50	5.00
North America	3.00	3.50	5.00
Rest of World	3.00	4.50	5.00
Additional cost per book			
UK	0.50	0.75	0.85
Europe	1.00	1.50	1.70
North America	1.00	1.00	1.70
Rest of World	1.50	2.25	3.00

PLEASE SEND CHEQUE OR INTERNATIONAL MONEY ORDER
payable to: HOUSE OF STRATUS LTD or card payment as indicated

STERLING EXAMPLE

Cost of book(s):...................... Example: 3 x books at £6.99 each: £20.97
Cost of order:...................... Example: £1.50 (Delivery to UK address)
Additional cost per book:.............. Example: 3 x £0.50: £1.50
Order total including shipping:.......... Example: £23.97

VISA, MASTERCARD, SWITCH, AMEX:

☐ ☐ ☐ ☐ ☐ ☐ ☐ ☐ ☐ ☐ ☐ ☐ ☐ ☐ ☐ ☐ ☐ ☐ ☐

Issue number (Switch only):

☐ ☐ ☐

Start Date: **Expiry Date:**

☐☐ / ☐☐   ☐☐ / ☐☐

Signature: _____

NAME: _____

ADDRESS: _____

COUNTRY: _____

ZIP/POSTCODE: _____

Please allow 28 days for delivery. Despatch normally within 48 hours.

Prices subject to change without notice.
Please tick box if you do not wish to receive any additional information. ☐

House of Stratus publishes many other titles in this genre; please check our website (**www.houseofstratus.com**) for more details.